Her Part
to Play

"A charming debut. Erlingsson hits the mark with this fun Hollywood-meets-the-South tale of love and healing and finding purpose."

Rachel Hauck, *New York Times* bestselling author

"Jenny Erlingsson's debut novel delves deep into the faith of a Hollywood actor and a makeup artist. As they develop a tentative friendship, Erlingsson weaves redemption, grace, and love so masterfully, the reader will reach the end before they're ready to. I'll remember the gospel truths and this sweet romance long after the last page."

Toni Shiloh, Christy Award–winning author

"Readers will care about these immensely likable characters from the very first page and find themselves emotionally invested in their love story and their personal journeys. Jenny Erlingsson has gifted us a romance that is equal parts celebrity glamour and small-town comfort, and while those two things don't always mix, the true power of Adanne and John's story is found in how beautifully these characters complement each other. I was deeply touched by this faith-filled story . . . and I also had a whole lot of fun. Fans of Denise Hunter and Toni Shiloh will not want to miss *Her Part to Play*!"

Bethany Turner, author of *Brynn and Sebastian Hate Each Other: A Love Story*

"In Jenny Erlingsson's *Her Part to Play*, an unlikely pair have as much to learn about themselves as they do each other. What they discover is a powerful lesson in relationships—with the Lord, among friends, within a family, and, of course, between John and Adanne. Erlingsson digs deep in her beautiful debut!"

Robin W. Pearson, Christy Award–winning author of *Dysfunction Junction*

"What a sparkling, stunning debut! Jenny Erlingsson weaves a Hollywood makeover tale into a hometown setting that warms the heart with—and opens the curtain on—star-crossed lovers faced with learning life's deepest lessons about who they are in Christ. Then, by faith, they can find their way to the meaning of a lasting, true love that honors him. A modern romance with old-fashioned courage and depth. More, please, from Jenny's pen!"

Patricia Raybon, Christy Award–winning author of the Annalee Spain Mysteries, including *Truth Be Told*

"Faith and romance are beautifully intertwined in Jenny Erlingsson's debut novel, *Her Part to Play*. Jenny breathes life into Adanne and John's transformative journey from conflict to connection, taking readers along for a unique ride with both Hollywood glitz and the warmth of a small town. Adanne's humor and her undeniable romantic tension with John kept me cheering for them throughout the book. Their story is a testament to God's faithfulness, a welcome encouragement that sits in your heart long after the last page."

Michelle Stimpson, author of *Sisters with a Side of Greens*

Her Part to Play

a novel

JENNY ERLINGSSON

Revell

a division of Baker Publishing Group
Grand Rapids, Michigan

Published by Revell
a division of Baker Publishing Group
Grand Rapids, Michigan
RevellBooks.com

Printed in the United States of America

Library of Congress Cataloging-in-Publication Data
Names: Erlingsson, Jenny, author.
Title: Her part to play : a novel / Jenny Erlingsson.
Description: Grand Rapids, Michigan : Revell, a division of Baker Publishing Group, 2024.
Identifiers: LCCN 2023056462 | ISBN 9780800745004 (paperback) | ISBN 9780800745851 (casebound) | ISBN 9781493445523 (ebook)
Subjects: LCGFT: Romance fiction. | Christian fiction. | Novels.
Classification: LCC PR9170.I23 E75 2024
LC record available at https://lccn.loc.gov/2023056462

Scripture used in this book, whether quoted or paraphrased by the characters, is from the Holy Bible, New International Version®, NIV®. Copyright © 1973, 1978, 1984, 2011 by Biblica, Inc.® Used by permission of Zondervan. All rights reserved worldwide. www.zondervan.com. The "NIV" and "New International Version" are trademarks registered in the United States Patent and Trademark Office by Biblica, Inc.®

This book is a work of fiction. Names, characters, places, and incidents are the product of the author's imagination or are used fictitiously. Any resemblance to actual events, locales, or persons, living or dead, is coincidental.

Cover image of woman: Arcangel / Nicole Matthews
Cover design: Laura Klynstra

Published in association with Books & Such Literary Management, www.booksandsuch.com.

Emojis are from the open-source library OpenMoji (https://openmoji.org/) under the Creative Commons license CC BY-SA 4.0 (https://creativecommons.org/licenses/by-sa/4.0/legalcode).

Baker Publishing Group publications use paper produced from sustainable forestry practices and postconsumer waste whenever possible.

24 25 26 27 28 29 30   7 6 5 4 3 2 1

To My Loves
—Bjarni, Nyema, Thor, Eyja, and Moses—
and to the Lover of My Soul.
John 12:3

1

*S*leep didn't come easily to the brokenhearted. Which was ridiculous. Since said heartbreak was too long ago to count. And had been a long time coming—according to John's mom.

Buzzing took over the silent presidential suite for what felt like the hundredth time. John groaned, wondering why he even bothered to set the alarm clock. He swatted at the appliance, hoping he'd managed to hit the off button before it joined the chorus of his invisible phone.

Licking his lips, he reached for the bottle on his nightstand. The room appeared opaque as he raised the bottle to eye level, peering at his surroundings through the remnants in the glass. Nothing left there either but a few drops. Just enough to frustrate.

He'd been nursing this bottle since early morning. A gift from the production studio, nestled among other sponsored items that had crowded his week-old welcome basket. Congrats after a year out of the limelight. Before that call, he'd ridden the fumes of an independent film that had awards-season talk all over it.

He'd meant for the fizzy drink to stay unopened. Preparation for his role included a strict regimen and diet. Which meant limited sugar. Especially his favorite specialty spicy ginger soda. But certain news had a way of weakening one's resolve.

John lowered the bottle and glanced around for his phone. The buzzing continued, but he couldn't remember where he'd thrown it last night.

Why did I even read that article?

Engaging in the gossip mills the night before today's challenging shoot had not been his intention. But that didn't stop others from sharing the news that sent him spinning.

A shaky hand ran through his almost-shoulder-length hair. He didn't know who he was more upset with, his manager for sending him the article link or himself for still caring so much. In a more orderly world, this bit of news would be the perfect way to bring closure, wipe hands clean of the past. But it felt like a scab being ripped off once again. No matter how many years passed, the sting of rejection still lingered.

Ultimately, ending their two-year relationship had been the right thing to do, even though it was mostly her idea. Somehow that knowledge wasn't enough to defuse the impact of this current development. He should've known that eventually his ex-girlfriend would have someone new.

But did she have to get engaged in just two months?

The buzzing continued to resonate in John's ear. He could only guess who was on the other end of the phone that seemed to be lost in some abyss. He glanced at the clock. Time to get up before he ruined this new opportunity. As excited as the producers were about him joining the project, especially after his pivotal role in last year's critically acclaimed movie, he knew they'd replace him in a heartbeat.

That was the way of the industry he called home.

A glimmer of remembrance came over him. He stretched

his left arm out over the bed, patting the surface of the down comforter until he felt a hard object.

"John! You up and ready?" The chipper voice of his long-time manager blared into his ear as soon as he slid his fingers across the device to answer.

The night had started too late, and he'd woken up way too early for that level of enthusiasm this Friday morning. Did Mike ever sleep?

He cleared his throat to relieve the telltale signs of his junk-food binge.

"Ah, I see. I hear the remnants of too much sugar. Hope you didn't already destroy all your preproduction work."

John gave a loud cough and finally cleared his throat. A glance around the bedroom of his presidential suite revealed a pizza box, the empty bottles of the spicy soda, and his favorite European salted-caramel chocolates. His body was going to make him pay for this binge. The days of teenage metabolism were long gone, but sometimes his lack of self-control forgot that.

"Good morning, Mike."

John placed the phone on speaker, scooting his legs to the side to ease out of bed while his manager continued talking. He paused on the edge of the firm hotel mattress, giving his head time to adjust.

This scenario would have looked completely different a few years ago. Back then, Mike would have already been pounding on John's hotel door. Or grabbing a key from the front desk himself, assuming his client was hungover from actual alcoholic beverages.

All that had changed two years ago. *Thank God it changed.*

However, the surrender of his life to the faith he'd tiptoed around as a child led to more change than he bargained for. It set off the downward spiral of his longtime relationship with fellow actress and singer Katrina Daline.

Despite the cost, and the news from last night, he intended to remain focused on building his career back up. He would do his best to stay in the limelight and on the straight and narrow.

• • • •

"Hey, you! Adanne, right?"

Her eyes flew open. *Oh no.* The bright sunlight filtering in through the branches of the tall oak had done nothing to keep her awake. Ugh, she should've taken the other makeup assistant up on her offer to grab her an espresso. It was a nice gesture, but she also may have been tired of Adanne's tenth yawn in five minutes.

The blame for her physical weariness wasn't on anyone but herself. For the third night in a row, she'd stayed up way too late cleaning at the community center. A good way to cut costs but not if she lost her job from falling asleep. Her role for most of the morning had been to stand by, making sure the extras' makeup stayed in place, darting in for last looks as needed before the cameras started rolling.

"Yes, you. Come over here." The assistant director motioned her over.

She squared her shoulders, making her way through the cast and crew gathered at different spots. She adjusted her makeup belt as she walked, checking her tools with just a few pats of her hand.

Despite the chilly January temperatures, the hum of her surroundings had lulled her to a light sleep as she leaned against the trunk of the wide-branched tree.

The movie set was a lot of hurry up and wait. Sometimes it was hard not to ignore the million other things on her list between applications, touch-ups, and everything else she had to do. And apparently, it was hard for her body not to think of dead time as a convenient naptime.

"Flying in," Adanne mumbled as she approached. She scanned the faces of the people around her in various stages of wardrobe and framing. Everyone's makeup was still in place, the key artist was posted by the monitors, and no one had called for last looks. She turned to the assistant director, Bo, which was short for something she couldn't remember at the moment. He certainly couldn't remember how to say her name. "It's Ah-dah-neh. How can I help?"

"Stand at this tag." Bo pointed to the cross-shaped gaffer tape stuck to the ground. "The lead is resting in her trailer. We need you to block a change to this scene so we don't mess up the wardrobe of the extras."

Her eyes rounded and her loose braids fell forward as she stared. "Do what now?"

"Stand here." Bo took her gently by the shoulders, facing her toward the doorway of an old general store. "He'll come from there, run out, grab your shoulders, and say, 'It's time. We are out of time.' Then you'll sway—not a faint. Just enough of a step back for him to keep you from falling. Got it?"

Adanne swallowed. How'd she go from a sleepy makeup artist to standing in as an extra? Most of the scenes were blocked before she finished applying the makeup. Surely someone else could do this with the stunt double instead of her standing in the last place she wanted to be . . . at the center of everyone's attention.

Before she could come up with a better alternative, the stand-in sauntered out of an office building adjacent to the general store. Except, it wasn't a double.

He approached her, adjusting the suspenders attached to his trousers as he listened to the production assistant who was walking beside him. Adanne blinked, swallowing down the bile rising in her throat. Surely the Lord would allow the Alabama clay to open and swallow her right up. Away from the man she'd been grateful to avoid since she'd stepped foot on set. The careless actor whose antics got her fired three years ago.

When she glanced back, her eyes landed on the curious gaze of the supporting actor.

He looked more like himself today, at least the version she remembered. According to today's call sheet, he'd be acting as a younger version of his character for this scene. He wore starched pants, a button-down shirt, and a bow tie to accent his professor-turned-older-vigilante look. He reached up but paused midair. A wry grin crossed his face. He probably remembered that the hair department wouldn't take it lightly if he ran his hand through his locks. As he approached, his fake rimmed glasses failed to cover the weary look in his eyes.

Adanne couldn't deny the twinge in her chest if she wanted to. She was her mother's daughter after all.

"You good?" The hushed words slipped out before she could catch them. His condition was none of her business. But the nervous energy pulsing through her had loosened her mouth. He blinked at her in question and scoffed without answering.

"Okay, John!" The assistant director stepped closer. Adanne pulled her eyes away from the actor, squashing the pang of compassion that had no business infiltrating her chest. He didn't deserve it anyhow. "Adanne is standing in while you run the lines. Saves us having to search through the extras. And she's the right size."

If Adanne hadn't been in shock, she might have given the director a side-eye. It wasn't anyone's job on or off this set to size her up for anything. Why in the world was she positioned opposite John Pope of all people?

Bo pulled away from John, who retreated back to his starting position. Adanne shifted toward the general store. Her stomach tightened in rebellion against the path her thoughts wanted to take. This should have sent waves of nausea or at least annoyance. Instead her core was tense with anticipation. John barreled out and stopped right in front of her. He grabbed her shoulders lightly and said the needed lines.

Adanne nodded, faltering the way she was told. Tingles rippled through her as John caught and lifted her, setting her firmly on her feet. She would not win a gold statue for this performance, but if it helped keep the schedule moving, she would continue. Because there was no drifting off after this. Her senses were awake and on high alert. Maybe it was a trick of the set lights causing the gleam in John's eyes of olive green.

• • • •

"Okay, we're ready to rehearse!"

John placed the woman on her feet for the fifth time. The lingering feel of her in his arms seeped through his long-sleeved shirt, her warmth still tangible on his skin. Her eyes were captivating, even with her gaze averted as much as she could manage.

A production assistant handed her a makeup belt. She snapped it around her waist, a slight tremor in her fingers. Having a stand-in block scenes was a typical part of the process. But something about her manner accosted his heart. And her question, "You good?" caught him off guard.

The wardrobe head stepped in, adjusting John's shirt while he chided himself for being immersed in the choices of his ex. Maybe his frustration wouldn't be obvious to a random makeup artist.

Of course his team wanted to make sure they prepped him for a response just in case. But there was no prep for having a Band-Aid ripped off of what you should be over.

And no reason why he should have been left reeling by

two words from a stranger with a disquiet in her eyes that seemed to match his own.

"Thanks for your help, we're good now." The AD placed a hand on the woman's shoulder, his nod of dismissal giving her permission to exit. She pivoted before John could say anything. Or even ask her name.

His gaze lingered on her from within the mass of wardrobe adjustments and crew instructions swirling around him. He shouldn't have been so distracted by her purposeful steps or the shoulders that looked like they carried a world of burdens. Or the warm press of her hand that still lingered on his arms.

2

Ugh, I'm going to be late.

Adanne scampered down the front porch steps toward her truck, wishing for the umpteenth time that she had a key fob. But she wouldn't trade her three-decade-old baby for too much else besides the one who used to drive it.

Fumbling with her keys, she yanked off the satin headscarf slipping down her forehead. Coffee would need to happen on the way as she listened to her Bible app in the truck. Maybe she'd hear something that would prepare her to conquer all the tasks on her call sheet and ignore her disconcerting feelings from last Friday.

Hopefully, it'd be the first and last time she found herself in John Pope's vicinity. Her stint in California three years ago left a bitter taste in her mouth. All because of him.

The truck door opened with a creak of protest. Adanne shoved her bag and snacks onto the passenger's side, careful not to snag her necklace in the process. The seat squeaked with age as she settled behind the wheel.

She rolled her shoulders, unsuccessful in diminishing the tightness in her back. She had enough to worry about without adding him to the mix. Her role as an assistant makeup artist should continue to keep her busy with the background cast and away from the leads.

Lord helping, she'd push through for the next couple months in exchange for the cushion to her bank account. She wouldn't even have this job if Celise hadn't suggested her to the film's key makeup artist. Having a cousin in the fashion industry had its benefits. Especially since she thought she'd never work on a film set again.

The brakes gave a small squeal of protest as she backed her daddy's Ford down the driveway. This little tucked-away neighborhood had once been a refuge, a place of sanctuary for her family. Over the last few years, the cozy town of Hope Springs, Alabama, had grown larger than the intimate place she'd grown up in. With several government agencies and technology companies relocating to nearby Huntsville, Hope Springs had caught the overflow of expansion. Houses filled the acres that had once been lengthy fields of wheat and cotton. Some streets had been widened to accommodate the traffic, a shock to the community members who'd lived in this area since before the first stop sign was installed.

Adanne didn't mind the new restaurants popping up or the better roads and venues. But she could do without the traffic complicating her commute to the set of the forthcoming film *Fighting for Home*.

The yellow light before her coming turn increased the tightness in her chest. The truck reluctantly pulled to a stop at the red light. Air whooshed out of her mouth as she leaned back against the worn leather seat. In all the scurrying, she hadn't taken a moment to be grateful.

"I'm sorry, Lord." Adanne leaned forward, shifting onto the highway after the light clicked to green. "I asked for *something* to hold me over a little longer. Now, all I can do is complain."

God had shown up right when she needed him to. Her desperate prayers the past few weeks had met with a surprise solution. Even so, it would only solve part of her problem. The letter from the bank a few days ago couldn't have come at a worse time. But she wouldn't let anything keep her from appreciating the provision that had come through a phone call.

Maybe, just maybe, he'd drop another miracle in her lap.

Adanne exhaled as her truck pulled up to the set with ten minutes to spare. The historical depot served as the main filming location, with its older warehouses and abandoned stores. Bittersweet remains of some of the small mom-and-pop shops on the outskirts of Hope Springs, unable to keep up with the town's growth. Reminders of long Sunday drives, buying ten-cent candy from glass containers that lined the shelves of the convenience store. But now, it was just a figment of the past as the residents moved out, leaving shells of memories behind.

She drove in the front entrance of the movie set base camp, giving the security guard her identification and what she hoped was a confident smile. He handed her ID back with cracked hands and a nod.

She maneuvered her truck past storefronts and houses that had come to life and others that looked to be in a state of disarray. Thankfully, the old store was still intact, just like she remembered it. Maybe if she peered long and hard enough, she would see her daddy walking out the front door, a peppermint stick hanging from his mouth. Grasping an ice cream cone in each hand, he'd have a twinkle in his eye because he knew good and well Mama had said no extra treats.

Adanne willed her memories to stay in a safe and controlled place like the rings hanging around her neck. She may not be able to bring her parents back, but what she did here was for them.

After parking in the crew lot near the main unit base, she headed to the office trailers to check in.

Alex, the key makeup artist, glanced up at the light knock. "Oh, Adanne, I was just going to call. You're moving from the backgrounds trailer." She gave a quick smile and resumed her scan of the laptop in front of her.

Adanne paused at the door of the trailer that housed the offices. "Why the change?" Though she tried her best, she couldn't keep the higher pitch from her throat or the sense of foreboding from creeping into her gut. "Is everything okay?"

The older woman shrugged nonchalantly as she tapped her papers on her desk. "One of the personal artists had to leave set. Family emergency. I need you in the main trailer to fill in."

* * * *

"Did I miss something?"

John pushed open the door to his assigned trailer expecting to see his personal makeup artist, the one who'd been with him to every set since his first feature film. She knew his face like the back of her hand. And he knew every cackle and wisecrack that she would recycle throughout their production schedule.

He couldn't say the same for the familiar stranger at his chair who had her back turned toward him. He leaned in, eyes traveling down the rest of the trailer.

Where is Doris?

Hesitating in the doorway, he vaguely remembered an unread text from Nora, his assistant.

Instead of the pink-haired grandmother of three he trusted to be all up in his business, here stood a much younger, smooth-skinned woman shifting toward him from her place behind the makeup chair. The woman who'd stood across from him during the blocking scene last Friday. The woman who had pierced him with her simple concern.

The makeup artist ran a hand over her hair, pulling thick, braided strands over one shoulder. Silver studs glistened from two holes in each of her ears, flanking the dimples that made a slight appearance in her cheeks as her mouth pulled downwærd. A silver chain hung from her neck with two metal circles—were they rings?—dangling in the center.

For the briefest moment, John wondered how deep those dimples would be if she really smiled. But instead, her lips poked out, as if a response worked its way to the front of her mouth, only to be swallowed up again.

John's need for an answer didn't seem to make her rush to give one. Well, he hadn't responded to her question the other day either. Come to think about it, that had probably come off as rude. Might be the reason why she stood before him in silence, full lips pulled into a kind of grimace. Dark doe eyes held his gaze warily, her cheekbones keeping their height despite the slight downturn of her mouth.

He sensed that he may be the source of her apparent displeasure.

When he cleared his throat, the makeup artist raised her other eyebrow. "I'm a last-minute change."

That's obvious.

She stepped around the chair, waves of tension coming off her as she stuck out her hand, her fingernails short and plain. So different from Doris's long, manicured nails painted a new color every week.

"Hello, *again*. My name is Adanne. I'm replacing Doris for the remainder of this location shoot or until she returns."

Adanne shook his hand after he reached out, then brushed off his touch like a spider had just crawled on her. She walked back to the chair, motioning him forward with a nonchalant flick of her hand.

Her lips tilted into a subtle smirk as John made his way to her with tentative steps. "I'm guessing you were not aware of her family emergency."

He swallowed the guilt niggling at his throat. The distractions of the past couple of days had kept him from getting the information about Doris. He'd call her later today to see how he could help. If he remembered to remind Nora to remind him to call her later.

He glanced at his new makeup artist, her face still pinched. In his career, it often felt like so many things were decided for him. Doris hadn't been his pick initially, but when he'd felt comfortable in her presence, especially after upheaval on certain sets, he'd asked for her to continue to be his personal artist. Maybe he would have suggested his own replacement too if he'd known. Despite the intrigue of this one's presence.

Adanne finished arranging her makeup tools and patted the chair. "All right, Mr. Pope, you can come have a seat if you don't mind. We have a long day ahead of us." She patted the chair again, the smirk gone from her face. "So, if you please."

John slung his backpack onto the leather couch by the door. He missed Doris already.

Maybe if Mike had done *his* job better, he would've made sure John knew about the staffing change. He didn't want to start over, especially when it came to someone who worked so close to him.

"What did you say your name was again?"

"It's Adanne. Adanne Stewart." Her voice dripped with slight exasperation, but still the tone flowed over him like rich honey. He ignored the warmth that spread in his core at the sound of her slight Southern lilt.

"Based on your accent, I assume you're from around here?" He held his arms to his chest like a shield. The arms that had wrapped her during that rehearsal, her shoulders tight with the tension.

"Yes. I am. Born and raised." She lifted an eyebrow, sparks in her eyes threatening to ignite. So different from the instinctive concern she had shown just a few days ago. "We can save the questions for later so you can get to your location on time. We've got a lot to do to get you camera ready. I promise I don't bite."

John wasn't so sure.

Adanne flicked a clean white towel across the padded leather chair, her gesture resembling a slight bow.

He sighed and sat down, praying this would not end in disaster. Thankfully, filming would only last for a couple of months, and then he could escape this town and its feisty residents.

3

*B*reathing against the rise of confusion in her chest, Adanne hurried to the forty-five-foot trailer that contained her makeup station, hoping the dim light of predawn would hide what must be a sour expression on her face.

Alex had reminded her to be a little more *cordial* to the talent. More cordial? There hadn't been a single complaint during her previous week on set working with the backgrounds. She spent *one* morning with John Pope and all of a sudden she was getting called into the principal's office.

I practically swooned in the man's arms for that doggone blocking scene!

Hmm. For whatever reason, he was bothered by her.

As she approached the longer trailer, she squared her shoulders before climbing up the metal stairs. It was all right. She sure didn't trust him either.

Unfortunately, John had arrived earlier than yesterday. When she opened the door, he swiveled his chair around with a smirk on his face.

How did he look so fresh at five in the morning? Even with slim athletic pants, a plain white shirt, and an athletic jacket, he looked like he just stepped in from a stroll instead of out of bed.

He lifted his chin toward the digital clock on the wall. "Caught up in traffic?"

Adanne swallowed her groan. The man knew good and well there were barely any cars out this early.

"Stepping up!" She called out the oft warned phrase, maybe a little too loudly. After breezing past him, she placed her bags in the cabinet under the makeup table. "No 'good morning' or 'how are you today'?" she chirped with her back to him.

His personal makeup artist couldn't come back fast enough. Doris, was it? Adanne's own family emergency hadn't garnered her any sympathy on that movie project three years ago, but she wouldn't begrudge the older woman's return. Then she could finish out her assignment away from John's vicinity and in the background as she preferred.

Oh God of mercy, I beseech thee . . .

"You know we're on a tight schedule, right? Every moment matters." His voice broke through, pulling her thoughts from heaven back to earth.

Adanne inhaled, willing herself to stay calm and reserved. No need to get frustrated over what she couldn't change. Including John Pope's exasperating nature.

She answered him with a small, tight smile. "Mr. Pope, if you would kindly give me five minutes, I'll be glad to get you ready for the day. And God willing, it will be in record time."

He crossed his arms as she placed the cape around his rigid shoulders.

"God willing, you'll be more prepared tomorrow."

To think she'd actually felt a bit sorry for him last Friday. "And hopefully, you'll be in a better mood when I get here." The mumbled words slipped out before she could hold them back.

Help, Lord, she prayed. *Before I get fired today.*

Adanne glanced at John's reflection in the mirror. She expected annoyance to cross his features, or even worse. But somehow, his initial sarcasm had melted into something quite different. His green eyes lit with amusement. As if he enjoyed getting her riled up. Which, in fact, aggravated her even more.

"Are you always this chipper in the morning?" He squinted at her playfully.

Still, Adanne willed her mouth to stay shut. Remain cordial, right?

She turned to assemble all the products she needed. A quick scan of the call sheet told her John had a light fight scene that he needed to look wounded for. She pulled out her "bruises and abrasions" wheel to mix the right colors.

He was lucky that it was just pretend. *Wait, what in the world am I thinking?*

Adanne shooed away the turn of her thoughts. Was she wishing violence on the man? Most definitely not. But goodness, he got under her skin while she did her best to prepare *his* for the day.

"You're shaking your head. Something more to say?" John turned his chair, almost trapping her in the small space between his seat and the mirror.

It wasn't intentional—the man was just so long limbed—but she backed up anyway.

Thankfully, the only other people in the trailer were on the other side of a partition, both the artist and actor wearing headphones as they worked.

"Nope, nothing to do with you." Although she tried to infuse her tone with lightness, she'd be caught in the blue-eyeshadow comeback from the nineties before she told him all the reasons why *something* did very well have to do with him.

"Have I offended you in some way? You seem a little cold

26

and strictly business . . ." He tipped his head to the side. She would have given anything to wipe that infuriating smirk off his face. "Except for when you were almost late this morning."

Yes, you have offended me! But instead of blasting the trailer with her grievances, she grappled for the fruit of self-control to tame her tongue. He obviously didn't remember the blip of their shared history that had bulldozed her career. She also didn't miss the twinge of something familiar in his voice. An inner struggle lacing his words. Especially evident since he seemed to care about the thoughts of an inconsequential makeup artist. It spoke volumes either of deep character that she had yet to discover, or of insecurity that the spotlight couldn't hide.

She almost felt sorry for him.

"I'm waiting."

Almost.

"Listen. I *am* doing my best to be cordial and professional. It doesn't make it easy when you walk in here acting like the world owes you something because a woman broke your heart."

Adanne glared at him, frustrated with herself that out of all the happenings of Hollywood she didn't care to pay attention to, she knew *this* tidbit of information. It tasted like a bit of sweet justice. But still . . . her words were out of line.

A shadow crossed John's eyes, but like the experienced actor he was, he seemed to tuck away any effect her words had on him. Much worse had been inflicted on her over the years, but her mama had taught her better than that. She flinched at the maternal tsk and side-eye expression still visible in her mind. Her experience on the West Coast should have softened her heart, but her words were stones, hitting their target.

"Sorry." She exhaled, straightening. "I'm trying my best to

do this job well and then stay out of the way." She grimaced. "Before I get called in to block a scene again."

John nodded, the clouds dissipating from his eyes. "I get it. Maybe we both need to focus better . . . and be friendlier." He gave a chuckle, releasing his own breath.

One of surrender, she hoped.

● ● ● ●

John opened the door of his personal trailer later that evening to a darkened sky and the grinning face of his manager. He groaned as the overhead light glinted against Mike's wide smile.

"Is it that Tuesday already?" he mumbled as he brushed past his manager. He'd been looking forward to a hot shower and maybe catching a game on TV from the comfort of his hotel bed. Not so much one of the monthly meetings Mike insisted on having with his clients.

Mike stepped back as John walked down the steps, almost stumbling down after him. "You know you look forward to every time you get to see my face in person."

"Don't know about that."

John lengthened his stride as he made his way toward his transport. He needed to pull the trigger for the rental car included in his contract. He was in no mood to talk to anyone right now after a long day of filming. Somehow, his morning in the makeup chair had altered his flow.

His new makeup artist bothered him a little more than he cared to admit. Her words subtle yet scathing—her scent lingering throughout the day. But he didn't want to start this process over. His capacity for change had decreased considerably in the past few years. If he could keep his mind focused and his tongue in check, he could push through this slight irritation.

28

The shoot would end in a few months anyway.

Although he was fit and only a few years older, Mike's legs pumped to keep up with John's pace.

"I've got a big idea for you today." He panted, blowing into his hands and stuffing them into his fitted coat. "Something I think will excite you—hey, slow down."

John smirked at the gasps coming from behind.

"What you need. Is to. Date. *Woo, it's cold!* Again."

John stopped in his tracks so fast his manager almost tripped. "You're kidding, right?"

Mike dusted off his shoes and straightened. "Whew, thank you!"

John narrowed his eyes and the amusement left them. "Those words didn't really just come from your mouth, did they?"

"Step out there again. Start another relationship. It'll get you back in the forefront and maybe put more pep in your step."

John cringed as Mike elbowed him in the side. He needed a break *from* drama, not for his manager to play matchmaker. *God, help me here.* He had no patience for any more of Mike's schemes.

"If I remember correctly, you were the one who introduced me to Katrina in the first place. And look how that turned out."

John resumed his walk to the hired car, arriving before his driver had time to get out. A quick rap on the door and then he made his way in as his driver released the locks. John tilted his head toward Mike as he climbed in and shut the door.

"Aren't you cold?" Mike rubbed his hands together.

John shrugged. "Alabama in January has nothing on Chicago. Buckle up."

He pulled on the shades that hung from the collar of his shirt, despite the dimming light of the setting sun.

"It's perfect timing, my man. I can see it all over your face. You're lonely. You need some companionship in your life."

John leaned into the soft leather of the back seat with an exhale. It would be great if the acting he did on-screen worked well off it.

"Mike, it's been a long day. I'm not in need of a relationship right now. Just my bed, to be honest."

"It's like that dude," Mike continued, undeterred. "That dude in the Bible, ah, what's his name? The one who had the big beauty contest for a new wife."

"You read the Bible?" That was news.

Mike brushed off the question as easily as the dust on his designer jeans.

"Not currently, but I admit I have a few years of Sunday school under my belt."

"Go ahead and preach to me, then."

Mike turned to face John directly. "Laugh if you want. All I remember is that the king—whatever his name was—got rid of his queen and then ended up gathering all the beautiful women of the city to find his next wife. Not too bad of a concept considering the number of attractive women in your circle."

Beauty didn't guarantee happiness. John knew that too well. He was a sucker for a pretty face like anyone else was, but he knew from unfortunate experience that if looks were the only focus of the relationship, it wasn't going to last. In fact, it would be detrimental.

The engine roared to life, John's preferred playlist wafting from the speakers. Something light and instrumental to help him clear his head of old lines in preparation for the new. Unfortunately, it had no effect on the words coming out of Mike's mouth.

"I can hear your thoughts, dude. Relax. Okay. Let's axe the relationship thing. You need a project. Something to do in this insignificant little town that will make you the hero and go viral in the media. Some nursing homes to visit. Stop by a food pantry, that sort of thing."

John shook his head. As much as he placed importance on giving back, the way Mike strung it together felt sleazy and insincere. But Mike wouldn't stop pummeling him with options until he took some sort of bait.

John lifted his glasses. "If I narrow my eyes enough, I can see all the ideas vibrating around you like ripples. What else do you have up your sleeve?"

"Back to relationships."

"Mike. Can we give it a rest for now, please?" *Wishful thinking.*

"Wait, hear me out. I have a better thought. Now that your last film has been nominated, what about the Oscars? Nora emailed about your reserved tickets from the studio. Have you thought about who you'll take?"

His thoughts flitted to the acquaintances he shared with his ex-girlfriend. The ones who'd been accessories to his fast-paced lifestyle more than the accountability that he needed. He wanted a safer option. "Maybe I'll take my mom."

Mike groaned. "Are you serious? It may be endearing for some, but we're trying to revive your career, not tank it. That will barely make a blip."

"It's worked for others. The more I think about it, the better I like it." His mom would have fun and he wouldn't have to worry about any drama. Most importantly, his heart would remain intact in the process. Even something as trivial as a platonic awards-show plus-one could go awry if it wasn't the right one.

"You're not a kid anymore, John. I'm telling you as your trusted manager, you need to be strategic about who you have beside you."

John turned to the window as they passed out of the gated

entrance of the set. The bare trees surrounding the winding road gave way to rolling fields. After a few minutes, these would eventually shift into the newer suburbs and establishments that were the sign of the growing town of Hope Springs. He'd resented this location at first—too low-key for his tastes. But after just a few weeks, he realized this Southern town was probably the type of medicine that he needed.

John turned back to Mike, who was scrolling through a stream of photos on his phone.

"I don't see why this is so important. There are industry members vying for a ticket. You can even place a seat filler."

"That's not enough," Mike answered without looking up from his phone. "The goal is to get your name back in the press by attaching it to another name of interest. Not some random, unknown person from God knows where."

"Like my mother." John chuckled under his breath at the exasperation in his manager's voice. "I guess my last movie's nomination is not enough to keep me in the press?"

Mike clicked his phone off. His arms crossed in frustration, leaving one finger loose to point at John.

"You know as well as I do that the audience loves speculation and drama. Something new. With your latest film up for Best Picture, this is the perfect opportunity to capitalize on it."

"I thought the audience cared about my intensity on film."

"Ha!" Mike scoffed. "They care about your face. And then who your face is linked with. At least for a moment."

"Now I feel like *I'm* the one in the pageant."

"It's all a popularity contest, man. But! *But.* It allows you to continue to do what you love. And then for the both of us to get paid for *you* doing what you love. You want longevity in your career, right?"

"Yeah, yeah. I guess I see your point."

But that was the question, wasn't it? That was what John's

struggle and frustration amounted to lately. If the love he thought he had for Katrina was so temporary, how did he know if his passion for acting was real anymore? Especially since his lead-actor status had shifted down a few notches over the past few years.

When he gave everything over to God, he'd started looking at each part of his life with new eyes. His acting career included. Everything shifted and he'd let go of his rising addiction in the process. Without that hazy filter, everything stood out in stark clarity with a raw edge that left him restless. But until he heard more or felt a clear direction, he would do his best to excel in the opportunities the Lord had given him. Which meant staying engaged with the people who formed his team and benefited from his success.

"Okay, Mike. Send me your ideas. For the project and the awards-show prop—I mean date." Mike's expression gave him some satisfaction. "But one condition. I will make the final decision of who I attend with. No manipulation or under-the-table deals. Got it?"

If Mike had hair on his face, he would have been stroking it now. That didn't keep him from staring at his client as if every scenario and implication were already running through his mind. This ultimatum may have adjusted a few of Mike's plans, but he always had different ones in his corner.

"Okay, John, agreed. I'll get in touch with my contacts and send some options your way."

*Y*ou didn't have to stop by, sis."

Daniel paused the forkful of spaghetti entering his mouth. Adanne watched sauce drip onto the table, but he ignored the napkin she slid his way.

"I wanted to come after reading the story the paper did." She shrugged, stabbing her fork back into her plate, getting a bit of salad and ranch in the mix. "Plus, this didn't take me long to do." She pasted on a smile.

Her brother squinted at her over his dripping fork. He finished his bite and then laid the utensil down.

Adanne averted her gaze from the knowing look in his brown eyes.

She hated seeing the sympathy in his expression. He and his family were the ones dealing with a crisis, not her. It should be his wife joining him at the table to enjoy this dinner instead of sitting at the hospital, watching their only son struggle.

"Just eat, Daniel. We go through this in some form every time I come over."

"Which is all the time because you're always over."

He laid one arm over the other as he took her in. He'd

been carrying a lot of weight over the past few months. No need for him to add more to his shoulders over her. Somehow this triggered an image of John's face looking at her through the makeup mirror. Still carrying the weariness that initially caught her attention, and the cockiness that had shut her down.

"Dee, I can't help it if I worry about my little sister."

The endearment sparked a smile, reminding her how he'd started calling her Dee as a toddler after hearing her full name for the first time. Adanne Denise Stewart. The nickname stuck and spread to the entire family.

"That's my job, no matter what else is going on in my life. Every time I see you, there are more shadows under your eyes. You can't cover everything with concealer."

She dropped her gaze to her dish, unwilling to let Daniel inspect her face anymore. Or the emotions his poking stirred.

"How is that new MAU job of yours going, by the way?"

Adanne cackled. "You mean MUA? For makeup artist."

"Close enough. You haven't done much of that since *LA*." She winced at his inflection. "And I know those set hours are long. You sure I shouldn't step back in to work at the community center?"

She gave a small shrug. "The center and my job are not for you to worry about right now. Jason is. You're right where you need to be." She waved a hand over the casserole dish. "It was a freezer meal, no big deal."

"You know Aunt Justine is more than willing to help."

"Did she call again?" Her head popped up. The mention of her aunt reminded her of the call she couldn't answer the other day, not intentionally but because she was busy. Which was always. And that meant she somehow never made it around to calling back. Because she forgot. Most of the time.

Daniel's forehead creased. "You say that as if it's crazy for a family member to check in."

Adanne grabbed her glass—she didn't like the taste of spaghetti laced with guilt. There was nothing to be ashamed of. Responsibilities had to be taken care of. She needed to be what her mother could no longer be for the family. Justine had enough on her plate as a school principal in the neighboring city of Huntsville.

Daniel sighed as Adanne put another chunk of spaghetti into her mouth. They sat for a few minutes in silence thick with words still hard to say.

"I don't want you to waste your life stressing about us. After you lost your job in LA, you jumped right into caring for Mama and now looking after us. You barely sleep, because I know all these meals you drop off don't just happen. Driving back and forth, picking up food and supplies, taking over my shifts at the center, handling all the paperwork. You stop by here or the hospital every other day."

"I told y'all I could move in and help even more. That would cut down on driving and bills."

Daniel tilted his head, giving her their family's signature look of irritation. "Adanne, that's not what we want."

Her eyes rounded. She swallowed the lump in her throat that hadn't formed from spaghetti.

"I didn't mean it how you're taking it. Monica and I don't want you to give up your whole life for this. We love you for your heart and willingness. But we want you to be happy too."

Daniel reached out to cover her wrist. Her eyes lingered on his hands. Stress and burden were slowly stealing the strength that used to be evident in corded muscle. Her brother, the star track athlete in high school and college. Leaping over hurdles and any obstacle that tried to keep him from his dreams.

Until Mama got sick. Daniel took over the management of the community center their parents had founded years ago.

Even with the pain of their mother's illness and her eventual absence, Daniel and his wife, Monica, loved working with the kids served by the community center. But that had shifted with their son's leukemia diagnosis.

Her gaze drifted to the walls of her brother's home. Various pictures of his little family were scattered around framed inspirational quotes. Most of the images contained the bright eyes and smile of her now-seven-year-old nephew as a baby and toddler, before disease stole his glow.

What made her happy was the least of Adanne's concern. What would that be anyway without the family and center she loved? The only thing that mattered now was for her brother not to have to work so hard to make ends meet. For her sister-in-law not to have to sleep in a hospital room. All she wanted was for her nephew to get better. And for her family not to lose the community center in the process.

Adanne stood up from the table, startling her brother. Her napkin crumpling in her clenched fists.

"Where you off to now, sis? Not going to stay a little longer to hang out with your big brother?"

"Oh, you know, places to go, people to see." Her singsong tone a sorry attempt at nonchalance. She piled up the serving dishes, tucking the ranch and container of Parmesan under one arm.

"I got it, sis." Daniel stood up and reached out in one fluid motion. She moved out of his reach, depositing the items on the counter before returning for the pot of spaghetti.

"I said I got it."

Adanne paused as her brother's hand put pressure on her arm. A divine echo infused those words, ripples from a different, deeper Source spreading through her chest. *Not now, Lord.*

No need to argue. He didn't need to see the emotions rising. She blew out a shaky breath. "Okay."

Adanne set the dishes down, gave Daniel one last squeeze, and headed out the door. As she walked to her car, she willed herself to keep it together while taking some deep breaths. She was at the breaking point. But she couldn't slow down now. There were things money couldn't buy. She needed to be available for her family. And because of that, she had to take advantage of her opportunity to earn more income doing what she'd been trained to do. If time were on her side, she would search for a more consistent job, but she had to work with what had dropped into her lap until then.

Adanne didn't have the heart to tell Daniel about the center's recent financial problems. If he knew about the letter from the bank, he'd be heartbroken. Losing the Hope Springs Community Center on top of everything else would be a devastating blow.

Enough to make them all crumble.

Her brother and sister-in-law's savings went to hospital bills and keeping their own home afloat. Financial support for the center had gone down over the years as other programs popped up around town, and now Adanne's bank account scraped toward empty. It took a lot to maintain the center. From mortgage payments to utilities and repairs, the aging facility felt more like a burden than a blessing. With the ninety-day ultimatum from the bank, it seemed like there was no lasting solution in sight. Adanne needed to create a larger buffer so that she and her brother didn't lose everything their parents had worked for.

Thankfully, no debt remained on the house her parents had left her. It would be there if everything fell apart. But if she didn't get the money she needed for the missed bank payments and more, she would have to face the hard choice of selling her home. The house remained her one bit of security, but the community center meant so much more. It was the epitome of her parents' legacy. Even after her father died when she and Daniel were young, her mother continued their work, expanding its reach. Not everything had been done perfectly, but she'd made sure that the center fed children, provided resources to strengthen families, and kept its place as a piece of Hope Springs history.

Adanne would do whatever it took to make sure *none* of that got lost. She just needed to push through and finish paying off the debts as quickly as possible.

That was worth anything she had to sacrifice. And it was worth hustling in her off time to make sure her brother's family had the resources and food they needed to breathe a little easier. Leukemia and loans didn't care about her happiness. And for now, she wouldn't either.

The small benefit that she barely let herself acknowledge was that she loved what she was getting to do with this new job. Her heart was to help her brother navigate this season with his son and to serve her parents' legacy well, but using her artistic skills was her passion.

She just had to stir up the enthusiasm she would need to deal with John Pope for the next couple months.

●　●　●　●

Lavender and the sweet smell of coconut lingered in the air as deft, slender hands worked their magic on the edges of John's face. He tried to concentrate on the task before him, but the ministrations of Adanne's brush work with his current wig were relaxing him to a distracting level. He would wear hairpieces every day of his career if the install always felt like this. Doris had been heavy-handed with her applications, doing her work with the familiar boldness of a beloved aunt. She maneuvered with too-long fingernails, patting and prepping with her lacquered weapons held away from his face.

Adanne's movements were just as experienced but gentler. She worked with efficiency and intention, her fingers moving across his face and forehead like a skilled dancer. Subtle chords rumbled from her neck in a hum that tickled his ear.

John swallowed, willing himself to wake up and focus. He still needed to review some lines for today's big scene but got further sidetracked by a text from Mike. The same one who reminded him to focus was usually the reason why he could not. His manager cared about this current role but seemed to put more emphasis on the impact of the awards-show appearance.

When John slid open his phone at the notification, the screen revealed a pdf of a few past co-stars who could attend the awards show with him. Mike was putting a lot of effort into something that shouldn't be that significant.

Why did he care so much?

The last time John had attended a high-profile event coupled up, he and Katrina had argued all the way from the hotel to the red carpet. He'd angrily consumed the provided beverages in the car, his attitude fueled by rejection. It had taken Mike weeks to salvage some of the media relationships John had ruined with his outbursts.

The horrible press from that night had been a wake-up call. Not because they had dragged John through the mud but because it'd all been true. Mike had no desire for that to be repeated.

John tried to believe it was because Mike cared for him as a friend, but who was he kidding? Mike wanted John's name attached to a well-known and well-liked starlet. For the speculation surrounding his love life to be like honey for the flies of the media and press. The more momentum, the more offers that would eventually trickle through. It didn't matter if the bait was tired of being just that and would prefer to watch the upcoming awards show in athletic shorts and a T-shirt. A bottle of ginger soda and thin-crust pizza on the side.

He sighed. This was the life he'd signed up for. But was it still the life for him?

"Got a lot on your mind?" John jerked as Adanne's rich rumble rolled into his thoughts. She chuckled but didn't move a muscle besides the rhythm of her application as she blended the wig edge with his facial makeup.

"You could say that." He closed his eyes, trying to push away the sullen thoughts that would not be helpful in today's scene featuring a happy reunification. Especially since Adanne's words were a sweet surprise. After their tense conversation last week, she had said little. He sensed her attempts to tread lightly, and he had to admit he was trying to stop being so uptight himself. He didn't need any more enemies in his life.

She motioned to his phone with her brush. "That's a long list of beautiful women you have there. In search of a new co-star? Girlfriend?"

John noticed Adanne's grin in the mirror. The genuineness of her smile, the hint of teasing sparkling her eyes.

As an MUA, she was supposed to pay attention to every detail on his call sheet and in her application. But the deep, sparkling orbs focused on him set off a twinge inside, loosening something.

He blinked away from her perusal, turning his attention to the link Mike had sent of potential candidates. He flipped the cell over, a sudden move that jiggled his chair.

"Sorry. Promise I wasn't snooping." Adanne's palms flew up, the brush held securely in the grasp of two fingers. John cringed at the guilt that shuttered her expression. "I noticed it when I leaned down to apply the concealer. Not trying to be all up in your stuff." She shifted around to the other side of John's face. "It's just *all up* in my face. Ha. It's none of my business."

John didn't want to lose the ease in the air that had empowered her to ask him a personal question. A welcome break from her usual distance. Plus, those dimples were too cute not to appear more often. But explaining the reason why he scrolled through a stream of women may be a little challenging.

He gave her a hopefully not-awkward grin. "This is the doing of my manager. Mike. My breakup happened over a year ago, but he's determined to connect me with someone to lift my spirits, so he says. Or at the very least, be a very marketable date for the Oscars."

"Aha."

"So, if you catch me scrolling, I promise I'm not doing anything weird. Just my job. Mike seems to think being connected with the right person will boost my profile."

"That may do the opposite. You *were* one of the most eligible bachelors back in the day."

John raised his brows, and Adanne tsked as she wiped away a smudge. Something about those words from her mouth straightened his spine.

"I'm intrigued that you knew about me. Back in the day." He grinned. "How long ago was that?"

She lifted one shoulder, avoiding his perusal through the mirror.

"I don't remember. My mom used to watch a lot of daytime shows, so we saw you appear at times. Noticed the magazine covers you were on. You were a lot younger, of course." She brushed a few granules of powder off the cape that covered his shoulders. "All that to say, I'm sure your current bachelor status is more of a boost to your career than you think."

"Your mom is my biggest fan, huh?" John couldn't wipe the pleased grin off his face. It felt like winning a small yet significant victory.

When Adanne didn't answer right away, John hoped she had accurately assessed his teasing tone. He looked up at the mirror to see her gaze shift to some far-off corner of the trailer.

"Maybe, at least until—"

"Until what?"

"It doesn't matter." Adanne cleared her throat, turning her attention back to him.

John chuckled carefully, trying not to stretch his face and mess up Adanne's work.

"Don't leave me hanging. I need to know how I fell from her favor."

John grinned, expecting Adanne's expression to ease with his intentionally light tone. But a shadow crossed her face. Her slender fingers fluttered to the delicate chain around her neck and then to her side.

"She didn't feel up to watching those reruns much when she got sick."

"I'm sorry." John fought the longing to ask her more. He sensed her struggle under the surface. But she was his makeup artist, not his friend. He didn't need to mess up this moment by digging too deeply into her personal life. He opted for silence to focus on his lines, even as curiosity stirred in his heart.

Adanne made a few more tweaks and then stepped back to inspect her work, a guarded but satisfied look on her face. She moved behind him to undo his cape, brushing off any remnants of the application with a larger brush.

"All done."

John hopped up, giving himself a quick glance in the mirror. "Thank you for making me look amazingly aged." He offered her a warm, tentative smile. It must have taken a lot for her to share the information about her mom. He wanted her to know that he didn't take that trust for granted. God

43

knew the things he had trouble sharing or even processing. Circumstances had a way of untangling some strings, only to reveal the knots that still lay below the surface.

Adanne's cheeks rose in response. The subtle beginnings of a sweet smile pulled at her gloss-covered lips. Her shallow dimple tugging at those tangled knots of his.

A rap on the trailer door startled him. Bo poked his head around the open door. "ETA?"

Adanne stepped back. "Good to go." She grinned at the AD's thumbs-up and quick retreat out.

"I guess it's time to film my part before I look for someone to play *this* part." John waved the phone at her before stashing it in his back pocket.

Adanne folded the cape and held it to her chest. "Well, if I see someone eligible around here, I'll be sure to send her your way. Maybe . . ." Her words were tentative, as if offering a wobbly olive branch with her coming suggestion. "Maybe what you need is a small-town woman who isn't caught up in all the glitz and glamour."

Adanne carefully placed the cape on the empty chair in front of her, wiping imaginary dust from the seat back with her slender fingers. His breath hitched for the slightest moment at the compassion in her eyes.

"Maybe someone down-to-earth will be less likely to make you fall . . . and break your heart."

5

*M*ike had a knack for moving mountains to get what he wanted. And what he wanted currently was for his favorite client—his words, not John's—to move on with his life and spread said life all over the top entertainment magazines.

He'd somehow managed to book a private plane to fly John to meet with his first choice for a short dinner. John couldn't even call it a choice. He'd mentioned to Mike that he hadn't seen Rachelle Fredericks since his daytime soap days. That was all the encouragement Mike needed to set it up. And lucky for him, Rachelle was passing through nearby Nashville for a long layover.

Mike sure did know how to make the most of every opportunity.

The problem was, John didn't quite know what to make of any of it.

Rachelle's mouth stretched in a wide grin as she turned her attention back to him, the light coming in through the windows of the Fifth and Broadway penthouse unit turning some of her springy curls golden. Although dressed casually, Rachelle still wowed in her fitted jeans, lace-edged top, and boxy blazer. Sitting across from John on a plush love seat, she crossed her legs, revealing a strappy sandal with a three-inch heel. He never understood how some women could wear those types of shoes for a long period of time, especially on an airplane.

Rachelle's brown eyes flashed with amusement. "Why do I feel like I've been pulled in for a job interview?"

"Because that's basically what this is." John grinned back, settling deeper into the textured sofa that served as a centerpiece to this swanky downtown apartment. Who knew what executive owned this piece of property? Stained concrete walls lined the foyer and opened into a well-lit living room with floor-to-ceiling windows lining two sides of the apartment. It seemed to be staged specifically for these types of meetings, each area designed to cultivate connection. He was thankful Mike had used *some* discretion. Instead of booking them a restaurant reservation, he'd opted for this flat with catering delivered. John didn't need headlines triggered before he was ready.

Rachelle pursed plump lips, a single beauty mark standing out against her warm skin tone. As stunning now as she was when they got started in the industry. Each of their careers had benefited from the popularity of that long-running daytime show kept alive in syndication. One of the storylines even featured a teenage romance between the two of them. Until she was killed off—or in other words, renegotiated her contract after a movie offer. It had been a popular plot at the time and, if her résumé was any indication, a smart move on her part.

"I was surprised at the invitation. But I thought it would be good to stop by and catch up for a moment." Rachelle leaned forward to assess the food offerings before them.

A lavish antipasto platter had been delivered, with sparkling citrus water on the side. John tamped down his craving for something else as he reached for a glass. Rachelle picked up one of the bone china dishes, selecting a few plump marinated olives, a slice of prosciutto, and a couple slivers of roasted tomato. John followed suit, eyeing the platter but settling on some focaccia and olive tapenade first. If he was going to have to brave these interview-ish dates, he would reward himself with bread.

"It's been a while." John swallowed a bite, taking a moment to glance out the window that showcased an impressive view of Nashville's downtown and surrounding neighborhoods. It had been years since he'd been in Tennessee's capital. Despite being born in central Italy, his mother had grown up in Music City long before it became the trendy spot with a steadily increasing population.

He turned back to his guest—if that's what he could call her.

"Whatever it's worth, thank you for agreeing to meet me like this. Not my usual preference."

Rachelle chuckled. "But usual for Mike."

"Exactly."

This didn't have to be awkward, did it? John tilted his head. Maybe that plot from over a decade ago could continue in real life, more or less? Rachelle had always been easy to be around. She resisted public drama, keeping her private life away from public scrutiny for most of her career. But even as he considered the potential for Rachelle to be the right fit, he had a feeling that she didn't feel the same. Her face remained friendly, but her eyes kept darting to the watch on her wrist. And then to her phone.

John shifted in his seat. "How've you been? Your career is going well. On season—what is it now—of your medical drama?"

Rachelle took a sip of sparkling water. "Season six. Can you believe it? Who knew breaking my daytime contract for that movie would end up this way? Best move I ever made."

She set down her glass gingerly, tapered nails clinking against the side. "What about you? Several films under your belt. Things look to be good for the most part. Maybe a bit bumpy here and there." Her eyes flashed with knowing.

John sighed. "Yeah, it's been a ride, but the road is getting smoother. Started photography on a project set in Alabama."

"Sounds . . . enchanting."

John crossed his arms. Rachelle's disdain made him uneasy. It wasn't unlike his own initial thoughts when he'd found out about his location. But in the few weeks he'd been on the ground there, he'd realized his perspectives had not been so accurate. The town of Hope Springs was small, just like any of the other towns filling the landscape around Nashville, but it had its share of charm. And compelling people.

"It hasn't been so bad. It's a welcome break. I've never had a film schedule so relaxed. It's given me a little time to breathe as I work."

Rachelle nodded and then checked her watch again. "Listen, about *this*." She waved between the two of them. "What exactly is our purpose here anyway? I'm glad to catch up, but I also would not mind getting in a little shopping before my next leg."

"Yes, that." John pushed his plate away, his appetite slipping. "Did Mike fill you or your manager in on what he's trying to do?"

"Not really. For all she and I knew, it was a movie idea— maybe a collaboration? Although I must say I am not interested in taking on something new now, but I was curious. John Pope stepping out of the shadows again."

John cringed, shifting his legs. No need to draw this out any longer. "Mike wants to set us up on a few dates, nothing serious, just like what we're doing now. Then maybe we can accompany each other to the awards show in March."

With every word he said, John felt his pride wisping away. He shouldn't have to beg anyone to be with him, no matter the setting or the place. Mike's suggestions and moves were always strategic. There was a reason why he placed Rachelle on the list, but from what John could see mirrored back to him, she wasn't ready to engage. And he hated the look of almost pity on her face.

"Not interested in this pitch either, I gather."

Rachelle plucked another olive from the platter, managing to smile demurely and chew at the same time. "You don't look like you are that eager for any of it. But the fact is that although I may appear unconnected, I've been dating someone for years."

That *was* a shock . . . and a relief. "You always did like your private life kept that way. I don't know how you managed to keep yourself out of public scrutiny for so long."

Rachelle grinned. "It's an art. But also, a necessity. I don't have the capacity to deal with so much drama. It's enjoyable when it's centered on other people, but I have little patience for it in my own life. I've got to take care of my mental health."

John stretched his right arm across the back of the sofa, collecting his thoughts as his eyes skimmed over the Nashville skyline. If only he could be so lucky.

"Why did you agree to meet me, then? To get an up-close and personal look at my own drama?"

Try as he may, he couldn't quite keep the bitter edge from his voice.

Rachelle's mouth tipped, her gaze more engaged than it was seconds ago. For the briefest moment, he saw solidarity there. Maybe what ailed him now was similar to what kept her from sharing the inner workings of her life with the public. After a moment, she lifted her shoulders. "I was curious with a little time to kill. And some favorite shops are close by."

"You chose to kill that time with me."

Rachelle smirked, leaning forward to place a hand on his arm. "John. Don't underestimate yourself. I may not want to be your date, but I've known you to be a dear castmate, even a friend. And those are difficult to come by these days."

John exhaled, his disappointment taken over by appreciation. "They sure are."

• • • •

"Okay, kids, y'all come gather 'round the table!"

Adanne's voice echoed across the gym where balls stopped dribbling and Hula-Hoops dropped with a clatter. She had Monday afternoon off after a change in the filming schedule and a trip out of town for John freed it up. Just in time for one of the center volunteers to call in sick. There were no real plans, just a container of construction paper, scissors, and glue, and then a Bible story video at the end.

At her call, ten pairs of feet made their way over, the children's eyes round with curiosity. It'd been a while since Miss Dee had taken the helm of their after-school class. And brought homemade chocolate chip muffins. This group held a special place in her heart because it was the one her nephew would be in if he wasn't undergoing treatment at the hospital.

Sheets of construction paper were spread across the table, and Adanne breathed a sigh of relief that there were enough scissors for each child to have their own. Nothing broke momentum like a child waiting impatiently for their chance to cut paper to bits.

"What we making, Miss Dee?" The raspy voice of Vanessa piped up, her thick, dark waves reaching halfway down her back. She had a face of cherubic innocence, but Adanne already knew a wild streak ran through her.

Next to her, blond-headed Pete bounced up and down on his squeaky sneakers. The light that used to flash from the soles wore down before his feet outgrew the shoes.

"How about we take a vote to decide. I'll write down three choices and we'll pick."

Considering she negotiated with second graders, this plan could backfire, but she trudged ahead, nonetheless.

She pulled out a sheet of magenta paper, grabbed a dark-green marker, and wrote down the numbers one, two, and three. Then she planted her hands on the tabletop, her gaze roaming around the circle.

Their faces all so different yet familiar. Their energy all at once amusing and a trigger for the bittersweet.

Jason should be here. He *wanted* to be here. But those weren't the words that needed to come out of her mouth at this moment. Because as much as she wished she could control what he experienced, she currently stood surrounded by the faces of children who carried their own burdens.

She forced a grin. "Okay, what will it be first?"

"Paper airplanes."

"Rocket ship."

"A book."

"A house."

"A boat that can go on the water!"

Adanne had to chuckle at that one as she wrote with large strokes. Never mind that this was way more than three, but at least all their suggestions were taking up some of the time she needed to kill.

"I think we're good now, we—"

"I know." The corner of Adanne's sleeve pulled down. She turned to see whose fingers were attached to it. Little Nia Carter looked up shyly, appearing surprised at the sound of her own voice.

Adanne leaned close, squashing the urge to wrap this little

bit in her arms. "What do *you* think?" She almost whispered, not wanting the timid girl to retract the words that had taken all her effort to share.

Nia glanced around the table then down, her lashes lying against her plump cheek.

"We should make a card. For Jason."

Adanne gulped, the marker paused over the paper. Her thoughts shifted to the article that had popped up in the town's paper over the weekend. A special interview with families from the children's wing of the hospital. An article that featured the words of her nephew. A little boy whose biggest wish was to be here with his friends. The rumble of the kids silenced for a beat, the break seeming to last for an eternity, as each child heard and remembered. Then time sped up with a chorus of voices.

"Yes!"

"Yeah!"

"Let's do it!"

"I can draw him a boat!"

Adanne put down her writing utensil. The decision was unanimous. She laid a gentle hand on Nia's shoulder. "That is a *great* idea."

Her gaze landed on each child. "A perfect idea. We can make him the best, biggest card he's ever seen and draw him all our favorite things."

The kids high-fived and scurried around, gathering their colors and scraps of paper. She could not imagine a more worthy project to create.

Two hours later, her Ford traveled the too-familiar way to the hospital in nearby Huntsville. Clutching the thick piece of construction paper to her side, she walked through the parking garage, following the route that had become so familiar to her. When she made it past the front desk, lifting her hand in greeting to a nurse she recognized, she moved quietly down the hall. She slipped on a mask, her eyes drifting over the bright colors on the walls. The lively artwork stood out against the severity of the diseases on this floor.

Although it wasn't quiet hour yet, she walked with light steps to her nephew's room. She gently rapped with her fingers before she stepped through the cracked-open door.

Adanne cringed. The shaft of hall light caused her sister-in-law to adjust in her seat within the darkened room.

"Hey. Sorry, did I wake you?"

Monica wiped her face with the back of her hand, ignoring the tissue wadded up in the other. "Oh, hey, I didn't know you were coming."

Adanne stepped in, closing the door carefully behind her. "Me either, but I thought I would make a special delivery of something the kids made today."

Monica used the armrests to stand up. She reached out to grab the giant card Adanne held out to her. "Oh Dee, he'll love it. I'll be sure to give it to him when he wakes up."

Adanne glanced at the still form of her nephew. "They were so excited to make it and will be happy to hear what he thinks."

Monica wiped under her nose, her eyes swollen with tears and exhaustion. She leaned over the bed to run her slender hand along the top of her son's thinning hair.

"Curls almost gone," she said more to herself than to Adanne. "Should have cut them off while I had the chance." She sighed.

"But the chemo is almost over, right? He should go home soon?"

"That was the hope, but there is something more. Some reactions they need to monitor. If things don't level out, he'll be in here much longer than he realizes. Than we want." Monica released a shaky breath. "Sorry. You just brought the sweetest gift. Thank you."

"Always my pleasure. And you don't have anything to apologize for." Adanne stepped back to leave but then placed a hand on Monica's shoulder.

"Do you need anything? I could sit with him if you want to take a quick break."

Monica gazed at her boy then glanced back at Adanne in gratitude. "What would we do without you? Yes. Yes, I think I'll get a coffee. One not hospital made. Do you mind?"

"Never. Take your time. Jason is gonna love sleeping in the presence of his Auntie Dee."

Monica chuckled. "Y'all stay out of trouble." She leaned to give Adanne a quick hug. "Thank you, sis."

Adanne blinked at her sister-in-law's retreating form. She shifted the card on the table already filled with other gifts and cards, positioning it so that Jason would see it as soon as he woke up. She leaned over the bed to get a good look at his face. Sleeping in peace, even with the equipment monitoring his vitals and the port in place to eradicate the enemy in his body.

"But no one can do it better than you, Jesus. Please."

Even that plea felt empty. It wasn't that long ago that she knelt next to a hospital bed, praying and pleading that the Lord would send healing. Or, at least, more time.

No. Not that bitter root again. But perhaps if she dealt with it, her doubtful appeals would be more effective for the little ray of sunshine lying in this bed. Maybe there would be more belief—more hope—fueling her prayers, and less fear clogging up the line.

She believed God could, but would he? *Would he?* He was good, that had been drilled in her since before she was born, said to her in a myriad of ways from the park bench to the church pew. But was he safe? Could she count on God to keep her covered? Would he keep her family well, even when those wishes hadn't kept her parents close, protected? Would he keep the community center from crumbling, her parents' legacy from being demolished?

Or was she destined to scrape for what couldn't be grasped? A promise that stayed ever out of reach. Things hoped for but never held, not fully.

Ugh, she didn't want to fill this room with those thoughts, but this triggered them in her. Assaulting her with doubt.

Her nephew deserved better than that.

So she did what would drown out her thoughts and fill the room with the hope she could barely feel. She perched on the end of the bed, grasping the strand around her neck. As she opened her mouth, she began to release the softest melody. "Amazing grace . . ."

6

*L*aughter and music filtered from the propped-open door of the makeup trailer as Adanne approached. The last Wednesday morning of January greeted their North Alabama town with higher temps, promising an unusually warm day. Spring was on its way. Slowly but surely.

Apparently some of the crew felt the shift too because everyone seemed to be cheerier than usual. Ronald at the front gate responded with a surprising smile when Adanne asked how he was doing. Maybe the honey-infused ointment she'd dropped off for him last week had helped smooth out his rough edges.

"Stepping up." Her words drifted into a chuckle. At the makeup station next to hers sat one of the supporting cast, a delightful teenage actress named Charlie. Trina, her makeup artist, stood behind, grinning into her phone.

"What y'all doing?" Adanne set her bags on the floor in front of her chair, no hurry to put her things away since John's call time wasn't until later. Until then, she'd help Trina with Charlie's application. But that seemed far from their minds at the moment.

Adanne grinned at the familiar melody that filtered

through the air. "Ooh, I remember this song." She crossed her arms, high school fun triggered by the upbeat tune.

Trina looked up, bobbing her head, oversized glasses in danger of sliding off her nose. "I thought you would. Been telling Charlie here that music these days doesn't compare to what we had in the nineties and early two thousands."

Charlie put a manicured hand up. "I'm still not convinced. Some of it sounds so dramatic." She scrolled and then pressed play on a song that elicited a groan from the two older women.

Trina stood with mouth agape and hand on hip, her lilac-hued layers swinging. "Nope. What we had was real singing, girl, without all that auto-tuning stuff."

"Or all the angst." Adanne grinned at Charlie's rolled eyes and stepped closer, peering at Trina's playlist. "Ooh, I love this one. This may convince her." Trina pressed play, drowning out Charlie's dour selection with a soulful rhythm.

She grabbed a curling iron, using it as a microphone as she shimmied from behind the giggling actress. "Don't hide your eyes now. You need to see what we were working with back then." She tossed a hairbrush to Adanne, who clasped it between her hands.

"Oh no, no, no, don't pull me into this."

"Oh yes, yes. We need to show this girl why her playlist does not stand up to our mixtapes."

Adanne hesitated, glancing back at the door. But this was Hope Springs, not Hollywood. She needed to loosen up. The set already felt so much calmer than her last experience. She chuckled in surrender. If Trina and Charlie felt comfortable enough to delay the application time, she would join right in—for a moment.

Because it had been a moment since she'd let herself have times like this.

She and Trina held their pseudo microphones to their

mouths, leaning their shoulders together as they belted out the song. Adanne didn't ease her voice into her sweet spot, instead she sang like they were at a karaoke joint. Their knees bounced in time, the vocal runs they remembered from past listens performed hilariously.

The song was a favorite, and from what she could recall, Daddy had loved it too. She remembered how he'd dip and spin, making Mama laugh. Then Adanne would join him, moving her hands to the high notes as if she could reach them.

As the music and memories took over, Adanne extended her hand, breaking off to face both Charlie and Trina, shaking her shoulders in time to the beat. Maybe if she could stretch far enough, even now, she'd feel her father near her, more tangible than a memory, wrapped up in the joy of the song.

She closed her eyes, swaying to the instrumentals, leaning forward to sing the last refrain. As she opened her eyes, the lyrics poured out of her mouth, more cackle than croon.

Trina stopped singing and Charlie's twinkling blue eyes looked beyond her. Barely suppressed humor teemed on both of their faces. Her voice slowed to a stop. "What?"

Adanne's stomach clenched with dread as she turned around too quickly, panting from her movements. She choked on whatever lyrics remained. John stood in the doorway, arms crossed over his chest, with an annoying smirk on his face.

"No, please, don't stop." His lips curved into a boyish grin, eyes flashing with amusement. "You were just getting to the good part."

"What—why are you here so early?" Adanne stammered, dropping the hairbrush on the makeup chair beside her.

"Am I not allowed to check on my favorite makeup artist?"

She rolled her eyes as the women behind her burst, their

laughs louder than the next song on the playlist. "I thought that was Doris."

"True."

Dread squeezed her chest, startling her almost more than his sudden appearance. "I would never have done all that if I knew you were here."

John tipped his head to the side, mock disappointment on his tan face. "Now, that is a shame. I think I like you even more like this."

A clatter came from behind Adanne. She turned to see Trina scramble with her supplies. John's co-star looked extra fascinated by her nail beds.

Just like that, she'd forgotten they were there.

"Okay, Charlie, time to work. Adanne, I'll need your help in just a moment." Their light snickers continued as Adanne turned back to face the man who flustered her around every corner.

John stepped in further, his playful expression defusing her frustration. But it did nothing to ease her embarrassment. Or the warmth that spread up her neck and into her cheeks as he looked down at her. "That *was* really entertaining. I should come in early more often."

"Ugh. Why me?" She groaned and stepped to the side but forgot about her bags. Her sneaker caught on her tote handle, catapulting her to what was sure to be another level of humiliation.

Before she could brace herself from crashing against the trailer floor, strong hands grasped her forearms, bending down to the level where she stumbled. John looked her over with concern, their noses almost touching. His eyes flickered to her lips and then back up again. No, surely she'd imagined that.

"You good?" John whispered, with a now mischievous glint in his eye, at the same time Trina hollered, "Girl, you okay?"

John held her gaze for a moment longer, not letting go of her arms until she was standing, steady.

"I've been better," she responded truthfully. Because she was most certainly not okay.

• • • •

After a few more hours of filming, John sighed with relief when the director called cut. Most of the crew had another hour or so to clean up. But all he could think about was eating, preferably something not catered in. It didn't help that some of the crew mentioned a famous barbecue spot a few exits down from their location. Mouths watering, everyone finished their tasks quicker than usual, ready to break free of the makeshift town for some modern pursuits.

"Give me a sec!" John called out to the group waiting to leave.

Adanne met him at the door of the makeup trailer as he walked up the stairs. "Oh, sorry, I just cleaned up. Did you need something?"

He didn't miss the way her eyes roamed his face, making sure.

"Just need to grab my hat."

He made a move to step aside and let her pass, but then shifted back. Her gaze questioned, eyes turning amber in the glow of the outside lights. Her soft twists were pulled up into a loose bun at the top of her head, high cheekbones on display.

John swallowed, something about the way she stood there expectantly putting pressure on him to say something coherent. It was different from Rachelle's persona, which oozed confidence built on the back of her celebrity status. Adanne carried herself in a way that some would call intimidating. Poised with undeniable grit. John wasn't easily put off by that kind of personality, but after the way they'd started off—and catching her in that highly entertaining moment earlier today—it wouldn't hurt him to tread carefully.

"I just want to make sure you're okay after this morning. I hope you weren't too embarrassed."

Adanne lifted one side of her lips, revealing a shallow dimple. "It's okay, no more karaoke for me. But I'm glad it brought you some joy."

Her long black lashes grazed her cheeks as she looked down and adjusted her bag strap. He didn't think she had a shy bone in her body, but here she stood shifting with discomfort at his words. Maybe it was because for the second time in the same number of weeks, she'd unintentionally found herself in his arms.

He swallowed, pushing down the swell in his chest.

"Well, hope you have a good night. I'll see you all tomorrow." Adanne shifted to step down past him, leaving her comforting scent of lavender and coconut in her wake.

The air suddenly felt colder without her presence. "W-wait." John grabbed his hat from the hook next to the door, banged it shut, and jogged a couple of steps to catch up to her. "You're leaving a little later than usual. Got some plans for dinner?"

Adanne slanted a look at him. "You could say that."

"That doesn't sound too convincing. A lot of us are grabbing barbecue. At a place called The Rib Shack."

"Hmm." Adanne grinned. "That place *is* good. One of my favorite spots."

"Then why don't you join us? A whole section is reserved."

Adanne stopped at the entrance to crew parking. "Thank you for the invite, but I'm not sure that's for me." She leaned to the side to look past him, taking in the group that gathered.

"Of course it is. You are as much a part of the crew as they are. You were even the co-star for twenty minutes when you blocked that scene with me." John grinned. "That counts for something."

Adanne chuckled and pulled her coat tighter. After fishing for her keys, she gave him an amused smile.

"Maybe so. But . . . I think I should pass." She pulled her tote strap to her neck again. "Thank you again for the invite. And for today. I think."

John decided right then that he really liked her slight smirk, the dimple that showed up when her lips twisted in that certain way. It gave her lovely face a more carefree expression. "It was fun. While it lasted."

Her hand lifted in a small wave before she turned from him to walk toward the parking lot, a solitary figure illuminated by a few tall spotlights. John gazed after her for a few seconds and then slipped his hat on as he jogged to the hungry crew.

● ● ● ●

Adanne scrubbed at a stain that wouldn't come off a plastic table in the main hall of the community center. Almost laughable since there was so much that needed to be done. The faded periwinkle paint needed patching. The gym floor that served as basketball court, activity space, and gathering place for meals was in dire need of resurfacing and new finish. Even these white plastic folding tables needed to be retired, but they had to keep on standing with no funds for replacements coming any time soon.

They weren't the only ones that needed a break.

Adanne tossed the sponge on the table and sat back on the bench behind her. Why in the world was she spending this night cleaning stains and not eating smoked brisket with the rest of the crew?

The welcoming look in John's eyes as he walked her out still surprised her.

Yeah. She had a lot of reasons why she didn't take him up on the offer. The main one floated to the top of her thoughts, lingering like the scent of citrus and sandalwood.

She should've skipped out on the impromptu jam session. Then she wouldn't have made a fool of herself in front of John. She was in his face and hair multiple times a week. But never had she expected him to hold her arms so tenderly, to show genuine care—and amusement—in his expression.

Too bad she couldn't scrub the memories away like this dried-up stain. Or the way her skin was left tingling after he finally let her go, making sure she was good. Ha, not when he was so close! The careful and respectful way he'd handled her disconcerted her more than if he'd done something inappropriate. It didn't fit what she assumed about him. The actor who hadn't seemed to care how his actions affected the livelihood of others, like her.

Adanne placed both hands on the table and dropped her head, her unbound twists drifting over her shoulder, reaching toward the floor. She loved this place, was thankful for the job, but . . .

Her eyes roamed around the facility her parents loved.

Adanne released a tight chuckle, shaking her strands from side to side. *What good did it really do, Lord? Did Mama do all this to suffer in the end and not see the fruit of her work?* Surely it wasn't for her daughter to refuse every bit of life she had to just run this place into the ground.

She needed help. But what did that look like with a brother going through so much with his son? Or extended family who had their own lives and careers? Who really cared if the Hope Springs Community Center bit the dust? Adanne sighed, her aching hands pushing her away from the table.

It was time to call it a night. Thinking like this would do her no good. The stains would be here tomorrow. But her

chances of experiencing life outside these walls were slipping away. Time to take her brother's advice more to heart
and prove it with actions to back it up. But preferably not
of the singing variety. She grinned to herself. "Okay, Lord,
next time I won't say no."

7

*J*ohn eased himself onto the bleachers set up against the
walls of the workout facility. His role had him acting as
both a twenty-five- and a sixty-year-old man, and both
characters needed to be in shape. Thankfully, today's later
call time meant he hadn't had to be here at the crack of dawn.

The trainer slapped him on the shoulder. "See you in two
days." He handed him his phone and a cold bottle of water.
"Have a good weekend but lay off the snacking."

John waved his towel in goodbye and took a long swig
of the crisp glacial water imported from Iceland. After polishing it off he leaned forward to check his cell for missed
messages.

The screen was full of notifications, the majority from
Mike and one from his mom.

MAMMA
Would love to come visit. Call later.

He grinned. It would be fun to have his mother visit soon.
Dating Katrina and intense film schedules had all but done
away with family time. Instead of holidays with them, he'd
whisked his girlfriend and their mutual friends off on exotic

getaways. All in the name of rest and relaxation but returning emptier than he'd left.

The longing for home hit with unexpected force. He could smell his mom's kitchen, tickling his senses with homemade lasagna, gnocchi, and zeppole. She fostered in him a deep appreciation for food. Made even more fun when his sister tried to fight him for the first bite.

John headed for the showers. His relationship with Katrina was over. He could honestly say he was thankful, even if her quick bounce back still felt like a shock. As if those years didn't matter. But letting go gave him the ability to focus on reviving his career and restoring his relationship with family. Whatever came after that, he would try not to worry about.

John slung his gym bag over his shoulder. After a shower and fresh clothes, he looked forward to a less intense day at set to review some scenes and then maybe catching a local event. The crew had been discussing some of the eclectic nightlife of Hope Springs and the surrounding area. The other leads were more interested in heading out of town to bigger cities for the weekend. But he couldn't afford to get caught on that slippery slope.

Nora. I'll call Nora. His assistant stayed up-to-date on his filming locations. Ah, but he'd given her the day off. His phone buzzed as soon as he stepped out of the locker room.

"Hey, you done yet?" Mike's tone was breezy. Something was coming.

"Wouldn't be answering if I wasn't."

"Great. First, have you given more thought to my suggestion?"

"You mean the unsettling task of prematurely opening myself up to heartbreak?"

Mike grunted. "You are in the right industry, my friend. All melancholy and drama. I'll get to that later, but no, the other."

John pushed open the doors of the athletic center to find

his hired car waiting. He pulled on his sunglasses and strode toward the black Mercedes.

"Refresh my memory, Mike, it's too full of melancholy and drama to think straight."

"The service project. Something potentially high profile. Well, let's face it, for that small town, the first-grade spelling bee would probably count as front-page news."

John rolled his eyes, giving a quick wave to his driver as he got into the car.

"I admit I haven't put too much thought into it. I can talk to Nora when I get a chance, but if you catch wind of something, let me know. You know better than me how to create the best publicity opportunity."

"Okay, fair. Next. Nora said you were free tonight."

"Okay . . ." John smelled trouble.

"I've got something lined up for you."

"That doesn't sound very appealing."

"Oh, believe me, *she* is."

"Mike. I beg you. Don't subject me to this again. It was good to catch up with Rachelle, I'll give you that. But we were already acquaintances, and it was still awkward. No one else—much less me—needs to be subjected to this. Finding a plus-one for the awards is not that serious."

"Okay, cross her off the list. But don't give up so soon."

"Mike." John's patience was wearing thin. He needed to run back to his trailer for a quick nap, not to plot out the next phase of Mike's matchmaking plan.

"Laney Price is on hiatus from her show, the one filming four hours away in Atlanta." Mike went on as if John hadn't said his name with exasperation. "I got to talking with her agent and get this—she's also recently single. With her career blossoming, she'd be a great match."

John hated feeling like a pawn in this publicity game. "I've heard of her, but again, not interested."

"Come on, John, the timing is perfect. She can fly over and be there this afternoon. With the rental car getting dropped off to set today, you could even pick her up from the airport. Have dinner, a little walk, and that's it. No pictures or paparazzi, I promise. Just a relaxing night with two young professionals."

At thirty-five, John didn't feel that young. Honestly, he would be touched by Mike looking out for his relational status if it wasn't attached to a possible uptick in roles and offers, and therefore a bigger cut of his salary.

"I can't, Mike. Sorry. Maybe another time. And remember, the deal is I have the final say."

Suddenly a more appealing thought bloomed in his head. And with it, snatches of a song wafting from a certain makeup trailer. "I actually have something that Nora didn't know about."

"Wait. What are you doing that we don't know?"

"Bye, Mike. I'm headed to set."

"No, don't hang up, I—"

"Oh, and thanks for the rental car."

John settled back with a smile on his face. It may not work, but he would give it a try. And maybe by the end of the day he could get at least one thing crossed off his list.

• • • •

Adanne hummed through her end-of-day routine, the rhythm instinctual and soothing. The muted chords echoed against the walls of the empty trailer bathroom. If only problems could be sorted, scrubbed, and rinsed away as easily as pigment from the bristles of her makeup brushes. Or tossed aside as quickly as the disposable sponges.

With the long day almost over, she looked forward to an evening of nothingness before running an errand for the community center later that night. Granted, it *was* Friday, so she should be doing something. At least that's what her cousins would tell her. But after finishing up on set, the only thing she would worry about before nine would be finding something to eat.

She continued to rinse and lay out brushes as the sounds of the door opening and closing filtered in.

The MUAs and hairstylists had been in and out all afternoon, cleaning up in preparation as sets shifted around. It was a rare five-day hold for many of the cast and crew. During the space between today's wrap and the next call time, several of the actors, including John, would fly back to their home bases for meetings. Along with studying looks for upcoming scenes, Adanne planned to spend those days researching other job openings within the surrounding area. Even though she couldn't wrap her mind around leaving the people she loved. She only hoped that if it came to that, she could find someone to replace her at the center. Maybe Daniel would get the miracle his family deserved and she could support from afar. Again.

"Because I already told you this morning." John's voice echoed through the almost empty trailer.

What is he doing here? Adanne peeked out the bathroom door to see John sitting in the chair at her station. There were couches along the wall and, of course, his own trailer to go to. And another assistant artist had cleaned him up an hour ago.

But there he was, wearing jeans, a T-shirt, and a leather jacket. His wavy, dark hair grazing the nape of his neck. John appeared to be relaxed, but the tight smile he gave toward the phone said otherwise.

"You're more than welcome to run my career, dude, but not my love life."

Whoops. Adanne spun toward the sink before she overheard too much. She miscalculated her location and smacked her elbow against the doorframe. A fistful of brushes fell to the ground with a clatter. She bit her lip against the sharp volt from her funny bone. Why did she have to be so clumsy at *this* moment? She didn't want it to look like she had been spying on John or admiring how he looked sitting in her chair. She envied his nonchalance and that the biggest problem he seemed to have to deal with was his too-pushy manager.

As Adanne crouched to clean up the tools, another hand met hers on the tiled floor. She looked up into John's green eyes, the color of his shirt deepening his irises even more. She saw the rim of golden brown and the faint scar that ran alongside his right eyebrow. She noticed the lingering smudge of makeup at his hairline that had somehow survived the removal process.

What she *refused* to focus on was the spark that popped as their fingertips met over the same brush.

John's eyes rounded in surprise, even as he continued to hold the phone to his ear. She could hear the voice of his manager on the other end.

John blinked, handed her the brush she'd promptly recoiled from, and then held his pointer finger up, walking backwards to the other side of the trailer. He held her gaze until he seemed confident she understood what he inferred.

She didn't know if she was more baffled by him asking her to wait or—Lord help—the ripple that went through her middle. Her senses acted as if she didn't make constant contact with his skin almost every day.

"I've got other plans, Mike," she heard him say. Then he paused before adding, "I said I was working on it, and I am."

Adanne wrapped up her supplies in a clean towel, her cheeks puffing out with the breath she didn't know she'd been holding in. She placed her belongings in her tote bag and grabbed her jacket from a hook outside the bathroom door. But she still had to walk toward John to retrieve the keys locked in the drawer at her station.

She pulled her long braid carefully over her shoulder to avoid snagging the thin hoops that swayed from her ears. Her stomach rumbled from lack of attention during a busy lunchtime. She'd fix that with a drive-through. Maybe a chicken sandwich.

John remained in the makeup chair, scrolling through his phone.

Adanne slid past him to unlock her drawer. When she grabbed her keys and clicked it closed again, she turned around to see him looking at her with surprising intensity.

"Yes?" She crossed her arms, keys dangling from her achy fingers.

John glanced at her key chain, his lips spread into a playful grin. "Lots of keys there. Do you use all of those?"

Adanne's smirk shifted to the shadow of a scowl. "Yes, I do."

He took in her expression and tilted his head, peering down at her hands again. "For an MUA, your nails are pretty plain."

Adanne placed a hand on her hip. "Better to not scratch you with, my dear."

John's laugh burst out, his eyes crinkling up in pleasant lines. "Ah, there's that fire."

A strange one, this man. "Was there something you needed, Mr. Pope?"

The amusement resounding in his chest puzzled her even more. "I can't tell if you are teasing me or judging me."

"Neither."

Adanne felt the drop in his pitch, the husky tone settling in her toes. He leaned forward, a gleam in his squinted eyes. "Doris had these long, killer nails that she changed out each week. I don't know how I survived all these years in her chair

71

unscathed, or unclawed. But I didn't have you wait to inter-
rogate you. Even though it's quite fun."

He stood up, his above-average height a nice match for
Adanne's frame. Other kids called her "thick" growing up,
whatever that meant, but over the years her form had settled
into lean curves. Legs that ran and hustled all over town.
Arms that lifted and carried, including a mother who had almost been too gone from late-stage kidney disease to care for.

She instinctively stepped back. Pushing the pain of that
memory behind the fire John seemed determined to stoke.

As if sensing the shift, he reached out his hand. But she
was in no danger of her feet stumbling this time. Just at risk
of falling into trouble of a different sort. In another place or
time, maybe she would've grabbed his hand to steady herself.
Wrap herself in his embrace, draw strength from his nearness. But she couldn't depend on anyone else for stability,
much less the man before her.

"I'm sorry, Adanne, I hope I didn't offend you." John put
his palms out. "That seems to come easy to me. But what
doesn't come so well is dodging the efforts of my manager.
You remember that matchmaking he's trying to do?"

Adanne nodded slowly, willing her shoulders to relax.

"He wanted to set up a date with a fellow actress filming
in Georgia. But when I saw you . . ." He smiled, the boyish
curve of his lips lighting up his eyes again. "I thought maybe
you would want to help frustrate him with me. Cut class like
we're in high school. Something that came a little too easily to me, although you seem like the type who never even
considered the thought."

Adanne gripped her keys, ignoring the press of metal into
her palm. "I don't understand."

"What I'm trying to say quite pathetically is, would you do
me a favor and show me around this town you call home?"
John ran his hand over his hair, which seemed more curly

than wavy at the moment but remained unruly, wasting his efforts. "I don't want more tabloid headlines. Going out with this actress would stir that up."

He looked at her with chagrin. "I've had enough of that for a while. I just want a few hours away from the fishbowl. I thought you would be the best person to help. And maybe you could give me some insight into ways I can help in the community while I'm here in town. Perhaps over dinner? If you are hungry."

Adanne's stomach had the audacity to respond in confirmation. She grimaced and placed her hand there to settle it.

John grinned. "I see someone agrees. I was just scrolling through my phone and saw this chicken place that looks good. Have you been there?" He turned the phone toward her. Of course it would be the very place she was about to head to.

Her hesitance melted. Probably in those flickers of heat taking up residence in her belly. Tonight she would let go, just a little, and take the hand that was being offered to her.

"Okay, then." She averted her gaze from the growing warmth in his eyes, shook the keys in her hand, and headed toward the door. With a slight lift of her lips, she looked back over her shoulder. "Follow me."

8

"Why are you laughing?" John's breath fanning on Adanne's neck was just about enough to dry up the amusement that bubbled in her as they stood in line.

She shifted, wiggling the tremors from her fingers. "It just feels strange that someone like you would stand in a fast-food line."

"I like chicken." John shrugged as if this was a normal part of his routine. As if he wasn't the most magnetic person in the room. He may have more of a supporting role in this film, but he couldn't shed his charisma so easily.

After they ordered, Adanne hunted for a less conspicuous table in the corner. She offered a smile or two to faces she knew, already regretting her choice to come out when several eyes widened as they focused on who she was with.

"Friendly residents you've got in Hope Springs." John flashed a smile to a couple two tables down and then slid into the booth across from her.

"You could say that." She organized her tray, unwrapping and setting every food item just the way she liked it, fork and knife at the ready, so she didn't look like an idiot stuffing her face in front of him.

John simply grinned into his sandwich, its wrapper peeled away and folded over his hands. "This looks so good." Before he took a bite, he sat up straight and set down his food.

"Wait, I should pray. Do you, uh—"

"Bless my food?" Adanne offered. She chuckled. "Yes, of course."

"Great, may I?"

Adanne felt incredulity rise again. They stumbled through such formality without a chair or makeup desk to turn to. She gestured for him to start. After removing his hat and tinted glasses, he reached out his hand but then retracted it as she intertwined hers in a death grip.

After whispering a mumbled prayer, he opened his eyes to her unbroken stare.

If he was surprised at her lack of eye closure during his prayer, he didn't mention it, just blinked and glanced around the room before digging in. "Hmm, I wish I could eat this more often."

Adanne placed a carefully cut tender into her mouth, washing down the bite with a swig of tea. "I thought there were franchises in California."

"There are, just not close enough to my condo."

John licked his fingers, eyes darting around. Adanne smirked and passed him one of her extra wet wipes.

"A condo, huh? I pictured you in a lavish home somewhere in those Hollywood hills."

He wiped his fingers—premature, really, since he had half a dripping sandwich left. "Not really me. If I decide to buy a home, I want it to be in a place that feels like it."

He scooped up his sandwich again and took another giant bite. Totally unaware of how this normal behavior, complete with sauce dripping off his chin, was unraveling her.

Adanne chewed on another tender dipped in buffalo sauce. She glanced out the window at her transparent reflection and the parking lot beyond, folding her legs far under her padded seat when his longer ones grazed her calves. His apology mumbled around another bite.

How did she go from barely ever going out to being tangled up with a celebrity at the local chicken place?

It felt like a publicity stunt of some sort, like she would look up and find a hidden camera lodged in the fake foliage lining the walls. Adanne Stewart, who hadn't been on a date in God knows how long, spotted about the town with actor John Pope.

"Hmm, that hit the spot."

Adanne turned back to the man at the center of her unease, polishing off crispy fries, grease lingering on his fingers like anointing oil.

"I'm not quite sure you even tasted the food, you ate so fast."

Adanne ignored the nervous ripple in her belly, and the voice telling her that he finished his meal quickly because he was ready to get rid of her.

John grabbed a napkin from the dispenser and wiped his mouth and hands. "Call it my sixth sense, but I tend to get a feeling. And when I do, I want to eat as fast as I can in case."

"In case of what?" She popped a fry into her mouth, but even as she said the last words, Adanne's ears picked up murmurs traveling through the dining room. John flashed a lopsided smile, despite his hat and glasses inviting more perusal, until the air buzzed with excitement.

"In case of this." He turned his grin from her to the mom approaching him with two kids and a reluctant husband in tow.

"I'm sorry to interrupt but I have to ask . . . Are you John Pope? The actor?" she drawled, glancing back at her husband, who shrugged in response.

John's smile went up a thousand watts. "I am."

And in that confession, Adanne found herself transformed from a hesitant makeup artist to a fumbling cell phone photographer.

• • • •

John half jogged to match Adanne's stride. She moved surprisingly fast for someone who had downed a plate of fried chicken thirty minutes ago. Her legs were not as long as his, but those muscles of hers behaved like they were used to leaving others in the dust, propelling her forward with surprising speed.

He would not doubt that she'd been some sort of athlete in high school, maybe even college. If she went to college . . . Now that he thought about it, he didn't even know how an MUA came to be that.

However, he wasn't speed-walking after her to determine her level of athletic or educational experience.

"I'm sorry about tonight."

Adanne shrugged, keeping up her brisk pace down the steps she'd parked next to. John hadn't intended to follow her on the next part of her night, but when he'd seen her face at the end of the meal, he hadn't wanted things to end on that frazzled note.

A baseball cap wasn't always enough to hide his identity. It wasn't necessarily the movies that kept him in people's minds but those pesky reruns of the daytime show he sometimes wished never existed. The same thick hair and smile as his Italian mom, paired with his dad's olive-green eyes, helped him become a household name over a decade ago. It also made him a memorable face among those old enough to remember.

He'd intended merely to put the slip on Mike, satisfy his hunger, and maybe glean some ideas for an easy service project that his team could pull off. He may or may not have stirred up a bit of an uproar in the dining room. A free dessert was delivered to their table with flair, and cashiers and more customers came up to the table to say hello after that first photo. He wasn't one to ignore a fan. They'd been the ones to help build his career, after all. Adanne had seemed to take the interruptions like a professional, impressing him with her calm. She took photos and tossed easy grins at some of the people she recognized, explaining multiple times that she was there as part of her job. Not for any other reason.

When they had been able to peel themselves away, she'd made a beeline for her car at the restaurant, not even taking the time to say goodbye. He'd hopped in his car before he could lose her. Maybe she didn't want to show him more of Hope Springs. At least he'd make sure she was okay. But now that he'd caught up with her, he wasn't so sure.

"Hey, where are we going, anyway?" John's question was met with silence. Never mind the fact that she brushed off his attempt to apologize. Adanne checked her watch and picked up her pace. Maybe it hadn't been a good idea to follow her. He glanced warily around at the buildings close to where they'd parked. It probably wasn't a good idea to do anything that would put him at risk. He was under contract after all.

John paused, contemplating a quick retreat to his rental car, but the alternative was his empty presidential suite at the hotel across town. And walking with her as the sky darkened was the chivalrous thing to do. Even though she could probably handle herself on the streets of her own hometown.

Ugh. He had no clue what she was doing, but leaving her at this point felt out of the question.

Decision made, John stuck his hands in his pockets, jumping down the last two steps.

Adanne stopped and pivoted so abruptly he almost ran past her.

"Don't you have lines to learn? Or a list of eligible celebrity date options to flip through?" She crossed her arms. "Maybe a groupie from dinner would suffice. You got a nice sampling of Hope Springs' finest at The Chicken Place. Ever thought about taking a soccer mom with you to the awards?"

"Ouch!" John shifted to mirror her stance, warmed by the fire in her eyes. The barrage of words from her mouth should have insulted him, but although there was a slight sting, the raw authenticity drew him in. "You may have just singed my eyebrows."

"If you don't like the heat, you are welcome to get out of my kitchen." Was that a hint of humor he saw in her eyes? A twitch of a lip, perhaps? He would take his chances with that twinge of hope.

"From what I see, we are far from anyone's kitchen. This looks more like a city park."

Adanne gave an exasperated groan as he laughed, aware of how corny that line was but interested in seeing if he could peel back more of her locked-down layers.

She ignored his feeble attempt at a joke, motioning to a four-story building down the path, partially hidden by tall trees.

"This is where I'm going. The botanical garden's event center. I've got some things to pick up. Since you're still here stalking me, you might as well make yourself useful. They are about to close. Come on."

She spun on her heels, resuming her brisk pace toward the entrance coming into view.

Warmth flowed from John's face into his chest. Adanne seemed to take solace behind her walls. It took a bit of fight to break in, but he couldn't help but enjoy the fire that burst through her now and then.

However, she had a point. He should go rehearse lines in the safety of his hotel suite. But something about the changing night sky hovering above the downtown park of this Southern town lit a spark in him. It was like watching a story unfold, knowing that somewhere, there were some words written here for him. More sparks that would set his passion ablaze again. Maybe that's what his career needed. Someone like Adanne to keep striking a match.

As he neared the building, a woman stood at the double-glass-doored entrance. She was dressed in all black with a tight blond bun at the nape of her neck and a badge pinned to her blazer. After handing Adanne what looked like a pastry box, she disappeared and returned with two bags that looked like they had more boxes in them. Adanne's words of gratitude wafted to him. He picked up his pace, making it to her as the main door closed.

Adanne turned to him with a look that said, "About time," and stuck out arms holding the bags in question.

"Of course!" He grabbed them from her, surprised at their heft. She settled the single box more securely in her arms and made her way back down the path. He guessed their evening was over, capped off by picking up suspicious items from a garden event center.

"You want to take the long way around?"

John glanced over. He hadn't expected her to say much more to him.

"Sure." He stepped forward, then reversed. "Wait. What does that mean?"

Adanne's clear laugh pierced through the darkening sky. The pink, orange, and almost purple hues of the setting sun would soon make their way to a dark shade of star-studded blue. Her eyes glowed, shifting in similar ways to the transitioning evening.

"We can turn around to head straight back to our cars or walk the loop around to them."

She tilted her head to give him another perusal, amusement

like flames in her eyes. "Maybe work off that fried chicken. Unless those bags are too heavy for you."

John gave her a wide grin, pulling the sacks up like dumbbells. "Never. I'm playing a super-skilled vigilante who is out to avenge his family, remember?"

"Okay, Mr. Vigilante. Just because you're skilled doesn't mean you're strong." Her smirk pulled another grin from him.

They walked in silence for several minutes, following the smooth sidewalk around the pond, through a winding walkway lined with cultivated bushes and trees, and down a path that led past a small bridge in the middle of the park.

Refreshed by the brisk air and already feeling the tension from the week slip from his shoulders, John let his eyes roam around the serene area for a few moments, then to the plastic bags swinging from his hands.

"What are these, anyway? Something in here that may be detrimental to my career?"

"*Tuh.*" She scoffed in an expressive way that John wasn't familiar with. But he liked the way it rolled off her tongue and all the attitude she seemed to put behind it. "If it bothered you for real, you wouldn't have followed me."

Adanne didn't look at him, but he saw the beginnings of a smile. "Don't worry, John. Nothing illegal in these bags. It's from a wedding. All safe and edible."

"Now I'm *really* curious. Anything in here that could get me in trouble with my eating plan?"

Adanne quirked her eyebrow, peering at him through the fall of soft twists that had loosened from her thick braid. "Not everything is about you, Mr. Pope. With all due respect. But if you must know, they are for what I do in the community. Nothing for you to be concerned with."

John gulped. One instant he thought they were teasing each other safely, and the next she erupted with just the right combination of words that called him out in the most disconcerting way. But her mention of community triggered part of the reason he had wanted to meet her for dinner. Before he could ask her more, she interrupted his thoughts.

"By the way, I thought I heard somewhere you are Italian. But your name doesn't fit."

"Pope is just about as Italian as you can get. Aka, the Vatican? Get it?"

She kept her eyes forward, but the side of her mouth tipped up at his cheesy joke.

Pleasure rippled in his gut at how she revealed another random fact about him that he never in a million years thought she would care about. "It's Pomponio."

"Huh?"

He adjusted his grip on the bags. "Pomponio is my official Italian last name. But when I started my career, a producer suggested that I shorten it. Make it easier for people to say and remember."

Adanne nodded, her profile contemplative. "Makes sense. But I think I would rather be remembered for who I am, not who I had to pretend to be."

John didn't sense any animosity or even tension in her words. Yet they highlighted his struggle. There she went again, with her authentic, unsettling ways. He cleared his throat.

"I'm sorry again, by the way. I invited you to dinner and it kind of got spoiled."

Adanne shifted her own package, rolling her shoulders back. "I'm not used to attention like that. But that's your scene. I get it." She turned her face fully to him. "No apology necessary."

They continued walking in pleasant silence. At what looked like the halfway mark, Adanne shifted a little closer, dodging a bench that straddled the path and grassy area.

John leaned in, his instincts ready to steady her if she stumbled.

But she recovered quickly, moving back to her original distance. "Are you sure you feel safe walking around the park with me tonight?"

John chuckled at her random question. "You don't think I can handle myself?"

"Yes. And no. You play an important role in this film. What if something happened to you?"

"I'm not worried."

"This ain't Beverly Hills, Mr. Pope."

He huffed. "I can handle myself. Beverly Hills may be where my current place is, but I grew up in Chicago."

Adanne scoffed. "What's that got to do with Hope Springs, Alabama?" She glanced at him, sizing him up playfully. "We have our own type of trouble here."

John paused. "And what kind is that?"

Adanne breathed in deeply, taking in his question with more intensity than he expected. He felt it too. A depth to that query that seemed to echo something in his core. What did he, a Chicago-raised, Beverly Hills–living, Hollywood actor, have to do with Hope Springs, Alabama? Why here? Why now . . . with her? Especially when he wanted to answer his inner questions by stepping a little closer.

"Not quite so sure at the moment." Adanne gave John an enigmatic look and turned to continue her walk. Like a magnet, he moved beside her, matching her steps. He could tell she wasn't comfortable with him so near. Working close to each other every day was one thing. It was for a specific purpose. But this felt different.

She fidgeted a bit with her box, rolling her shoulder back again, focusing on anything around her but him. Searching, so it seemed, for a polite, conversational word to say.

"On a lighter note, how is your beauty hunt going?"

John laughed with genuine humor. Maybe she was more focused on him than he thought. "Is that what we are calling it now?"

"You've got to admit that's what it is." She shrugged, sneaking in a smile. "Basically. Without the ladies in front of you to give a crown to, or a rose."

"That's fair." He dug his hands into the pockets of his jacket, the bags from the botanical garden hanging from his wrists and brushing against his legs. John watched Adanne's dark locks glow golden at her crown as they strolled under the park's lamplight.

"The prospect of all of this should excite me, especially since my last movie earned an award nomination. But I don't know—"

"You don't seem that passionate about any of it." Adanne's face remained focused on the path in front of her, but her tone unexpectedly raised his defenses.

"I wouldn't say that. This is part of what we actors work toward."

"Okay. If you say so."

Her simple answer continued to unnerve him. He didn't like the way her questions poked at his issues. She often said little, but there was perception in her eyes that laid him open more than he liked. But if he were being honest, maybe his frustration had more to do with his longing for her to say more, for her to trigger a response that would help him process the restlessness he couldn't define. Instead, her unspoken words left him dissatisfied.

"Enough about me. What does a makeup artist do on the weekends around sleepy Hope Springs?"

Adanne chuckled. "You're not going to follow me again, are you?"

"Wasn't planning on it."

"Good." She sniffed with chin lifted, her nose and full

lips creating a lush profile. "Wouldn't want you cramping my sleepy style."

He coughed out a laugh. "I don't think your style could ever be in danger of that."

Adanne gave him a sidelong glance. The chink of armor she carried so close parting for just a moment. Appreciation flitted across her gaze as their eyes met, the tiny slice of pleasure setting off a buzz in the air between them.

A subtle wave of something about her here in this open place with him made him crave a bit more.

Where did that come from?

The thoughts that tumbled into him excited and sobered him. Why in the world would he think about any of that in relation to Adanne? He needed to keep his head clear and concentrate on the reason he was in Alabama. Even though it wasn't to build lasting friendships, he couldn't deny that he longed for that, even here.

They arrived at their cars too soon. To her relief, most likely, but his disappointment was hard to dismiss.

As she unlocked her truck, John shifted the bags he carried so he could open the door. After setting the items inside, he turned to go but halted his steps when she touched his shoulder.

Adanne's eyes skirted to the side, her face dissolving into a shy expression when she looked back. "I go to church on the weekends if you really want to know." She jingled the set of keys in her hand, then grasped them tight as she looked him in the eye.

"Maybe. If you are interested . . . that's somewhere you would like to be?"

9

*J*ohn straightened his collar, not sure if his quick work with the ironing board had been enough. *Maybe I should wear a tie.* But that seemed too formal. He wore a button-down shirt, open near his throat and tucked into slim dress pants. He took another look at himself. *Maybe jeans?*

It had been so long.

In the mirror, he saw the face of a child who still mourned unanswered prayers that his dad would come back home. And in his mouth the bitter taste of the teenager who pushed it all down. The dress code had probably changed considerably in the years since he'd last attended a church. Funerals and the occasional wedding didn't count. At least that's what he convinced himself of when he was invited into a sanctuary for those moments. Despite the opportunities to visit church services in the past, faith felt safer in the comfort of a living room. More authenticity, less hypocritical performance. He'd never said yes to corporate worship. Until now.

He didn't need to spend any more time thinking about what he would wear. Or why a simple invitation from his

makeup artist tipped him over the edge into church attendance. Nope. Today he'd focus on connecting with God,
nothing more. There was no part to play here. He'd rely on
the practices he'd learned in his West Coast small group and
do his best to drown out the surroundings. But there was
no denying the pull he felt to make a good impression, at
least for Adanne's sake. He didn't want to lose the rapport
developing between them.

Watching her face Friday night as she mustered up the
courage to tell him about her church had been a study in
will versus—what—compassion? She extended an invitation
into her world, giving him the chance to connect on a spiri-
tual level. This morning he would push aside his hesitance
to follow through.

Glancing back at the mirror, he walked to the closet and
pulled out another option. If he was going to keep it together,
he needed to be himself. Adanne's words from that night still
echoed, dropping into areas of his life he hadn't inspected in
a while, the dust lifting and settling around what needed to
be cleared away. When it was all said and done, would John
only be remembered for what he pretended to be?

He grabbed his keys, tossing them up in the air and letting them land noisily in his hand. Requesting a rental car
in his film contract had been a savvy move. He appreciated
the freedom to explore during his time off, especially in a
small town like Hope Springs.

The morning was colder than he expected, his leather
jacket a welcome addition to the button-down shirt and jeans
he finally opted for. The long stretches of fields interspersed
with fresh developments and established tree-lined homes
were air to his lungs. The skyline wasn't cluttered with building after building of distraction. Just wide-open space and
sky to let his thoughts roam for more of that dust-clearing.
The scenery soothing to his soul.

Or was it more than that?

His GPS directed him to turn off the main highway and into an area not too far from where he had been on Friday night. He pulled into the parking lot of a building that didn't resemble the churches he'd sat in growing up, but the sign greeting him at the entrance told him he had indeed arrived at Hope Springs Bridge Church. Trees lined the walkway that led to the entrance. The trees, though bare, continued the spirit of welcome as he found a parking spot.

After shifting the car into park, he kept his hands gripped on the wheel.

What was he doing? Adanne had also mentioned that he could meet the pastor, a man named Ben Southerland. Maybe set up an appointment if he wanted to talk more. But the pastor was just a man. The congregants just more of the regular people he encountered during his time here.

That didn't keep doubt from washing over John the more stepping into the church became a reality. How long had it really been?

He didn't know how to do this anymore. Whatever it meant to *do* church. This wasn't some red-carpet event where everyone arrived glossed over for the cameras, a place he could simply smile and wink his way through with some liquid courage on the side.

Gatherings like this had been special to his heart long ago. Now they were the source of his greatest disappointment. Too bad his father never saw it the same way. Marco Pomponio had seemed to have no issue breaking his wedding vows and then making new ones in the same church he used to volunteer in. As if enough years had passed to make his unfaithfulness okay.

John swallowed down the rising bile. Maybe coming to an actual church today wasn't the best idea. He still had time to leave and apologize to Adanne later. Right as he pressed his foot back on the brake, a knock sounded on his driver's side window.

John turned to see Adanne standing just outside the door, her truck parked one car over from his Audi. She lifted a cautious hand, offered a small smile.

He shut off the engine and opened the door slowly as she stepped back.

"Good morning." Her tentative smile blossomed into a warmth that eased the tightness of his chest.

"Morning," he croaked back.

Adanne's twisted braids hung loose over her shoulders. Mauve earrings dangled from her ears. Her long dress flowed over distracting curves. The morning light bounced off high cheekbones, melting her dark-brown eyes to a shade resembling honey.

A vision of both wariness and calm, she stood by his car, the two bands that hung from her necklace rotating between her fingers, her silhouette framed by the sun.

When he saw her shift her weight to one foot and glance nervously to the side, he realized with slight embarrassment that he'd been gaping at her.

"Are you ready to go in? Service is about to start." She glanced at her watch and bounced slightly on the balls of her feet.

John ran a hand down his throat, stepping out of the car.

"Lead the way." He straightened his pants and willed himself not to look in her direction as they walked to the front, the ease in conversation from Friday night lost the moment he saw her.

He focused on what felt easier, nodding at the congregants raising a hand in greeting. Some eyes widening as they recognized him.

With dread, John considered that his presence at Adanne's church may not be the most comfortable thing for her. This was a part of her personal life, where he imagined she filled up to turn around and deal with people like him throughout the week.

A few steps from the front door, John guided Adanne to the side, stepping among the shade of the trees that stood as sentries along the front entrance. She looked up at him with confusion, especially after noticing his arm around her waist.

He grimaced. His arm moved back to the safe spot at his side. "Didn't mean to startle you."

"It's okay"—she turned toward the doors, her hand lingering at the place he'd held her—"but the service is starting soon."

"That's exactly why I wanted to stop here. I may be having second thoughts. I don't want to walk too far into your personal business."

"Too late." Adanne's lips barely twitched, but the humor in her eyes invited him to continue.

"You're probably right, but you don't have to do this today, or any day, really." He moved his focus to the brick exterior, away from her distracting gaze. "You should be allowed to enjoy a weekend away from the film set without me here as a reminder. I hope you didn't feel pressured to invite me."

He'd stumbled through it, but there it was. Permission to let him walk away.

Friday night had shifted something between them. They'd traipsed into a strange place of familiarity. But he still couldn't assume he had the right to force her to be his friend if she didn't want to be. He didn't need anything else in his life to become complicated.

Adanne tilted her head, her eyes assessing him. Hesitance mingled with—was he seeing it right—a kind of longing?

"I didn't feel pressured into anything. I wouldn't have brought it up if I did. Church should be a safe place for all of us." She brushed a piece of lint off his shoulder. "Actor or not."

"Good to hear." He jammed his hands into his pockets. Maybe then he wouldn't be tempted to grab her slender fingers. Hold them and the rest of her close.

She held his gaze for a beat, then her berry-stained lips tipped into an approving smirk. She turned toward the door, the skirt of her dress swaying with the movement. She glanced back, tossing him a smile that dried out any other objections. "Okay, John. Come on, then."

His nerves melted away as the heat in her eyes took up residence in his veins.

● ● ● ●

"Forget the former things; do not dwell on the past."

Pastor Ben's voice boomed over the sanctuary. The hum and rhythm of the ancient words vibrated in the air, setting off a buzz of expectation. He paused, looking out over the hundreds gathered. He grinned, nodding slowly as if to assure everyone that these words did indeed apply to them. Leaning forward, he placed a hand in one pocket of his slacks and emphasized the remaining words of the verse with his right hand.

"See, I am doing a new thing! Now it springs up; do you not perceive it?" Pastor took one step down from the platform, his increasing proximity to the crowd heightening the potency of the verse. "You see, family, the question is not if God is doing something new. The question is, will we position ourselves to see it? Are we willing to take the blinders off our eyes, to shake off the shackles on our feet and get into a position where we can *see*?"

Although several years past midlife, Pastor Ben jogged back up the steps to the podium. He leaned over his Bible, grinning wide at the text he obviously cherished. "Let's keep reading."

As the words from Isaiah 43 continued to pour out over the crowd, Adanne adjusted her cardigan for the thousandth time. Why did it feel like Pastor was all up in her business this morning? The words coming from his prepared message kept hitting her with a prickly sensation, making her squirm more than usual. And why now, when she sat next to John Pope, of all people?

The light scent of aftershave and citrus wafted to her in steady waves. She snuck a glance in his direction after keeping her eyes forward for most of the service. It was hard enough to sing during worship with him standing so close. Something that usually brought her joy felt too conspicuous now.

His self-awareness and concern about her needs right before they walked in stunned her. She'd determined to let this be a normal Sunday, despite his attendance. How could she anticipate the honesty in his gaze, how right it felt when his arm circled her waist. The moment was so much more jolting than when she'd blocked that scene with him on set. All the safeguards of a professional film environment were not available here in the wilds of Hope Springs.

It was different, and crippling awareness had displaced her intentional focus.

The way he leaned forward pulled his shirt tight across his back, revealing athletic shoulders and arms. The arms that had no trouble lifting her or keeping her from stumbling. She could still feel the press of his arm around her waist.

As if John wasn't attractive enough with his thick, dark hair grazing the collar of his shirt and the hint of stubble around his jaw and cheeks. His rapt interest in the sermon moved her. John took in the message like a hungry man, following the pastor's movements with his intense gaze, eyes wide and engaged.

Ugh, why was he here working his charming way into her too-full life? It was impossible. They were so different—their childhood, upbringing, culture, career, and even skin color. She didn't have any problem being with or around a man outside of her race, but not *this* man. He wasn't the one to be with, no matter how good-looking or devout he was, or how close he sat next to her on the cushioned pew.

John's last high-profile relationship was with an actress who spent her off time releasing chart-topping hits. Not to mention that his occupation and presence were a constant reminder of what Adanne lost those years ago. Plus, they worked together. It made sense for John to mention not wanting to cross the line in any way, shape, or form. But . . .

The words Pastor shared echoed in Adanne's jumbled thoughts. Past time to open her eyes to the new things that God was doing. This job and all that came with it were variables she never would have expected that were thrown into her busy routine. Who knew what God would do with it all? At the very least, it couldn't hurt to gain a pseudo friend. Even if that friend had started his acting career on her mother's favorite daytime soap.

As if drawn to her inner turmoil, John turned his head to the left. He caught her gaze, trapping her with eyes full of gratitude. "Thank you for inviting me," he whispered.

She leaned closer. "Only right to invite you to the church house after you followed me around town."

A grin crinkled his eyes and the lining of her stomach. "It was worth it."

Before she could think of a response beyond a blink, a more attentive member in the row before them scolded with a muttered shush over her shoulder.

John's eyes widened, his Adam's apple working overtime

to stymie the rising laughter. Adanne turned her face away, but not before a giggle escaped. He coughed, turning his attention as best as he could back to the message.

She still felt the buzz, the hum in the room from hundreds of hearts in agreement as they worshiped and listened to the Word of God preached. But it took up residence in her belly, warm, gooey, and seeping into cracks and crevices that lay barren for so long. Stirring thoughts not too far off from the man sitting next to her. She leaned toward the back of the pew in front, hands folded in sincere supplication. Her whisper muffled by the press of her fists.

"Lord. Help."

•   •   •   •

Is this what help looks like?

Adanne watched as a crowd formed around John. A group made up of mostly women, some with their husbands standing nearby chuckling at the commotion. She was glad they found it funny. For her it was just another public display of gushing like she'd experienced two nights ago.

John's camera-ready grin flashed over the heads of most of them as he answered questions. He caught her eye for a moment, put his palms up with a shrug, and flashed his smile back to the group. Cell phones popped out as he leaned in for selfies.

After he met the pastor and accepted the invitation for a future coffee chat, news about John's presence at the church spread among the attendees. Most residents were aware that a film was shooting close by, but he'd kept a low profile.

Until the other night.

Adanne leaned against the doorframe of the sanctuary entrance watching the scene unfold just like it had at The Chicken Place. She wasn't his bodyguard or assistant. Yet he'd kind of come here *with* her, or at least as her guest of sorts.

It wouldn't do well for the movie or her job if one of the main actors didn't show up to work because he got attacked by an adoring mob . . . *at the church*.

Adanne shook her head, a sickening feeling inching up her throat. She didn't need to be remotely jealous when she had no stake in the man.

Maybe God *had* answered her prayer. There was no temptation to be with someone who seemed to belong to everyone else.

John Pomponio Pope was definitely not her new thing. Any extracurricular activity with him was just a distraction. Her focus had to remain on getting her family and finances settled.

Tossing her paper coffee cup in the trash next to her, she turned on her low heels toward the exit doors. John appeared right at home where he stood. Soaking up the attention that he never seemed to grow weary of. She would leave him to that and reclaim the rest of her day.

Thank you again for that word, Pastor. She'd keep moving forward one determined step at a time. And John Pope and his fan club were not invited along for the ride.

10

*L*ooking out the window from the high-rise office, John couldn't help comparing the smog-tinged view of Los Angeles to the clear skies that had been his canopy lately.

Every time he flew into the city, a surge of excitement rushed him for what would be next. He had only been away from the West Coast for a few months, and next month he'd return to this side of the country for the awards he'd rather avoid.

Despite the short time he'd been there, Hope Springs had marked him. The peaceful pace of the Alabama town was the respite he hadn't quite known he needed.

Narrowing his eyes against the sunrays fighting their way through the haze, he didn't feel any kind of elation at being here. Instead, the lingering notes of a sermon hummed through his veins, turning his attention away from the next big thing to the possibility of something new.

John swiveled his chair to the conference table, putting his back to the afternoon sun. His gaze roamed from face to face while they waited for Mike to re-enter the room. Nora, his executive assistant, sat on his right, her paper calendar spread out before her, with her phone and tablet synced up. She'd been a recent hire, referred by Mike after she moved from the East Coast and away from her former client's home base. Her experienced opinions and friendliness with his contacts were an asset. She'd rebuilt many of the bridges John had unintentionally—okay, some intentionally—burned over the years.

Across from him sat his agent, Peter, instrumental in getting him the role for the movie filming in Hope Springs. He'd also been the one to introduce John to his small group leader, Garth, the man who eventually led him back to the Lord. Peter had a knack for seeing beyond what his clients wanted, matching them with roles that steered them in the right direction for their careers.

Next to Peter, John's stylist, David, had his laptop open and fabric samples sticking out of his leather portfolio. His tattooed arms flexed as he punched keys with thick fingers. At six-three and with the build of a wrestler, he gave John the best of two worlds—a bodyguard with a keen fashion sense. David had a pulse on styling options that remained classic, masculine, and comfortable. John credited him with keeping him off the worst-dressed lists and away from sacrificing his sense of propriety.

Mike finally burst through the door, the energy level picking up as he set his phone on the table. He plopped in the chair next to Tanya, his director of publicity, who rounded out the group.

"Okay, what's next on the agenda?" John exhaled, preparing himself for a barrage of information that he would process later.

Although it'd been great to catch up on his schedule, discuss potential jobs, and look through style ideas, he was ready to grab some food and head back to his hotel. He wouldn't mind getting a good night's sleep before the early morning flight the next day. And the fact that he was ready to get back to not-so-sleepy Hope Springs was not lost on him.

"We've covered almost everything, I think." Nora's finger flowed down her pdf. "I inserted the dates on your calendar. Peter's assistant has already sent me some details for the developing project he mentioned. What I don't have yet is the assistant contact for who you are going with to the awards. Has that decision been finalized? Or are you going solo?"

Solo was a funny word when it came to anything that took place in the entertainment industry. No one really did anything alone since some entourages outnumbered the cast members of his film shoot. John liked to travel light, however, and considering what Mike had in mind, he hoped he could get away with traveling as minimally as possible.

"I'm still working on that," John answered at the same time as Mike said, "Definitely not going alone."

The agent and stylist exchanged looks. David returned to cataloging design ideas with an arched eyebrow while Peter leaned back in his chair, a lopsided grin on his face. His dark-brown eyes sparkled with mischief. "Now, this is interesting. Shall I get involved? Since this seems to be playing out like a casting call."

John didn't know whether to scowl in annoyance or give his agent a high five in agreement. Peter had a remarkable ability to read the room. And anything said in his Nigerian-tinged British accent added a level of precision to his words.

Mike scoffed. "I've got more options lined up. Just need John here to pull the trigger so we can move forward." He tilted his head toward Tanya. "Hit me with some of your data."

She tapped on her tablet with her long, pointed nails. "John's social media engagement has been down by thirty percent since last year, due in part to the focus on his current role and his time *away*. However, it did spike last month with the news of Katrina Daline's engagement."

John rolled his eyes, then shared a pointed look with Peter. Peter grinned, his leather swivel chair gently rocking.

"John's name is not showing up as frequently and as high up as we'd like in search engines. I've already contacted several publications that will feature him in a few months. There will also be the standard interviews with the cast at release. Our goal now is to get his name to perform well on platforms by attaching it to an actress who is currently trending. That should amp up searches and subsequent search engine optimization. From there Peter should see an uptick in casting opportunities in the next season."

"So, just like that, my career hinges on who I date."

"No pressure, right?" Peter directed his smirk toward Mike. "And apparently no need for a savvy agent who doesn't depend on one's relationship status to get his clients jobs."

"It can't hurt. It's been a quiet year for John, but this will help."

Tanya nodded in agreement with Mike. "And let's not forget a well-timed social-justice project that will strengthen our efforts."

"Of course, can't forget that." John smirked and glanced at David, who made a sound from behind his laptop. He kept his bearded face lowered, however.

Tanya slid a stapled stack over to John. "Here is a list of community centers, hospitals, after-school programs, food pantries, and shelters within a thirty-mile radius of your base camp. I've sent more details to Nora, who will determine the best fit based on your needs and shooting schedule."

"Good to know you all have this figured out." John pushed his chair back from the lacquered table. "If there is nothing else, I'm going to turn in early."

Mike reared his head back. "At four p.m.? What about dinner? We catered from Reginald's."

John stood up. He folded up his paperwork and jammed it into his back pocket.

"Sorry. Hate to change plans. I seem to have lost my appetite and feel a headache coming on. Nora will take any other pertinent notes for me. I'll see most of you next month. And I'm sure I'll see you in a few days, Mike."

John gave a quick nod to Peter and kept his composure when David looked up at him with his poker face. John felt his rising heat defuse when David raised his hands slightly, bringing them together in silent claps. As a veteran, David usually had no patience for the frivolous parts of the entertainment industry. Which made John's stylist an oddball in the industry but the perfect fit—pun intended—for him.

John didn't exhale until the elevator doors closed. He rode down to the main level and walked through the turnstile door of the building entrance. Lifting his face to the warmth of the sun, he dug his hands into his front pockets. He shouldn't have felt like he was suffocating, but he found himself unable to breathe deeply in those spaces anymore. Having dinner with some of his discipleship group guys two days earlier had been great. Three of them in town at the same time was nothing short of a miracle. But something was being triggered inwardly that he needed to deal with sooner instead of later.

It didn't help that talking about his career in such technical terms bugged him, a constant buzzing that he wanted to smack against the wall.

Speaking of . . .

When he pulled out his phone, a forgotten business card fluttered to the ground. He bent to pick it up, half expecting the call to be from one of the team members upstairs asking him to come back. *Nope.* No cajoling from them would make him return.

The caller ID displayed a different kind of problem.

"Shannon? Long time." John winced at the memory of the pixie-cut-wearing media darling whose voice flowed from the other end. She'd seen him at some of his worst moments, and that wasn't a good thing.

"I heard you were in town for a few days. Are you still here? Why don't you come see us? I know someone who would love to see *you*." Shannon's words oozed out, barely giving him a chance to process each question with an adequate response. All he could focus on was getting off the phone.

"I have an early morning flight back to my location."

"Aw, come on, Johnny. You guys can catch up. Everything is just water under the bridge anyway."

He could only think of one person those words would refer to. The only other person, besides Shannon here, who called him Johnny. But why would Katrina even consider seeing him again when her future was pledged to someone else—at least for now?

The pull was torturous. Not because he wanted to enter back in but because he wanted to assure himself that he was fine. But his craving for a drink after the meeting he'd just left would be amplified in a gathering of familiar faces. He couldn't just step back into the flow with some of those people like things hadn't changed.

Because things hadn't just changed. *He* was different. At least he hoped.

And many of them didn't realize how much. He couldn't allow himself to be put back in a position that would derail his progress. It didn't matter if they thought he wasn't over her or if he offended them.

"Shannon, I appreciate you thinking of me. Now is just not the best time for me to catch up. Maybe another time when my schedule isn't so pressed. Wish you all the best."

John hung up right after her dismissal and breathed in,

finding himself in desperate need of some oxygen. The card stock in his left hand bit into his palm as he clenched his fists. He opened to a familiar logo and the words "HSBC, Hope Springs Bridge Church, pastored by Ben Southerland" printed in raised text.

• • • •

"Pastor Southerland, thank you for meeting me. Especially on a Saturday. I hope you didn't have to go out of your way."

"It's my pleasure. I'm glad you took me up on the offer for coffee. Meeting our church guests is one of the things I enjoy the most. I assumed your film schedule would be tight, but coming straight from the airport is another level."

John shrugged, trying to make himself comfortable under the pastor's assessing gaze. "Tight, yes, but it ebbs and flows. This film set is more relaxed than others I've been on. But it may have to do with the town it's filmed in."

Ben Southerland grinned. "Hope Springs has that effect. How are you liking it here?" He leaned forward, giving John a conspiratorial wink. "We only allow two answers, by the way, that you love it and if you don't, we'll do our best to change that."

John chuckled, already feeling his shoulders drop. "I'll have to go with the first answer, then."

"Smart man."

"And an honest one. My drives to and from set have given me an appreciation for the area. And one of your members, a makeup artist on our crew, has shown me around as well."

What the pastor thought of that comment he wasn't sure, and maybe he shouldn't have mentioned her, but the pastor's expression remained clear and open.

"Good to know you're being treated well. So"—the pastor tilted his head, eyeing John with unguarded curiosity—"is there anything specific I can talk with you about? Something I can agree with you in prayer over?"

John leaned forward, his elbows on his knees. "Not necessarily. At least not yet. I've got some things I'm still working out how to communicate, if that makes sense. Things over the years I'm coming to terms with. But your message last Sunday gave me a sense of assurance that it will all unfold in God's time."

The pastor nodded. "That it will."

John leaned back in the soft leather chair, his eyes roaming the comfortable office. Books and Bibles were strategically placed on the shelf with other trinkets that must have held meaning to the graying man across from him. A man who remained quiet, reassurance that he was engaged and available to listen.

"I feel like I should get counsel to unpack what is rising to the surface. For whatever reason, I trust in my gut that you're the best one to give it."

Pastor Southerland chuckled, putting an arm on the back of the leather tufted sofa he sat on. "I wouldn't say I'm the best, but I will surely *do* my best. Sometimes it's enough to have the room to breathe and process outwardly without judgment over what we struggle with internally."

John nodded. That alone was a gift. He didn't need a yes man or convenient answers. Those could be easily paid for. His thoughts flitted to his meeting from yesterday. Not really any yes people there. Just team members pushing him to go in a certain direction, for his benefit, maybe, but also for their portfolios.

"Since I'm here, I also wanted to see if there are any areas you know of where I can be of service in the community. A place to give back while I'm in town."

As John said the words, he cringed at the insincerity he felt. It wasn't about the acts of service, but the way in which his manager wanted him to go about it. Just like the search for an awards-show date. He wanted something to develop naturally, not be manipulated or contrived. At least he could find out for himself instead of picking a project randomly from a curated spreadsheet.

The pastor rubbed his chin, assessing John for a few beats, compassion filling his gaze until it overflowed in the room.

Finally, he leaned forward, placing his palms on his lap. "I may have an idea for you if you are up for it. You want to take this talk and coffee to go?"

11

*a*danne wiped the droplets accumulating on her forehead. Alabama in February did not compare to the humid heat of late spring or summer. But with a high of sixty-two degrees and a central heating system that never worked right, the community center felt all too stuffy on this Saturday morning. At least the mild temperatures and clear skies were a good reason to hold the monthly community meal outside.

In all the changes to her schedule with her contracted makeup job, she'd forgotten to lock in volunteer teams for this month. Something that Daniel handled with flair but she stumbled at.

Stopping this community tradition in East Hope Springs was out of the question. Her grandfather started this brunch from his restaurant, donating food and services to gather and feed the community around him. The Stewarts kept it going, enlisting the help of other restaurants and organizations, widening the circle of those who could be involved. Now it was a pseudo potluck, a random assortment of goods and snacks. That was something that had shifted under her as time grew tight and resources diminished. Instead of getting full-scale meals, she gathered as much as she could from local restaurants and filled in the gaps that remained.

Maybe if she had been here during those times instead of chasing her dreams in California, this would be easier.

And now, with Daniel out too, she had to play the role of bustling honey bee *and* hostess, stepping into shoes that felt overwhelmingly too large for her to fill.

Adanne closed her eyes, pausing with a platter of chicken biscuits in her hand—coveted breakfast sandwiches left over from The Chicken Place's morning rush. She saw her mom in her mind's eye, rushing about, telling those stepping forward to "come on up here, baby, don't be shy." Delia Stewart hadn't stressed about the food because her focus was on the people. On serving them well and making them feel welcome.

"Okay, Mama," Adanne breathed. "I hear you." She opened her eyes, but before taking another step she tilted her mouth. "And I know you're here, Lord. Help me remember this is ultimately about you."

"You talking to yourself now, cuz?"

Adanne nearly dropped the platter on her tennis shoes. After glancing over her shoulder, she hurried to put the tray of biscuits on the plastic-covered table outside the entrance. Her cousin Kenya pulled her into a hug before she had a chance to dust crumbs from her sweatshirt.

"It's so good to see you!" Adanne felt the swell of emotion in her chest. She couldn't help feeling like this unexpected appearance was an answer to unspoken prayers. "I didn't even hear your car pull up."

Kenya stepped back, but not before swiping a pastry from the table. "Is this from the bistro?" She took a bite, rolling her eyes back into her head. "Oh, I know it is. And why would you be talking to yourself when you could pick up the phone to call the family you barely see?"

Adanne ignored the wave of guilt, knowing that her cousin always said what she thought but her heart stayed consistently pure in the process. It wasn't that she didn't want to see her family. It just became increasingly hard to take the time to drive out to see them in Huntsville and commit multiple hours there. Hours that would be soaked in memories she didn't always want to recall.

"What are you doing here, Kenya?"

"I'm here to help, of course."

Adanne gave her a pointed look. Her younger cousin was dressed in fitted slacks, a silk blouse tucked in at her slender waist, and heels that were not the best mix with the uneven pavement.

Kenya waved off the question in her cousin's eyes. "I can run a marathon in this. I'm good." She finished off her pastry, snapping dust off her fingertips. "Plus, I finished early with a client downtown and remembered what day it was. So I thought I would see if my cousin still existed, and if she did, I could give her a hand since she never asks."

Adanne chuckled, rolling her eyes. "I told you I would call when I needed help. I had it covered." Her throat revolted at that bit of untruth, but it felt more uncomfortable to admit the state of her true emotions of five minutes ago.

"Mm-hmm, I'm still waiting on that call to happen." Kenya pursed her lips, stepping past her but not before giving her a loving bump on the shoulder. Adanne watched Kenya step into the foyer of the center, looking around for a safe place to stash her phone.

She continued placing trays and platters on the table, work made quicker with Kenya's presence. As her cousin placed and shifted, Adanne wondered why she hadn't called her earlier. Kenya had a busy schedule as well, overseeing events and parties for organizations across the region, but she was still family. And this member of the Stewart clan had the gift of organization and planning, with the flair of style that made her sought after.

"By the way"—Kenya straightened the last tray on the table—"I heard from my client that Anthony is coming into town."

"Anthony?" Adanne furrowed her eyebrows as she mentally counted the number of paper products they had, hoping it was enough.

"You know, middle-school-talent-show Anthony. The one we called Ty."

"Oh yeah. He coming to perform?"

Kenya tore open a bag of fruit snacks, popping one in her mouth. "Hmm, the ones with juice inside."

"Speaking of middle school. Did you not eat today?"

"Do you even need to ask? Anyway, when my client found out I knew him, Anthony sent a text to say hi. And he offered two free tickets to his set at Plantain and Pies. It's a month away. You need to go."

"P and P? That's nice of him. I do love that place, but maybe I can give mine away to someone."

Kenya put a hand on her hip, her mouth full of juice-filled gummies tilted in disgust. "You will do no such thing." She gulped. "You're going. *And* taking someone with you. I would join, but I have an out-of-town event that night. Plus, he asked for you to be there."

Adanne arched her eyebrow, waving at some teens making their way toward them. "Why? I haven't spoken to him in years."

Kenya shrugged, moving to stand behind the desserts. "I guess you'll have to go to find out. You deserve a night out."

After half an hour, everything was set up and people started making their way to the center, some with baskets ready to be filled. Although the stash was dwindling, the community center collected paper products, toiletries, and nonperishable food items to give out as needed.

"Hello, Ms. Bernice." Adanne greeted the older woman who'd been coming by for as long as she could remember. Over the years her home had stayed full of kids who needed a safe place, so Adanne's mother had kept her pantry stocked with things from the center.

After receiving a hug from the petite grandmother, Adanne noticed a car pull up. She blinked rapidly. She knew the car but not the person in the passenger seat—or, at least, she couldn't reconcile who he seemed to be within her familiar surroundings.

"I've got something for you, baby." Adanne forced her attention away from the two men stepping out of the vehicle to the sweet face of the woman in front of her. Ms. Bernice held out an envelope, her veined hands causing the paper to quiver.

Adanne took it, her smile questioning as she opened it. Her own hands trembled as she took out a check. "What is this?"

Ms. Bernice grinned, her eyes moist and twinkling. "Now that I'm moving in with my oldest, don't need as much as I used to. Wanted to give a little back to y'all. Y'all've given so much to me over the years."

Adanne shook her head, glancing down at the amount. She held a gift that would be little to some but was a generous treasure from this selfless woman. Pulling her hands to her chest, she held the check there next to the memories around her neck, soaking in the unexpected offering. It wasn't enough to ease the financial burdens, but it would give her the ability to replenish some needed resources.

"I don't know what to say."

Ms. Bernice reached out and placed a hand on her wrist. "You know we love your family." She tipped her head toward

Adanne, her eyes flitting to the silver chain before she gave a pointed look. "And that includes you."

When Bernice released her, Adanne turned to blink away the moisture threatening to undo her composure. She ended up face-to-face with Pastor Ben and—

"John?" She hadn't seen him since last Sunday, but it felt like weeks. He was dressed casually in jeans and a zip-up hoodie, a sheepish grin on his face but some weariness in his eyes. What had happened this past week while he was away?

"What brings you here, Pastor? It's good to see you but . . . it isn't your turn to serve this month."

Her question was directed to Pastor Ben, but she couldn't take her eyes from John, who looked at her with interest, his gaze deepening with warmth. She brushed off the tremor tickling her skin. Probably felt sorry for her with how disheveled she looked. Nothing like the polished and professional women he had been around during his trip to LA.

Adanne averted her gaze. That thought alone filled her with disgust. Who cared who he was around in Los Angeles? She sure did not. His time there had nothing to do with her here in Hope Springs.

She placed the envelope from Ms. Bernice in her pocket. John opened his mouth to say something, but Pastor Ben beat him to it. "Tell us what to do, I've got time to spare. Had coffee with this young man here—"

John chortled. "Depends on your definition of *young*."

Ben grinned. "Much younger than me counts. Thought I would show him around and looks like we came at the perfect time."

Pastor pushed up his sleeves and rubbed his hands together. Before she could give a suggestion, he stepped away to greet a young family walking up.

"Yes, please, put me to work." John unzipped his hoodie in turn and stashed it under the table, clearly not caring that it could get soiled. Before he could shift back to her, a voice called from a few people down. "Hey! You look just like so-and-so . . . what's his name? . . . from that show in the mornings."

People turned their heads toward John in curiosity, including Ms. Bernice, who was in conversation with Kenya at the other end of the table. Adanne gritted her teeth, hoping today wouldn't turn into another scene.

John laughed. "Yes ma'am, 'so-and-so' is me." He ducked his head. That rare display of awkwardness surprised Adanne and so did everyone's response.

Each person resumed their movement down the line, engaged in their conversations, as they picked up other food items from the table.

John glanced at Pastor Ben, who was already at work loading supplies into the car of one of their guests. Adanne hoped Kenya would stay preoccupied for a while before she inquired about their additional volunteer.

Adanne leaned toward John when he drew near. "I'm impressed."

"That I was recognized?"

"No, that you know how to say 'ma'am.'"

John followed Adanne's lead, placing a biscuit on the Styrofoam plate of the next person in line. The middle-aged man with leathery skin and a horseshoe mustache didn't give John a second glance as he continued down the line.

"My mom was raised in the South. I know what's up."

"Do you, now?" Adanne said, her eyes teasing.

"Actors generally make it their business to." He smiled genuinely at the child who stepped in front of him, putting her at the center of his gaze. "And for you, my dear, what may I offer you this fine afternoon?"

The girl Adanne recognized from one of the after-school groups giggled at the lilt in his voice, her pointer finger darting out at a fruit snack. Adanne tucked in her lips before a full smile threatened to break through. John picked up the package of gummies like it was a crown nestled on a velvet pillow. Leaning down, he presented it to the curly-haired girl, her snaggle-toothed grin wide. "Your fruit, candy . . . thing, *madam*."

His enunciation wasn't lost on Adanne.

The little girl received the fruit snack with great care, and her eyes lit up with delight.

"Well played, Mr. Pope. I see your skills are put to good use on and off the set."

"That, I assure you, was genuine. No *skilled* acting involved."

"So, when you're not acting skillfully you just pop in with a charming British accent?" Adanne smirked, hoping her voice came out more even than her thoughts were. Standing here next to him was getting her all "twitterpated," as her mother used to say.

"So, you think I'm charming, huh?" He placed another fruit snack on the plate of a waiting child.

"I—uh," she sputtered, turning her attention to the next in line. "Well, hello, Mr. Timothy, can I offer you a pastry from the bistro?"

"That from Alonzo's place?"

"Sure is." She grinned at the man whose springy white hair poked out from each side of his tweed flat cap. She placed a croissant on his plate, and after looking both ways down the line placed another one down with a wink.

He grinned like a five-year-old getting a second helping of dessert. Then, as Adanne expected, he leaned over the table, tapping his cheek. Adanne chuckled, shook her head, and gave him a peck.

"Well, now I'm jealous." John leaned closer, eating up any space between them with his firm upper arm.

"Over the second pastry?" She focused on the parking lot, refusing to look at him, most likely already betrayed by her dimples.

"If you say so." His husky response was warm against her cheek.

"Young man, what you think of our rocket city?" The ache stirred by John's words was cut through by the next person in line. John looked from the older woman to Adanne, confusion on his face.

She grinned. "Ms. Nathaniel here is talking about Huntsville. Technically, we get roped into it because we're in the metro area, but we take the benefits where we can."

"I think I'm still lost."

"NASA. Space Camp. Rockets. Did you not do any preproduction research on your location?"

"I usually just fly in and out . . . wait, Space Camp is here! I always wanted to go."

"Um, you may be a little on the older end to attend." Ms. Nathaniel pursed her lips, holding her plate out to John. Before he could finish placing fruit on her plate, another person called out.

"Hey you, pretty boy, come taste this pound cake. Bet you never ate something like this in ole Hollywood." Adanne recognized Francine, a longtime East Hope Springs resident who lived two blocks down. The older woman pulled John down to the other side of the table where Kenya was positioned behind the drinks.

Now this was the kind of attention she liked to see. Nothing like getting lovingly bossed around by the residents living near the center.

Adanne hid her laugh behind her hand, lingering on John's tall frame until she pulled her glance away . . . right into the knowing eyes of her cousin. *Oh goodness.*

"I'm gonna start making you pay for those," Adanne

hollered as Kenya popped a gummy into her mouth, her eyebrows raised.

Pastor Ben stepped up next to Adanne as John left her side. "You think he's gonna be all right?"

Adanne put her hands on her hips. "Yeah, he should be good. Hopefully. Miss Francine is harmless most of the time."

She peered after John, her lips tilted at the way the woman piled down a Styrofoam plate with things for him to try.

Turning back to her pastor, she crossed her arms, grateful for the help despite the weird tension of it all. "Thank you again for coming out. I—um—it's good to have y'all here."

"It was a perfect way to show our newest community guest the heart of our beloved Hope Springs."

Adanne beamed, the genuine compliment lifting her chin.

Instead of stepping away, Pastor Ben lowered his head, putting a hand on her shoulder.

"You know that, right? Anytime you need help, you call, even if it's outside our regular schedule. Yuh hear?"

"I'll try to remember that, Pastor."

"You be sure to."

Adanne nodded, feeling like she could breathe deeper. At least a little. "Now, Pastor, you better go rescue Mr. Pope over there before the producers sue us for giving their actor a sugar coma." She couldn't help the chuckle that released. "Looks like Miss Francine is trying to get herself a new boy-friend."

12

*a*danne rolled her eyes as she stepped into the main room from the bathroom on the following Monday, tweezers in hand. John seemed to enjoy popping up when she least expected him. According to her call sheet, he was several minutes early for his turn in front of the mirror.

Waiting for her in the makeup chair with a ridiculous grin on his face.

"Why are you looking at me like that, John?"

"What's that in your hand?"

"If you must know, they are tweezers. For removing the facial hairs I'd rather not have you see while I'm in your face."

"Ah, okay. Just making sure you weren't planning on attacking me or anything."

Adanne released her breath, doing her best to keep a smile from fully escaping. "Don't you have your own trailer that you can hang out in? Take a five-minute nap, run through your lines. Eat breakfast?"

John chuckled, dragging his feet on the ground to face the mirror as she made her way toward him. He looked like a child on a merry-go-round. A very grown, long-legged one.

His dancing eyes teased her from the mirror. "And why are you here so early?"

"I'm the utmost professional." Adanne set the tweezers to the side and, like clockwork, moved all her items into place. She scanned the list of what she needed to do for the day's scenes.

"By the way . . . it was good to be there on Saturday. At the meal? And I forgot to say how much I enjoyed church the weekend before."

"Mm-hmm."

"The message really hit home for me. And the people. So welcoming."

"Yep." *I'm sure they were.* Adanne's eyes didn't leave her list. John could be as chatty as he wanted, but she wouldn't let his charm distract her. She had work to do. Flirting with the actor who caused her to lose a past job wasn't part of it.

John must have taken her silence as a hint. He turned on music on his phone, settled back in his seat, and closed his eyes as she worked.

Familiar notes wafted up to her. A worship song from church poured out of the Bluetooth speaker. John usually listened to instrumentals but as she applied his makeup for today, they listened to an entire worship playlist, the styles ranging from hymns to urban gospel.

Her stomach tensed with approval despite her resolve to ignore all his wonderfully intriguing ways. She added the last few touches to the sides of his face and then stepped back to compare her work to photos from last week to ensure continuity.

John opened his eyes at Adanne's light touch on his shoulder. "Ah, perfect." He grinned into the mirror, intentionally searching out her eyes. "Thank you. And again, for last week. After hanging with the pastor, I want to go back to the church again."

"Wait." Adanne held up a brush-wielding hand. John playfully lifted his own palms in surrender, ducking his head a bit.

Adanne struggled to keep her face straight, although a tickle in her throat threatened to undo her. "I don't know how comfortable I am with us spending time together outside of here."

Even these words felt like a confession. His eyes rounded as he slowly put his hands down.

"There are a lot of great churches in town. Maybe it's better you received food from another table, if you understand what I'm saying? Would feel less awkward?"

His lips tipped up on one side. "I like being fed at yours."

Adanne bit the inside of her cheek. He made this difficult. She didn't appreciate the way his innocent comment made her stomach flip. Such a sincere expression that soon turned into a bit of pink spreading from his neck to his ears.

"That is, I, uh, I know it's not your table, specifically—like you personally—but uh, my mom will be happy to know I attended a service. She's been trying to get me back to church for years." His embarrassment somehow made him more endearing. Made her want to silence his stammering with her lips. *Adanne Denise Stewart!*

She needed to regain control of this conversation before her willpower failed. Adanne dipped her head, making sure he saw her eyes.

"John, it's time for you to go, but hear me out. Thank you again for dinner the other night and for your help Saturday and so on. But you're too well-known to traipse around Hope Springs with me."

The Italian lifted his dark eyebrows, currently made to look salt-and-pepper from age.

"Why is that?"

"Because you have an image to protect, and I have a life I

want to keep private. There are already posts of you circulating. You know how tabloids are. I don't want anyone getting some idea about you." *About us.*

Adanne sighed and turned around to prepare her tools for cleaning. If only she had her own bath of lavender-and-peppermint-scented soap to soak in.

She turned her head to speak over her shoulder, her eyes directed toward the floor. "I'm here because I was hired to do a job that I want to do well. There are actual issues in my life that need real money. It may be hard to understand, but I don't want to mess things up because you want to follow me around town."

John sighed, his shoulders slumping against the chair. "Does every little thing have to be taken so seriously?"

Adanne did her best to tamp down her frustration. He had no idea how much his public persona had set her own life off course.

"Why shouldn't it be? You have lines to learn. A call time to show up to. Contract to abide by."

John chewed on that for a bit. "Maybe. But sometimes I wonder if this job is still the perfect one for me."

He sat up, jostling the chair with his movement. "Seems like everything you do carries an extra touch of sincerity. The care you put into every detail. The way you meticulously fold my cape. How you organize your workspace. Your focus when you check photos and supplies and time. I saw the same intensity as you served others at the community center."

Her cheeks warmed at his roundabout praise. His words defused the tension building in her shoulders. She'd been close to telling him off and here he was noticing things she'd stopped paying attention to.

"How did you get into this? Makeup artistry? If you don't mind me asking." Irritation gone, his eyes lit up with genuine interest.

Adanne closed her eyes for a moment, lifting her cheeks as the warmth spread inwardly. If the man wanted to be late to his call time, that was on him. Maybe he wasn't so much the perfectionist today.

"I watched my mom drive to Hope Springs Community Center day after day to serve. She styled hair for women in our neighborhood. But Mama didn't just do physical makeovers."

Her hands rested on the back of the chair, fingers light against John's back. "She loved them so well. Every stroke, every brush, changed them from the inside out. Caring with the tender love of Jesus." Her laugh was soft, an escape of air from her lightening chest.

"I wanted to do the same. Maybe it's selfish or impatient of me. But I wanted to see the physical transformation. The immediate fruit of my efforts. Maybe in not so noble of a setting. And when she passed . . ."

Adanne swallowed, removing her hands from the seat and their proximity to John. Reality crashed into her, abrupt and cold, dousing her awake from memories that still felt so tangible. She was suddenly grateful for the mornings of John's extra-early call times, when no one else occupied the trailer. "I guess I lost the fire for that, dealing with—everything."

Adanne looked up at the mirror in time to see an arresting expression come to John's face. Compassion. Respect.

"I see it still. The passion is there, Adanne."

●   ●   ●   ●

John needed to get to his scene location, but he didn't want to leave. His heart burned from Adanne's words. The fire she said she longed for, he felt warmed by in her presence. Adanne's expression was thoughtful, her pause pregnant with more, but in her typical way, she refrained from talking further. The window to her soul closed off until the next time.

She set her tweezers in her personal makeup bag and turned to wipe down the tall table. Her shoulders drew up toward her neck, looking tense under the clasp of her necklace. Like they carried invisible burdens that he sensed she still held tight to.

John wanted to know more, to gently turn her to him with his hand. But all he could do was clench and unclench it on his lap. Adanne had a story and a deep well of pain that seemed to be more than a match for his own. But they had to keep things professional, at least for her sake. Even though he fought it as he dealt with his own loneliness, he knew she was right. He couldn't cross the line of familiarity.

However, he could pray and ask the Lord to help him encourage her as he could. To soothe the heart of the woman he was starting to care about. Yeah, caring for someone was still safe. It was part of his duty as a follower of Christ. A step up from his behavior on past movie sets.

Long after John left the chair and after several hours of filming, he still hadn't forgotten about his conversation with Adanne. Her presence on the outer edge of the set. Her words swirling around his head, adding a punch to his delivery that the director called "inspired."

Adanne wasn't his muse. He didn't even believe in that stuff. All he knew was that the warmth in his chest hadn't left since the other day at the community center, even with the walls Adanne erected. He couldn't blame her. His track record didn't really scream dependable. Even though they spent a lot of time together, the connection mostly revolved around the components of this job, this movie. When filming wrapped, any type of growing friendship would dissipate.

That thought left him feeling bereft. He dragged his feet

as he made his way through the lobby of his hotel, almost forgetting to respond to the greeting of the receptionist.

He ran his hand through his wild hair as he walked into the elevator that would take him to his suite. The Southern humidity was seriously no joke, even in February. His normally obedient waves were transforming into the unruly curls of his childhood, his Mediterranean heritage unwilling to be tamed.

The elevator opened and John walked slowly to his door. Another lonely night in his hotel suite. This kind of night was preferable to being caught up in his past lifestyle, but walking the straight and narrow wasn't without its moments of isolation.

As he approached the door, the aroma of something familiar floated to his nose. It smelled like . . . home?

"Mamma?!" His mouth dropped as he unlocked his suite door. His mother, Giulia, wearing the apron she never cooked without, moved about the small kitchen area, miraculously whipping up one of his favorite meals.

John crossed the foyer in three long strides and buried his petite mother in his embrace. He leaned his head close to her curly, salt-and-pepper hair, thankful for the scent of cooked onions and spices that already clung to her tresses.

"But how? When?" He mumbled into her head.

Mamma chuckled, giving him an extra pat on the back before releasing him. "Your team called ahead and told the hotel I was coming. They gave me a key, delivered groceries, and here I am to check in on you, gioia mio."

John's heart soared at his mother's term of endearment for him. He hadn't always been a source of joy for her, but she never stopped calling him that. "Sorry it's been so long since I've seen you."

She placed her soft hands on either side of his scruffy face. "It's been a minute." Her lips poked out, but then she flashed the same smile that had placed him at the top of casting calls.

Her Italian-laced Southern drawl pulled him in, reminding him of the years before his life became public consumption. The Chicago suburb that formed him had been more lively and vibrant because of his Tennessee-born, Italian mother. And because of the charm of his father—well, before he decided to find his happiness elsewhere.

John released her, watching her move back to the stove. She tilted her head to look up at him, stirring. "Look at you. I see you're still skinny. Do they not feed you? How's craft services? You have enough money to buy half the restaurants on this block. Are you not eating?"

John laughed and grabbed a cucumber slice from a platter she'd already laid out. "I've been waiting on you to cook for me, of course."

His mom beamed, swatting at him with her wooden spoon. "Oh you. Wash those movie-star hands and help me stir the lamb stew."

An hour later, John sat next to his mom on the sofa that overlooked the outdoor shopping area below. He leaned back with a full belly and gratitude swelling his chest. The early morning gym session would be brutal, but it was worth it.

As he watched the people below him scurry around sidewalks and into various stores, longing was a lump in his throat that he had a hard time swallowing. Leave it to family to make you more vulnerable than normal. Now that he was healthy—more or less—and single, his chest ached with a desire that he couldn't pinpoint. All he knew was that it felt soothed, somehow, when Adanne was in the room.

His mother leaned her shoulder into him. Cooked onions still mingled with the perfume she'd worn since he was a kid, probably since before he was born. He turned his face to her, giving her a tilted smile as her hazel eyes assessed him.

"A tiramisu for your thoughts?"

"No. Please." He groaned, holding his stomach. "Mamma, you may have single-handedly ruined three months of my workout regime with dinner. I've got nothing left to give."

She raised one eyebrow, a semi-satisfied twinkle in her eye. "Okay then, son, tell me your thoughts for free."

She turned toward him, leaning against the end of the couch with her feet tucked under her. That picture triggered memories of many a night when he and his sister snuggled with their mom on the couch, ignoring their struggles and escaping into a book or movie. It's where it all started for him. The pull to create something that would help another person escape from circumstances they couldn't control. John gave his mother a grateful smile and leaned back himself, air escaping his lungs in a drawn-out exhale.

"I don't know if I can put words to it yet, Mamma."

He turned his gaze out toward the courtyard. Now he mostly saw their reflection in the patio pane as the sky continued to darken. "I've been thinking about the past."

"Hmm." She hadn't been fond of his relationship with Katrina. He shifted his position on the couch to face her, although he kept his eyes forward.

"I'm reminding myself that I don't need to stay there. That God is doing new things, even for me." He sighed. "But if that's the case, what does that look like?"

"Some deep thoughts for my boy. Have you been to counseling?"

He smirked. "Not exactly. But I met with a pastor after going to church last week."

John chuckled at his mom's gasp. "Mamma, I gave my life back to God. You know that."

"Yes, but I thought it would be at my funeral when you stepped into the doors of the church again."

"Mamma!"

"I'm joking, but really"—she leaned forward and held his scruffy face in her hands—"don't lie to me. Who is the woman you followed to the church house?"

John would have laughed out loud at his mom's expression, but her hands were like a vise, so all he could get out was a small saliva spray and cough.

He pulled her hands down, wiping the moisture off her forehead. "It's not like that."

"What's her name?"

He groaned, rolling his eyes to the ceiling. "Adanne."

"Bellissima. Especially the way you say it."

"Mamma!"

"Okay, *okay*. The deep thoughts. You know, I read a story about a little boy the other day."

John's brain experienced whiplash adjusting to his mom's shift in conversation.

She cleared her throat, settling back against the armrest on her end of the couch. "It popped up on my feed. The friend of a friend, you know."

John nodded, encouraging her to go on with the story that had nothing to do with him.

"Anyway, a little boy in this area needs a miracle. Has been dealing with a troubling diagnosis, but all he wants to do is get well enough to spend time with his friends at someplace called the Hope Springs Community Center."

John perked up. "Adanne!"

His mom glanced at him curiously.

"I mean, that's the place my friend volunteers. Or works. What are the odds?"

His mom gave him a knowing smile.

"Ah, I knew it would interest you."

"What do you mean?"

She reached up to lay a gentle hand on his cheek.

"You need to shave, gioia mio. Other than that, I know

what kind of heart beats under that muscle of yours. I remember the things that moved you when you were young. Your quiet, compassionate generosity to others during those crazy years to serve as penance for your mistakes. Like supporting your brother-in-law's business." Her head tilted. "Or sponsoring how many kids to attend summer camp those years ago?"

She put her hand down while John's gaze flitted back out through the glass. She repositioned herself to look out the patio window too.

Mamma sighed, a gush of air that came out almost like a melody.

"I don't know what a new season looks like for you, son. But remember to *anchor*. If you know who you are in Christ, you won't have to worry about the in-between. Do what you know. Remember your first love. Engage in what makes your heart sing. You'll see God unfold everything else from there."

Long after his mother went to bed in the guest bedroom, John sat up, alternately looking outside and at his phone, where he pulled up a story of this kid and others. It sounded like the perfect way to fulfill his manager's request. And at least this idea had come from his mother and not from data. He didn't want there to be any hint of manipulation, but either way, no child deserved to suffer. And at least for now, he had the means to bring some joy into this one's life.

And he knew *just* the person to help him.

13

*J*ohn swallowed as Adanne walked through the front entrance. He stood near the sanctuary door, waiting. For what? For her? *Of course you are.*

Regardless of her halfhearted attempts to keep him away, and because his mother was off visiting friends in her hometown of Nashville, he'd felt compelled to leave his empty hotel suite. And maybe the part of Adanne that did want him near would win out . . . eventually.

She approached him with purposeful steps, her long braids held back in a simple ponytail. Her blouse was tucked into wide-legged pants that dipped in at the waist. The only other adornment was the delicate chain with the thin bands that never seemed to leave her neck. Her eyes sparkled as she drew near.

Focus on why you're here, he chided himself. But it was getting harder to discern.

He *was* really enjoying the atmosphere of this church, welcoming and open, with people from all walks of life, it seemed.

When Adanne stepped close, his skin rippled with warmth.

"I didn't think you would show up here again. After our *table* talk."

"It's Sunday," he responded with a shrug. "I have issues. Seems like the best place to be to get *un-issued*."

Adanne's lips twitched as she nodded.

"Oh, I saved you a seat. If you don't have one already."

Her eyes lit up, dimples exposed in a full smile that he'd never seen before. "Oh, did you now?" Her laugh vibrated against his ear with rich, melodic tones. "No fan club? Or what about the friends I may want to sit next to?"

Heat of another kind crept up his neck, moving toward his ears. *I saved you a seat?* It did sound ridiculous. How in the world did this woman transform him into a nervous schoolboy in an instant?

Adanne's dimples reappeared. "Just come on, John."

"That did sound middle-schoolish of me." He dug his hands in his pockets, looking off to the side to find anything to rescue him. Maybe that fan club she mentioned.

"It's okay." Adanne tucked her smile back in, the light still dancing in her eyes. She placed her hand on his arm. He glanced down at the light touch, her gentle reassurance seeping further under the surface than she could imagine. "Of course I'll sit with you. I don't have many friends, anyway."

● ● ● ●

Adanne wondered if John had anything better to do on the weekend than to take another stroll through downtown Hope Springs with her. Especially since they spent almost every weekday together. But she couldn't say she minded as much as she had the last time they walked around the park. John intrigued her more than she cared to admit. He was not the same man she'd encountered those years ago.

She pulled her eyes away from his profile to take in the path before them. Who was she to even judge? Back then, she hadn't really known him. Just the result of his actions. What would people say about *her* now?

Her comment earlier at church about friends came out in jest, but her only consistent ones were probably her cousins. Busyness over the past few years had kept her from making room for anyone else. There was barely any time for this walk, considering the prep work she needed to do for the center before the week started. But it was getting harder to resist John's attempts to pull her out of her shell. Or the gratitude rising toward him for even trying.

And a girl had to eat. Giving John a taste of her favorite local eateries hadn't been a bad way to pass an hour or two. To her relief, it had been a calmer time at church and the restaurant. Perhaps Hope Springs was getting used to having the actor around. Or maybe she was determined to ignore the buzz.

"How did you like church today, John?" Adanne turned toward him and blushed when she saw his eyes were already on her. Her belly tightened under his perusal, and she felt the intensity of his gaze down to her toes.

He shifted forward, reining in his grin. "A lot. I admit it was hard for me to go the first time. A few things I need to work through."

"You mentioned that earlier. Got some church hurt?"

John made a deep sound in his throat, putting his hands behind his back as they continued their stroll. "I wouldn't call it that. Maybe more like disappointment." He looked up to the white clouds that streaked across the otherwise clear blue sky. "With my father."

Adanne peered at him under her lashes, expecting him to say more.

"That's an interesting addition."

She turned in surprise toward the direction of his gaze. He peered at the bright-blue bridge that connected the two sections of the Hope Springs Downtown Park.

"I didn't notice this the other night. Hard to see this color in the dark."

Adanne gave him a small smile as he shifted from the turn their conversation had been about to take. She knew the cost of releasing too much at one time. The stories that still hurt to tell.

"That's Hope Bridge. Lots of pictures and proposals happen there."

Adanne led John down a sidewalk toward the bridge. She hugged the street side, giving him room to walk on the side flanking the park. Suddenly she found her steps shifted by John's gentle touch. He'd traded positions with her, a buffer between her and the road.

The move was subtle, but that simple act of chivalry about made her stumble, his protective touch lingering on the small of her back.

When they reached the bridge, she spread her warm hands on the cool of the lacquer. She stopped at the inscribed metal welded onto the middle of the railing. Her fingers grazed the bronze plaque where two hands clasped an olive branch.

John leaned forward, dark hair falling into his face as he read the inscription.

HOPE BRIDGE, APRIL 6, 1975

On this day, in the center of our beloved town,
we declare that we will place God's love at the
center of our hearts. When others choose to divide,
we will remember that we are centered on Christ.
From that equal footing at the cross, we will choose
to move forward with peace, hope, unity, and love.

John straightened, letting his own fingers touch the engraving. "You don't see that every day." His hand bumped against the fingers Adanne didn't move fast enough. She grasped them to her belly, looking out over the east side of the park.

"Yep. Our town is special."

John nodded in agreement as he let his eyes drift over the scenery, his hair lifting and settling in the cool breeze. "I can see that. More and more each day."

Adanne heard the tease in his voice. She didn't try to hide the smile that attempted to make its way out so often in his presence. "This bridge is one of our most beloved landmarks."

"Tell me the story. Sounds like a good movie." John gave her a friendly bump on the shoulder and then leaned with his forearms on the railing, looking at the small number of fish that swam around the fountain in the middle of the pond.

Adanne leaned against the railing to face him as she recounted what all local Hope Springs residents learned when they started school. "Our town is obviously way older than 1975. Much of the Civil Rights Movement of the sixties took place further south, but we had our own share of issues to tackle here in North Alabama."

John turned his head to her, interest in his gaze.

Adanne cleared her throat. "But in the seventies specifically, tension increased as schools and neighborhoods became more integrated in the Huntsville area. Many feared Hope Springs would move back to the way things were, just to make it easier. But two ministers met and decided to fight for a unified future. They pastored different racial congregations but felt that change needed to begin with the church. So they started holding prayer meetings out here, hosted rallies and services. My grandfather gave his life to the Lord during that time. Together they served the community, listening, meeting needs, helping each other. It wasn't without its hiccups or naysayers, but they persevered. They made such an impact in the city, a wealthy donor commissioned this bridge in honor of their work. And so they made this sort of covenant, in honor of God. In service of this city."

Adanne took a deep breath and turned to lean over the rail in the same fashion as John. The chain around her neck hung out over the water. She tucked it into her blouse before continuing.

"The pastors eventually formed a church, the one you attended with me. Many years later, this inspired my parents to purchase the Hope Springs Community Center to continue that heart of unity and service."

John straightened, clearing his throat. "Those are some amazing roots you have. An incredible legacy."

Adanne's heart swelled at her history. At his words. "And I'll do whatever it takes to preserve it."

14

*S*hould I be worried about what's in that box?"

A shiver ran up the arm Adanne used to deposit sealed envelopes on the makeup station counters and seats. The familiar voice bunched her cheeks, her dimple probably already on display.

"Nothing illegal in these envelopes, Mr. Pope. Just a Wednesday morning pick-me-up."

She paused her deliveries to shoot a look over her shoulder. That was a mistake. John's presence spilled into the trailer. The scent of fresh soap drifted toward her. His hair, curly and dark, left wet patches on the shoulders of his fitted T-shirt. He often arrived at the makeup trailer straight from workouts. But today . . . *Jesus, be a fence.*

She continued her drops until she made it back to her station with an empty container, trying to ignore John as he wandered around the empty trailer, observing each placement. But her eyes would not be deterred from following him around the room. She snickered as he lifted the one on Trina's station. He bounced it in his hand, an eyebrow lifted.

"Okay, nosy!" She retrieved the envelope from his hand.

A chuckle vibrated from his chest. His palm was warm, heat radiating from his entire frame.

"Humph." Placing the packet back on Trina's desk was a much better alternative than facing the way his eyes lingered on her when she approached, a mischievous gleam in his golden-green gaze.

"Is that for me?" Stepping in front of her chair, he picked up the envelope she'd dropped there while he was meddling. He grinned, eyes narrowing playfully. "Can I—"

"Yes, yes." She flapped her fingers at him as she turned to arrange her brushes and heard paper rustling. She hadn't expected absolute giddiness to be a by-product of her simple gift.

"A Valentine's Day card?!"

Adanne turned, bracing her hands on the desk behind her. "I bought some for the kids at the center to give out later today. Thought I would drop off my extras here." She offered a shy smile. "No biggie."

His expression was so genuinely delighted it hurt. He tore the wrapper off the red sucker that came with the card, jamming it in his mouth as he plopped in the chair. Adanne gave in to a bit of indulgence and leaned over his shoulder to get a better look at the card he held.

"You are beary special," he read around the lollipop, holding the turquoise card with a cartoon bear as if it were a golden ticket.

He swiveled around and, before she could back away, Adanne found herself inches from the candy in his mouth, the handle the only barrier between their lips. His green eyes flickered, his strawberry-scented breath warm.

If only . . .

John bit into the candy and the crunch startled her to reality. Adanne cackled, her nervous energy finding release. He kept his eyes on her as he chewed the remnants of the sucker like a coffee grinder. She pulled back, turning away from his face.

"You done with that sucker yet?" She glanced up at the photos taped onto the mirror before grabbing a couple facial wipes.

"Yup." John pulled the lollipop stick out of his mouth. Adanne stepped around him to cleanse his face. "This reminds me." He paused as she wiped around his mouth. "I want to do something for the kids at the St. Jude clinic in the hospital nearby."

Adanne's hands stilled. "That's sweet. But where did that idea come from? Valentine cards and candy?"

"That and an article my mother showed me." John placed his hand on top of hers. *Oh God, surely not.* Adanne willed her fingers to keep themselves together as he pulled her hand and the wipe away from his face. He looked so serious, probably in response to her shock. He dropped the half-chewed stick into the used wipe. She rolled her eyes and tossed them both in the trash.

Her application today was simple, translucent powder for a no-makeup look and groomed eyebrows. But despite the simplicity, her heart continued its increased tempo. "Can you repeat what you said again?"

"I want to do something fun, like a party, for the kids in that part of the hospital. And maybe throw in something for their families."

"You want to plan a party, and help the families of the kids too?" Adanne gulped through the anxiety that tried to squeeze her throat shut.

"Is there an echo in here?" John relaxed into the next part of the makeup routine, unaware of the tension on the other end of her powder brush. "Yes, a party that will give them a sense of connection and fun activities—doctor-approved, of course. If candy and a bear on a card can brighten my day, imagine what a themed celebration would mean for those kids."

His words swelled within her, affection simmering too close to her surface. "Why does this matter to you, John? There are hundreds of kids with similar stories all over the country."

He closed his eyes as her brush moved around his forehead. "Because Hope Springs is my current location. I don't know, what if God is leading me? I haven't been able to get this story out of my mind, knowing that I can help in some way."

Her mouth dropped open, then she closed it. Words squeezed within her tightening throat.

"With that, I have a favor to ask." He placed his hand on her arm before she could say more. "One of the kids mentioned Hope Springs Community Center. What are the odds?"

Adanne's wide-open eyes managed a blink. *Say something!*

She couldn't risk it. Stepping away from her job in California for her family had cost her. It had been worth it to be with her mom that last year of her life, but could the same thing happen again?

Don't be silly. For all she knew, this could just be some publicity stunt. Devised by the same manager who wanted John to attend the awards with the right woman just to place him in the spotlight. Fodder for the headlines. Experience she knew all too well.

Something inside told her to trust his character. To lean into what she had been sensing about him over the last few weeks. She felt the tug of the Holy Spirit, inviting her to put down her reticence. Yet, her experience from the past kept her mouth shut.

John continued, oblivious to her inner turmoil. "Will you

help me plan this party? Not too complicated. It could also be a time that parents can get a break. Maybe we can set up a spa day or a nice lunch out."

He caught her eye in the mirror. His mouth tipped into a timid grin, as if it embarrassed him to share his ideas or ask her for help.

"I know I have assistants and a team who could do this." He glanced at her over his shoulder. "But I don't want Hollywood involved," he went on. "I want the touch of a woman . . ."

Adanne arched her eyebrows. John didn't break contact, sending his disarming gaze her way with disconcerting intensity.

"A woman whose love for her town is palpable. Someone who would know better than my team the best way to pull this off." His smile leaked into his eyes, sending tingles of awareness up her spine. "What do you say?"

Adanne slowly shook her head. More in disbelief than denial. His passion for this and his trust in her were dismantling her objections.

"I don't know . . ." Something subtle pulled her to agree. She *would* have dismissed this as a shallow publicity stunt if she didn't see the authentic compassion in his eyes.

"But I'll say yes. I'll help you."

John smiled broadly, clapping his hands together. The sound echoed off the almost empty trailer. "Yes! I will cover the cost and my team will do whatever you need. And you can recruit any local professionals that you trust."

He stood and pulled out his phone, motioning it toward her. "Can I have your number? To send your contact information to my assistant."

After grabbing her cell from her bag, she spouted off the digits, gazing warily at the screen as John dropped contacts her way, pushing aside another chunk of her resistance. This

136

man was giving her the keys to his little kingdom, all so he could bless her nephew and the friends he'd made in the hospital. Except he didn't know that this was *her* family.

"John. I need to ask. I mean—I need to talk with you about this more."

He stepped closer, pocketed his phone, and then placed a hand on each of her shoulders. "Adanne. Believe me. You don't have to worry about anything. It will be fun, and the press will eat this up. Help me do this. Then I promise I'll leave you alone."

The pressure of his palms spread currents down her arms. All her protests and her confession turned to liquid. Adanne felt the pull deep in her belly, even as apprehension made her want to secure her defenses. His green eyes focused on her.

"The last thing that I want"—*is to be left alone*—"is to say no." She didn't care about magazine covers or celebrity status. Her concern was for her family. And here was John, moving his mountains to do something for those *she* loved. "But maybe, for the sake of the families, it should stay more private than public. Keeps it about the kids."

"Okay." He hesitated, but then nodded, blinking away the uncertainty that had briefly crossed his face. "You have my word."

Her stomach tightened at his genuine smile and the glow in his eyes. He gave her arm a light squeeze and hurried out the door.

Adanne swallowed the lump in her throat and turned toward the mirror. The fluorescent bulbs highlighted the worry in her eyes that no amount of makeup could hide.

She needed to remind herself that this was good attention. This wasn't the haphazardly posted video on a celebrity's social media feed. The girlfriend of a certain actor giving her followers exclusive behind-the-scenes footage of his set life, her camera capturing his comments about an assistant makeup artist. A woman, unbeknownst to them, on her way to see her ailing mom.

Adanne sighed. She hadn't been on social media since.

After cleaning up, she pulled out her phone. Her cousin answered on the third ring.

"Kenya, I need you."

"Well, those are words I never thought I'd hear from my long-lost cousin."

"I just saw you last week and live twenty minutes away from you."

"*Exactly.*"

Adanne groaned, placing the phone to her forehead. She didn't have the time or energy to give any excuses for her absence at Sunday dinners or for forgetting to return messages. Kenya took the pause as an opportunity to pounce.

"So, who is the man?"

"Come again?"

"I remember you saying that you would enlist my help for something that mattered, like a man. Who is he? Maybe that actor at the center on Saturday?"

What could she say? There was no word or definition she could use to describe John and what they were falling into. Could she even call it a friendship? And it wasn't like he was her direct supervisor. He was almost like an upper-level coworker. With a very upper-level salary.

It didn't even matter. No explanation would move Kenya off the trail of romantic curiosity. Adanne would just have to let her form her own ideas and deal with them later.

"Well, it *is* about a man, but not like you think. He has enlisted me to help plan a party. It's a little complicated and I don't know where to start."

"Well, you definitely called the right person."

Adanne let out a sigh of relief. "He wants to plan something fun for the kids at the hospital."

"Aw, that sounds great."

"More specifically, the St. Jude's clinic in Huntsville."

She gasped. "Ohh, I'm gonna cry. I can already see costumed characters spread out. Hmm, nontoxic balloon displays. Interactive backdrops . . . ooooh, what about a mini carnival? Like we did on field days at school. I know just the colors that will make it pop. Jason and the others will love it so much and—"

"I don't really want Jason to know I'm there," Adanne blurted out.

"What? Why? Won't he see you?"

How in the world would she explain the layers of what she couldn't quite vocalize herself. "I-I haven't told John I have family there."

"So . . ."

"So?"

Kenya scoffed. "I don't see the problem."

A notification went off on Adanne's phone. A reminder to head to the set to prep for last looks. "Gotta go fly in, but we'll talk later. I just want Jason and the other kids to have their moment without Auntie Dee hovering."

"Whatever you say," Kenya agreed without much enthusiasm. "I'll work my event-planning magic and be in touch."

● ● ● ●

"Cut!"

John stepped back, narrowly avoiding the cone at the edge of his scene. He had to get his thoughts straight. He was costing the production time and therefore money, but he couldn't make his mark. He usually had no problem shutting off his personal life to engage in whatever role he found himself in.

After his mom shared the article, he couldn't get it out of his head. He felt a strange pull to make sure he executed this well, like he was being called to step in. The plan made him feel more alive than he had in a while. And he would have a palatable way to satisfy the machinations of Mike and his publicity team. Maybe that would lift the pressure for a while.

Yet he wasn't necessarily getting warm and fuzzy vibes from Adanne. He'd expected her to be more excited since the event involved kids from her community. He thought about her pinched features speaking to the multitude of thoughts passing behind her eyes. Did she doubt his motives? Did he doubt his own? But she didn't open up enough to share those sentiments with him. If he was being honest, his fervor may not have even given her an opportunity to. He should have let her unpack the idea more instead of letting the shadow of her conflicted thoughts sneak into his scenes.

Gray, the director, stepped away from video village to walk toward him, hands in his pockets. "John, you're wound up today. I need that energy *in* this scene, not locked up in your brain." He leaned in close with a chuckle. "Do I need to get one of the runners to grab you something? Help you relax?"

John shook his head emphatically. "I plan on staying sober."

Gray nodded but still held the offer in his eyes. "Got it. But whatever you need to do to hit this so we can move, do it. Let's take ten." Gray stalked back to his chair, swirling his hand in the air. "Ten one!"

John placed his hands on his hips, looking up at the early morning sky. Wisps of salmon-pink and saffron melted away from the rise of the sun. There were other ways to push through besides the drink that almost cost him his career.

Lord, I need a little help here. Help me focus today so I can take care of what you've trusted me with. Amen.

15

So, what's up, man?"

Mike slid into the booth across from John, his lips curling after a quick glance at the tabletop. If he had it his way, lunch would be at a five-star restaurant. But that was hard to find around Hope Springs.

John's thoughts flitted to his early days here. He'd been frustrated and troubled over Katrina. But this small community softened his jagged edges. He felt the space to breathe deeply here. To be authentic to who he was becoming. No longer missing the expensive perfume that Katrina wore, he craved the scent of earthy coconut oil and lavender with a dash of lemon from freshly cleansed makeup brushes.

"Man, you're distracted. I thought your mood the other week in LA was just some hangry phase."

John looked away from the window that had carried his thoughts. Their booth stood apart from prying eyes, but there was never any escaping the perusal of his manager.

"What do you mean?" He took a long swig of water and settled back into his seat to get his own good look at a stressed-out Mike. The exuberance of Mike's early years in the industry had dissolved into a constant drive that left little room or desire for his manager to rest.

Mike cut his eyes away.

"Don't give me your concerned, I'm-praying-for-you look." He clenched the menu, eyes narrowed. "The word on set is you've been a little off your game the past few days."

John laughed, shaking his head. He shouldn't have been surprised that his manager's tactics hadn't changed. Recruiting someone on the film sets who earned a little extra commission for keeping tabs on Mike's clients.

Considering Adanne's face the other day and the waves of tension coming from her lately, it wouldn't have been a shock if she graced Mike's roster. "Let me guess. My new MUA is your latest spy. Did she already tell you about my hospital idea? Was the whole Doris departure a cover-up for your latest recruit?"

He almost spat out the words. Usually, he just laughed off Mike's attempts to stay ahead of the curve. But speaking of Adanne in this context tasted bitter. His stomach rolled in unpleasant waves.

Mike sniffed, unbuttoning and pushing up his sleeves. "I won't reveal my sources."

John drummed his fingers on the tabletop. His manager didn't know. So much for keeping things private.

Mike tilted his head.

"But kudos for the community service. Very good to know. And maybe we *should* talk about this makeup artist." His manager's tight smile didn't reach his eyes as he crossed his arms on top of napkins he placed on the tabletop. "I see I've hit the mark. Unlike you the past few days. How many extra-curricular activities do you plan on having with this local?"

"Bro. Do you hear yourself? What I do on my minuscule off time is none of your business."

Mike put his hands up. "I haven't accused you of anything.

I'm just scratching my head to figure out why you've gone from laser focused to slipping off your game. There's a lot riding on this role."

"Then maybe you should take my place, since you care so much."

Mike pressed his lips together, his face a portrait of exasperation. The server took that moment to take their orders. John hadn't even noticed him step up.

After the server departed, John ducked his head, running a hand through the wavy curls he desperately needed to trim. He didn't mind his hair being on the longer side, but having to keep a certain style for a role always made him feel boxed in. He released a sigh. "I'm not trying to be difficult. I'm grateful for this role. And while we're at it, thankful for you being my loyal manager for ten years. Even though I don't say it enough, I'm sure."

"Yeah, yeah, no need for sentiments here, bro. Tell me what the *but* is."

"Come again?"

Mike took a swig from the glass of Coke before him. "Ah. Tell me what you're plotting to say after your syrupy speech. The words that will destroy your previous compliments."

Irritating his manager always made John laugh. "Chill. I just want to build my career more on my terms, not just on the whims of the audience. Or the tactics of my maybe *too* loyal manager."

Mike harrumphed.

"I'm not the same guy I was two years ago. A new man. This probably sounds as crazy as it did the first time I told you, but God has to be at the center of my decision-making. I need you to be patient with me. My career matters, but I need to figure out how to do this better. Be me better."

John pulled his glass of water closer, though he wished it were a Coke, like Mike's, or a ginger ale. "You can pass that message along to your spies. And if my makeup artist is not one of them, leave her out of your investigations. She's good people. And she's not a distraction." *Because she sure does feel better than that.*

"What is she, then?"

John wanted to say inspiration. Spark. The oxygen in this town of Hope Springs that he wanted to breathe in more of. But their meal came, silencing any coherent response that would make sense of what he couldn't quite comprehend.

He rubbed his hands together, looking forward to this splurge. The fresh-baked roll that encased his burger. Crisp, golden fried-potato rounds overflowed on the plate with three little dishes of dipping sauces to choose from.

Before he could dig in, Mike slid the plate away from him. "Hey!"

Mike shrugged, stabbing his fork into a potato. "This is the stuff *old* John would eat. Thought I'd do you a favor since you're a new man and all."

· · · ·

"I really don't have time for this." Adanne ambled past the rows of color-coordinated items in the party supply store, drifting her fingers along the streamers hanging from their hooks. Kenya trailed not too far behind, pushing an overflowing shopping cart.

"I always have time to spend someone else's money, *honey.*" Kenya whizzed past her toward the balloons while Adanne paused at the superhero-themed party items.

Her tension eased as she thought about the upcoming party on Saturday and the looks on the faces of all the kids. The pediatric oncology floor at the hospital was filled with children who needed something to brighten their day as their families prayed for the vicious intruders to leave their bodies.

This event would not shoo the cancer away, but it sure would stir up some hope. *It has to.* Adanne could tear up right there in the party aisle. But one thought dried it up real quick.

She'd already heard of a few television stations that had gotten wind of the story. Her fears about this becoming too public were growing into a concerning reality. So much for John keeping his word.

"Girl. You gonna get your head out of that display?"

Adanne threw her armful of decor into the buggy her cousin pushed. With a quick swipe of her hands, she straightened the items thrown askew.

"Just tell the man, Dee. It's not that big of a deal, for real."

Adanne didn't appreciate her cousin's clairvoyance or the nonchalant way it flowed from her lips. "Get out of my head, Kenya."

"Nope, cuz, you get out of yours." She stuck out a hip, crossing her arms. "I still don't understand why you think this should be so hush-hush. So what if a few reporters show up? It's something the community can rally behind. And Jason will recognize the both of us immediately." She gestured toward the hero-themed decor. "It's not like you'll put on a pair of glasses and, bam, 'That's not Auntie Dee!'"

Adanne's eyes bugged out at her younger cousin, who placed a hand over her mouth in mock shock.

"Those kids don't need paparazzi breathing down their necks," she huffed. "And we'll be wearing masks, not glasses."

"There are no paparazzi trying to come to Hope Springs, Dee." Kenya leaned back, narrowing her eyes. "I'm not buying all this. You know Jason will love you being there. You're making this too complicated, and you hate fuss."

Adanne rolled her eyes at her cousin, who was trying to look serious but failing spectacularly with the multicolored balloons floating around her face. Her slick ponytail, striped blouse, and navy pencil skirt made her look more like a lawyer than a children's party planner. But with the way she'd deftly handled John's team and local vendors in the past couple of days, she wasn't too far off from that. Kenya had hit the ground running in her four-inch heels as soon as she got the word.

"Seems like you're letting some minor issues keep you from enjoying the fact that your favorite movie star wants to spend his money on your *favorite* nephew."

"He's not my favorite movie star. Just the talent on a job that will eventually end. I know this will mean a lot to all the kids. I just don't want them in a spotlight they didn't ask for."

Adanne averted her gaze from her perceptive cousin. Her mask was slipping, and she knew it. She couldn't reveal her fears without processing her feelings. They were all tangled up in a flashing smile and green eyes.

Kenya perked her eyebrow up. "If he doesn't matter, as you say . . . confront the man and move on. It's not personal." She paused, a sly smirk crossing her lips. "Unless it is."

16

*a*danne couldn't keep from smiling when she saw the decorations in the main activity room of the hospital. Kenya and her impeccable party planning, as well as John's small but efficient team, turned the place into a dream for any child.

Familiar tightness pulled at her chest—her eyes blinked away rising moisture. *Don't lose it, Dee.* There was too much at stake today. She needed to get through this as together as possible, to not ruin things for her family.

They had already lost so much.

"Well, we did it!"

Adanne turned. Kenya was exuberant, her heels click-clacking on the linoleum floor, straight, shoulder-length hair swinging with her steps. Adanne grinned. They couldn't have been more different. Kenya had been into makeup, fashion, and design since childhood. She loved keeping up with trends and experimenting with her looks as much as she enjoyed hitting the gym. But Adanne hardly prioritized her looks, even when she ventured deeper into the makeup profession. She just enjoyed the way her craft contributed to someone else's confidence.

Or at least she used to. Until life squeezed the joy out and her work became fueled by necessity. She clenched her hands, dry and achy from all the work beyond makeup. But this wasn't the time to bemoan her appearance. It was a day to celebrate.

Kenya stood beside her, observing the room with hands on her hips. "Not too bad, huh?"

"Not at all." Adanne gave her cousin a bump with her hip. "Thankful for your help, cuz." Her gaze skittered away, growing blurry.

Kenya placed an arm around Adanne's taller frame and bumped back. "Always ready to help, Dee, you know that."

Adanne felt something inside of her snapping, tight cords loosening bit by bit, but before she could respond, a warm, male voice drew her attention.

"Has the dance portion started already?" John stood in the doorway of the activity room with an older woman next to him. They were joined by a man from the hospital staff.

Kenya stiffened beside her, eyes on the grinning doctor, the color of the scrubs actually appealing against his smooth skin.

Before Adanne could assess *that* further, John's gaze landed on her after casting his eyes about the room. An appreciative smile spread across his face as he strode to where they stood. Her body stiffened at his approach. It was the only way she knew how to contain the emotions she didn't comprehend, especially as they stirred up around him. She forced her lips into a smile when he stepped close.

"The room looks fantastic!" The pleasure on his face gave Adanne a traitorous sense of satisfaction. She gestured toward her cousin, unsuccessfully defusing the charged atmosphere with her limp wave. But Kenya's attention was not on John at all. At least not fully. Her eyes darted at the doctor who led him into the room. The one who seemed more fascinated by the room change than the woman who couldn't take her eyes off him.

John coughed, hiding a grin as he tipped his chin in Kenya's direction. Adanne couldn't help the smirk that crossed her lips in response.

"Ahem. This is my cousin Kenya. The event planner that I hired. You may have seen her at the community center that Saturday you stopped by. She's the one mainly responsible for planning and setting everything up alongside your team." Adanne leaned toward her cousin, bumping her back into focus. "Kenya, this is John Pope. Aka Mr. So-and-So at the community brunch."

Kenya's lashes fluttered as she sent a coy smile his way. "Nice to meet you, John. Officially. This will mean the world to our—ow—!"

Adanne gritted her teeth, keeping her smile tight as Kenya turned to her in disbelief. But that dissipated when Kenya assessed the glint in her older cousin's eyes and the threat to get pinched again if needed.

"Uh, it will mean the world to these little community members of Hope Springs." Kenya pursed her lips, her composure recovered. Adanne wanted to smack her forehead but kept her face straight.

John chuckled, to his credit. "Nice to meet you, Kenya. I appreciate your work to make this happen."

He stepped aside and placed an arm over the shoulder of the much shorter, older woman who had walked in with him. "This is my mother, Giulia. She is the one who inspired the idea."

"Oh, I wouldn't say all that." A warm gaze, hazel eyes framed by long lashes, greeted Adanne, showing off the magnetic smile she'd passed on to her son. Her dark, almost-black hair hung in a stylish bob, her curls streaked with silver. Instead of shaking Adanne's hand, Giulia Pomponio pulled her into a warm embrace, causing her eyes to sting a bit.

Adanne's shoulders relaxed, just for a moment. Maybe this was a good time to tell John what she couldn't bring herself to say before.

"Ah, there they are." The melodic voice of the doctor ended the brief embrace, drawing their attention to the opening doors. Adanne breathed a sigh of relief. Her heightened emotional state and John's friendly mom had almost weakened her resolve. Giulia gave Kenya a quick hug and walked to the other side of the room to talk with the nurses.

The kids filed in with shuffled steps, some in wheelchairs, a few led by the hands of their nurses and other hospital staff. They all wore bright handkerchiefs as blindfolds. Huge grins were plastered on their faces as they waited for their surprise. Adanne didn't bother wiping away the tear that trickled down her cheek as she watched her nephew enter.

Kenya leaned over to whisper into Adanne's ear. "Jason has lost so much weight since the last time I saw him."

Adanne nodded. "I hate this disease." Cancer and the subsequent treatments were to blame.

Kenya squeezed her arm. "Gotta head to my next event." After one last look at Jason, and a side glance at the doctor, she headed out the door.

John replaced Kenya at Adanne's side, his mouth a grim line as he surveyed the kids. He swallowed and rubbed a hand down his neck. "I hate this disease too. But I hope they don't have to think about it at least for today."

He grazed his shoulder against Adanne's. It was an innocent gesture, but it almost sent her reeling. *Dear God, I need to get out of here.*

John cleared his throat. "By the way, I'm sorry about the press. One mention to my manager and—"

"One word is all it takes." She flinched at the edge in her voice.

He paused. "I assumed he already knew since he'd encouraged me to find a community project here to get involved with."

I knew it. She thought of how he'd helped at the community meal. Probably for publicity too.

"*But* I didn't make any moves until my mother talked to me. I meant it when I said that the article"—he grinned with boyish charm—"and your Valentine's Day gifts inspired me." Adanne felt the fist in her gut loosen. Perhaps she didn't know that much at all.

"Well, either way, I'm thankful they weren't allowed in." Adanne scanned the room. "I just want the kids to enjoy themselves without any interference."

John leaned closer, looking relieved. "I know you mentioned helping with snacks around the corner. Sure you don't want to stay in the room? At least until after they take off their blindfolds?"

"No, no." Dark-brown braids swept across her back, punctuating her decision. "There will be plenty of people in here between the staff and characters in costumes." She looked pointedly at the men and women dressed in a variety of superhero, princess, and cartoon outfits. "My skills are better used in the kitchen. Out of sight." She took one last glance at her nephew, her heart fit to burst.

Adanne turned back to John, allowing a self-deprecating smile to grace her lips instead of more tears to cross the threshold. "Plus, I wouldn't want any of the kids to mistake me for a character."

John stifled a laugh, but then his voice grew soft, dialed down for only her. "How could anyone mistake you for anything but a queen?" He lifted one shoulder, jamming his hands into the pockets of his jeans as he turned to greet the kids.

Those words lingered in Adanne's thoughts as she scurried in the background, popping in and out of the small kitchen area the nurses let her use to set up the snacks. She watched her nephew's cute face from afar when the blindfolds came off, his joy overwhelming her until she had to breathe deep to contain herself. But that didn't help the sinking feeling in her belly. Somehow keeping this detail from John burdened her more than she wanted to admit.

She had to thank him. Honestly.

Brushing a few bits of sugar-free cookie crumbs off her gloves, she made her way back to the party area. A portion of the wall jutted out, giving her an excellent position to view the festivities without being seen. The costumed characters engaged the children in gentle dances, assembled balloon animals, and led some carefully around the mini-carnival games. Nurses stood at various points in the room to help as needed. Some dabbed their eyes as they meandered about, and others cast starstruck glances at John.

Adanne didn't blame them. It was hard for her not to be starstruck at the moment. He was down on one knee, eye to eye with her nephew. Jason's grin bloomed wide in his thin face, his weariness swallowed up by delight. They both had mini basketballs in their hands and John seemed to be getting basketball pointers from the seven-year-old.

Adanne's heart soared with pride. Her nephew was so giving, even in his sickness. He was the reason they were all here. She took one step forward, the scene of them captured in her mind.

John threw back his head, laughing under his mask, carefully moving his toned arm against Jason's narrow one. No acting here. He was even more authentic in this setting than when he'd stood next to her handing out biscuits and fruit snacks. She'd been around John enough times to notice the difference. At least, she hoped. Because she could fall for a man like that.

"So good to see him like this."

Adanne sucked in her breath. She hadn't noticed John's mother approach her from behind, eyes on her son.

Adanne turned her attention back to the pair at the basketball goals. "He really shines in these settings."

"Yes, that's for sure, but there's been something different the last few weeks."

Adanne shifted to see Giulia's focus on her now, a knowing smile lifting her cheeks.

"A glow from another source, perhaps?"

Adanne opened her mouth but the words left her as Giulia walked away, her comment hanging in the air.

She could attempt to read between the lines, run with the subtle meaning trying to rise to the surface. But John's interaction with her nephew was too captivating to entertain any other enticing thought.

On what seemed to be the count of three, basketballs spun through the air, landing simultaneously through their respective nets. The hoarse whoop that came out of her nephew cut something loose in her. She released a strangled cry but muffled the end of it immediately behind her hand.

At the same moment, Jason looked around, victory on his face. He almost missed her, but before she could duck back behind the corner, his eyes widened, his arm went up in a wave. "Aunt Dee-Dee. Is that you? It's me! You're here too?"

Could he grin any wider? Or could her heart drop any lower? The satisfaction that framed John's face shifted to shock and then confusion at her nephew's words.

Adanne swallowed, waving back, pulling the mask down from her nose and mouth. No place to go but forward. Jason's eyes sparkled with welcome. She focused on his radiant joy to distract herself from the intensity rolling off John as she approached.

"Mr. John, my auntie Dee-Dee is the one who taught me how to shoot. She's the best."

"Is she now?" John's eyes sparked, and Adanne averted her gaze.

As she knelt on the other side of her beloved nephew, she prayed for the strength to face John at work on Monday.

Or better yet, she might as well prepare a resignation letter.

17

The sound of the basketball echoed off the floor of the empty gym near the hotel. John planned to get a few more shots in before heading to his suite. His mom promised him brunch before she flew back to Chicago that afternoon. But he didn't know if it would be enough to rid him of the frustration building since yesterday.

He threw a bounce pass against the wall, the ball slapping soundly as it ricocheted back to him. Yesterday was amazing, the hospital staff gushing over the party and the response from the kids. And watching Jason's sweet spirit shine through the ravages of his disease had been overwhelming. He wanted to do more to help.

Adanne's face floated through his thoughts, dragging up disappointment he couldn't brush off.

He didn't know what bothered him more, the fact that Adanne had kept her relationship to Jason from him or the pang in his heart from her lack of confidence. She wasn't required to disclose all her family information to him. So why did he want to earn her trust so badly?

That question haunted him on his way back to his suite and the mother waiting on him. What was it that made so many push away from him? After a quick shower and slipping into comfortable jeans and a T-shirt, he joined his mother at the mini-kitchen counter.

John's words were minimal between the bites of homemade zeppole and berries. Even a plateful of his favorite Italian pastry couldn't diminish his melancholy. He didn't bother looking up when he sensed his mother had stopped eating.

"Son. I know you wish she'd been more open with you. But don't you think it's interesting that this young boy I told you about is the nephew of your lovely makeup artist?"

He gulped down his bite. "Mamma."

"Don't 'Mamma' me. I saw the way your eyes lingered after her. How you found her across the room. I may be getting older but I'm not blind."

"You know I'm not going there with you, right?"

"And I'm not trying to take you." She patted his knee. Her legs cracked a bit as she stood and stretched.

"Just saying that you shouldn't be so hard on her. Or on yourself. I believe you were an instrument of God's love for those kids and families. And who knows why God placed her in *your* life? Maybe to help you too."

John's mother dusted off her hands before wrapping her arms around his neck. "John, I know you've been hurting. But Adanne is not Katrina. Stop cutting people off and out when they fail you. Or you *think* they do."

He groaned. Her tone took on an all-too-familiar note. "Is this going to turn into another try-to-talk-to-your-dad conversation?"

"Nope, I would never force my grown son to do something he doesn't want to do."

"Ah, but you underestimate your powers of persuasion."

His mother laughed, releasing his neck. But not before planting a kiss on his scruffy cheek. "You need to shave again. Or grow this out a little longer."

She stepped to the side of him as John leaned back in his chair. "Why does it matter to you so much, Mamma?"

Her lips curved in a small smile as she took the dishes from the counter and put them into the sink.

John stood up. "Let me get those while you answer." He regretted saying that almost immediately as she drew her hands out and sent droplets of soapy water his way.

John bobbed to move out of the line of fire. Or water, rather. A throaty giggle bubbled up as she headed to the seat he vacated.

"So." He scrubbed one platter and placed it carefully into the dishwasher.

"John, you've been forgiven of so much."

He felt his forehead tighten, but he scrubbed in silence.

"We all have, gioia mio. Because of that, we must forgive others as well."

"I've forgiven him. That's not an issue." He placed another dish in the dishwasher.

"But have your actions shown that? Not by what you do toward him. But how you carry this within yourself." She sighed, lingering weight in her exhale. "Your father never intended to hurt you. I know that doesn't amount to much and it doesn't justify his actions, but it's true. He just got caught up in finding his own happiness and convinced himself that it wasn't to be found with me. The issue is that this hurt you still hold affects your view of others. Ready to push people away before they disappoint you."

John paused, his hands still in the water. "You forget *Katrina* is the one who decided to leave first."

His mother's sympathetic look annoyed him. He didn't need all the extra compassion in her gaze, even if she'd earned this conversation with her zeppole, prosciutto, and fruit brunch.

"But you were always afraid of it. You went the extra mile

buying her the world while guarding your most precious commodity. Your heart."

John considered her words, chewing on them slowly, the bitter taste melting into probably needed medicine.

"I'm not saying you need to beg Katrina back into your life. I had no great like for that woman, honestly. Nor am I saying you need to go play a game of pickup with your father."

She gave her son a soft smile.

"I just want to make sure you carry grace along with your boundaries. That you hold mercy as tight as your need for justice. And that you let forgiveness keep the door open to whoever God has for your future."

· · · ·

Daniel's shot was sure as he aimed for the basketball goal. Adanne wasn't really in the mood, but she couldn't say no when her brother asked her to hang out with him the Sunday after the party.

"Jason can't stop talking about the fun he had. It made his whole year."

That was something to be thankful for, but even her family's excitement over the party didn't push away the shadow of regret for Adanne. Fear had held her back from being transparent. Worse than that, this heaviness revealed more to her than she cared to admit to herself. She cared about what John thought of her. But why should she, especially after what happened three years ago?

"Sis! You still here? Or do I need to throw an unexpected chest pass to wake you up."

Adanne gaped at her brother standing several feet away, the basketball held between his palms.

"I'm sorry, Daniel, what were you saying?"

He made a sound in his throat. "If I didn't know better . . ." He shook his head, deflecting his own question with the skill of an experienced sibling.

"I was saying that Monica wanted to send a basket or something to say thank you. To that actor of yours?"

"He most definitely is not mine." Adanne leveled a gaze at her brother.

He smirked and passed her the ball in response. "At least now I've gotten your attention."

"Humph." She broke contact with his discerning gaze, taking a shot that bounced shamefully off the backboard.

"By the way, Justine has been stopping by more to visit and bring food." Daniel recovered the ball, dribbling it back to her. "You know they ask about you too. How long's it been since you've gone over there?"

"I've lost track."

She *did* know. So much for being transparent. She still remembered what she'd eaten that day. Her sweet aunt had cooked for everyone on the two-year anniversary of her mom's death. For some reason, the abundance of family and the memories of her parents that lingered in the house were too much to deal with. It was also the last good memory of her nephew, a healthy Jason. A couple weeks later, Daniel and Monica received his diagnosis.

Adanne stopped in the middle of the community center's court. She watched Daniel run to the basket before powering into a layup. He caught the ball bouncing up from the floor after his successful shot and dribbled back to his sister.

A long hand waved in front of her face. "*Hello.* I know you didn't just miss me showing off."

Adanne blinked. She bounced the ball in her hands once but tucked it back under one arm. "Sorry. I'm so distracted lately." And heavy. And worried. And stressed. She could make a list of every emotion.

Daniel stepped toward his sister. "That's exactly why you need to stop by Auntie and Uncle's house. Mama would want that. She hated that her sickness caused you to stop everything you were doing." He chuckled, his lips lifting into a wistful smile. "She always said your hands were made to create beauty. Whatever that means."

She rolled her eyes at his expression of feigned disgust.

"But maybe those hands have forgotten what that means because they've been so gripped in control."

Adanne stiffened, shifting away from his sharp words.

Daniel touched her shoulder, bringing her vision back to him. "Dee, hear me. You gotta get to the point where you can live out your God-given purpose without being burdened by things you aren't supposed to carry by yourself. Just because you honor a legacy doesn't mean you have to walk it the same way. You keep trying to fill mom's shoes. But you can't, sis . . ." Adanne reared back, the flush in her face as hot as a physical slap.

"Because you weren't meant to. Our parents forged a path for us, but we gotta walk it out in our own way. With God and the ones he's called to come alongside us."

Adanne sighed, shaking her head at her big brother. The words swirled around her, stinging but settling on her shoulders with soothing warmth. "When did you become so wise?"

Daniel laughed, the sound weary and relieved at the same time. "Circumstances have a way of doing that, don't they?"

He placed his hands on Adanne's shoulders, the dropped basketball echoing around the cavernous room. "*When* we get our miracle, I want to move forward from this place well. And my hope for you is that you don't stay locked behind your *own* walls. Don't forget how much you're loved. You gotta do the things you're passionate about from that place. Trust God with the things you can't control."

Adanne wanted to trust that God would take care of her family, her friendships, and that, whatever the outcome, he would remain faithful. But it was so hard to let go. So hard not to let the experiences of the past dictate the here and now.

"Okay?" Daniel leaned his head to his sister's forehead.

Adanne leaned toward him. Soaking up the strength her brother offered. "Okay."

18

*W*hat's this, Adanne?"

She turned from the bulb-lined mirror to see the envelope that contained her resignation flopping back and forth in John's hand. Her stomach somersaulted, his pained expression surprising her.

"Where did you get that?" She wanted to grab at it but kept her feet planted near her station.

John paused for a beat, assessing her response. He seemed to deflate as he took a slight step forward.

"Why didn't you talk to me first?"

Adanne scoffed, willing her stomach to loosen. "Why are you here? It's Monday. Today's scenes don't involve you, according to my call sheet. And it's not your job to handle staffing issues."

"But you work mostly with me."

"Occupational hazard."

"Working here is hazardous to your health, is that it?"

"You tell me."

John worked his jaw, the laugh lines around his mouth deepening. She looked down to deflect his gaze when she noticed that she was not as far away from him as she had been when he walked in. When had he moved forward?

She sighed, putting down the towel she'd been using to wipe the desk surface. Preparing the area for the person who would take over for her.

"What I need you to tell me is why you're quitting. If I hadn't stopped by to look through some takes, I wouldn't have known until tomorrow."

"That should have been private."

"Then get with the twenty-first century and send an email. A text even. When Alex told me that she might need to find another MUA to fill in, I was obviously curious. So she showed me this. And just about begged me to use my daytime charm to convince you to stay."

Adanne bit the inside of her cheek. *Daytime charm, huh?*

"John, why do you care? I'm replaceable. Let me leave."

"Adanne, why do you keep asking me questions like that? Finding another person at this stage in the process costs time and money. And I thought we were becoming friends. I'm not that cold or heartless to not care."

"But aren't you?" She couldn't believe what was coming from her mouth. But she needed to know what this all meant to him. Maybe if she threw enough words at John, he would give her a glimpse of his true nature. Reveal a part of him that would give her a reason to stop falling. For him.

"I hope you know that's not true." His tone quieted as he stepped closer. Close enough to pause her frantic thoughts and quicken her heartbeat. For her to take in the scent of cinnamon from the mints she left for others on the table, which he sometimes pocketed on his way out. To notice the crumb on his otherwise blemish-free shirt—most likely a remnant of his breakfast. She lifted her hand for a moment but clasped it behind her instead. She glanced away, toward her purse and the keys inside that could carry her home, instead of lingering on his intense gaze. Disappointment mingled with something else she didn't want to name.

John placed his hand on her face to turn it back toward him. It took all her self-control not to close her eyes at the feel of his palm. It sure was a heady feeling to be at the center of his attention, under his searing touch.

"I just stuck around to pack up my things." Adanne moved out of his reach but paused as a whisper pricked her heart.

She turned, her cheek still warm from his tender touch. "I *am* sorry, John. I didn't lie to you. But I should have told you about my nephew from the beginning of your idea."

He sat down on the couch next to her purse. His arms draped over the back of the sofa looked too much like an invitation. She pressed against her mirror, positioning herself between it and the shield of the makeup chair.

"Why *didn't* you tell me, Adanne?"

Her breath pulled into her chest in shaky measures of one, two, three.

"I think because I was afraid I would mess it up for him. For me." She sighed, her shoulders slumping. "That saying too much would bring attention our family didn't need."

"But the initial article is what brought this together. Publicity doesn't have to be negative."

Adanne smiled as she held back tears. "Yes. And it meant the world to him, John. The way his face glowed . . ." She turned her head, dashing away the drop of liquid that dared to cross her lashes, escaping from the aching throb in her throat. She swallowed. "We haven't seen that on him in so long. Thank you. And to your mom. I'll always be grateful just for that."

At the sound of the door opening, Adanne gripped the table.

Trina and another MUA walked in, lifting their hands in quick greeting. The trailer soon filled with the sounds of items being organized and put away. Adanne forced her fingers to move her things around. The struggle to keep her emotions under control was taking too much mental effort.

"I wish you had trusted me." John's voice sounded closer, intimate.

She looked up and took in his reflection in the mirror, only a couple of feet behind her own. A quick glance to the side revealed the other artists were engrossed in their own conversation at the other end of the trailer.

"Do they teach spy moves in acting school too?" She brushed against the counter, turning around to face him. Not the best idea, though, as she noticed his forearms perched on the chair that no longer worked as a barrier.

His lips curved, but the eyes staring at her were tinged with something she couldn't define. And maybe if she was being honest, she would say that the same look probably reflected in her own eyes.

"What do you think I would have done?" he whispered fiercely. "Thrown you out because you have a sick nephew?"

"It happened the last time I worked with you. Except that time, it was my sick mom."

His eyes widened as he straightened, shock written on his face. "What?"

Adanne placed a finger to her mouth, her eyes pleading with him to keep his voice low.

John ran a hand through his hair. "I would never have someone fired for that reason. That's what Doris is doing and why you're here now. And when did we ever work together?"

Now was as good a time as any to tell him. Then she could move on. Deal with whatever consequences came after. "A few movies back. The one about time travel."

His mouth dropped. She placed her hand up as the other

two artists walked past them out the door, carrying their travel bags to head to an offsite shoot.

"I was just one of the assistant MUAs. Real low on the ladder. But on my way to a promotion after that job." *And representation.* She'd worked her tail off at smaller jobs, sometimes for free, to get her foot in the door. So close to joining the agency that would help make sure that door stayed wide open.

"Go on." John crossed his arms, leaning against the counter. Adanne automatically shifted to give space to the strain between them.

"My mom had been sick off and on, but then got worse. I had already been so distracted, fumbling with some of my applications. I was so stressed then." She closed her eyes, unsuccessful at shaking away the lingering shame. "Then when Mama got worse, I left as quick as I could. Right before I was assigned to use a specific technique."

"On me," John breathed, remembrance lighting his eyes.

"On you." Adanne nodded, her gaze flitting to the couch.

"I thought it would only be a few days." Her chest rose and fell. "The doctors diagnosed her with end-stage renal failure. And it was that diagnosis that eventually killed her. I sent a message to the department head and . . ." She tried to shrug away the rising tears that betrayed her outward composure.

John tensed, the regret in his eyes palpable.

"You know how film schedules are. They'd already gotten a replacement. And based on complaints from one of the actors—live on social media—the agency didn't want to represent me anymore."

• • • •

John had gotten Adanne fired. Or at the very least, temporarily blacklisted. All those years ago.

He wasn't always the easiest person to work with in the past, had burned through several relationships, both professional and personal. But he never experienced the tangible outcome of his behavior on set.

Until now.

Producers and directors, he waved off. Headlines, he didn't care about. But the woman standing next to him now? An entirely different story.

Adanne turned back to him. "Everyone knew you then for being particular about the people who surrounded you. I assumed I was too far removed. I didn't expect to be dismissed without a word more. But after your ex-girlfriend did that live stream in your trailer, recording your complaints . . . it was over. But I get it. There was a schedule to keep. Ultimately, that's on me for forgetting what kind of industry I worked in."

It took all the fruit of self-control for John not to pull Adanne into his arms. But this revelation of his past character wasn't the time. Nor was the place this makeup trailer at the base camp of his film location.

He remembered those days well. And that one in particular. During one of the most tumultuous seasons in his and Katrina's relationship, despite what they tried to present to the public. He also drank the most then and was so demanding and perfectionistic to cover up his weakness.

John didn't remember Adanne—many of the hair and makeup crew wore masks—but he remembered pressuring Mike to influence the chief makeup artist's decision when the assistant artist didn't show up three days in a row. It wasn't the first time he'd gotten someone fired. He often let the pain of his past and present hurt the lives of people like her.

His mother was right. He still had a lot to learn about forgiveness. He needed to fix this.

John reached out, laying a hand softly on her arm. "I'm sorry, Adanne. Please forgive me."

She bit her lip for a moment, her rounded eyes dampening. She clutched her necklace. "Already done, John. Honestly. I . . . I sometimes have trouble with the trust part . . . no matter who it is. Working on that."

Adanne patted his hand on her arm and then gently pulled it away from her. His fingers buzzed from the lingering warmth of her touch as she gave him a clunky handshake. "For what it's worth, I will be as open as I can with you in the future." Her eyes twinkled into a grin. "If it's your business. And if you are okay with me retracting my resignation. I'll send a text to Alex this time."

John released a chuckle, relief flowing out. Something shifted in the air. He felt the pull to get closer, to hear more about the stories Adanne hid behind her dark doe eyes. As if sensing his mental approach, she jumped back, bumping a container of setting powder. A smattering of it landed on her black shirt.

"Ugh." She frowned at herself in the mirror. John bit back a smile when she muttered, "Serves me right," under her breath.

Her clumsy frustration amused him, even if he still wasn't sure how he felt about how things had gone down, or his part to play in it. Adanne gently unclasped her necklace and laid it on the counter. She excused herself to the bathroom, a pack of makeup wipes in her grip.

John peered at the necklace, which looked a little gritty. Pulling out a couple wipes from the pack, he picked up the chain to get a closer look as he wiped it down. A simple silver strand holding two similar gold bands—one thick, one thin.

After a couple minutes, Adanne walked out of the trailer bathroom, a playful grin on her face, until she saw what John held in his hands.

"Messing with my things, Mr. Pope?" John looked up from the jewelry, the two bands pulling at his chest in an inexplicable way. They triggered faded memories of the wedding bands his mother had placed on a Bible on her nightstand. Rings she'd guarded fiercely for a long time, afraid to lose them, as if that would have had the ability to control the outcome.

In normal circumstances, he never would have picked Adanne's jewelry up, but his curiosity over the necklace she never removed compelled him.

He lifted the strand, the metal swaying and glinting from the bulbs surrounding the mirror. But instead of snatching it from him, she dried the last remnants of moisture from her hands with a paper towel.

After tossing it in the trash, Adanne placed her hand under the swinging bands, the rings resting on her soft palm, and breathed deep, gazing at the jewelry as if seeing it for the first time.

"May I?" John straightened, the necklace still held carefully in his grasp. Adanne nodded without a word, turning her back to him, pulling her braids over her shoulder.

John moved with a tentative step, not willing to disrupt this moment that felt like the most sacred invitation. He paused, fascinated by the soft, tight curls at the edge of her hairline, and then lifted his arms over her head to place the necklace around her neck. She held the bands in both hands as he secured the clasp in the back. He didn't realize until he finished that he'd been holding his breath.

The release of air tickled those textured tendrils, causing Adanne to turn her face with a closed smile, a dimple making an appearance. If he were somewhere else—or someone else—he may not have thought twice about leaning down close to that exposed neck and the lips that tilted shyly toward him.

Instead of following the flow of his thoughts, he stepped back and dropped in the makeup chair, clearing his thickening throat.

"What's the story behind the necklace?" He infused his voice with as much playful charm as he could, hoping it would dispel the longing in his eyes, distract him from the awareness in hers.

Adanne adjusted the necklace, holding the bands out with two fingers. She averted her gaze, looking toward the side. "Belonged to my parents. Their wedding rings. My mama started wearing Daddy's around her neck when he died. And then I wore both when she left too."

As much as Adanne seemed to hold parts of herself away, tucked in a safe place, John couldn't help but be impressed with how she wore her grief. Like the rings around her neck, she held her memories dear to her but open enough for others to see. He wished he had that level of courage. The ability to not choke on his words. To speak his peace as fluently as he did the lines of a scripted page. But life itself followed no script. It did what it wanted to, ebbed and flowed with sometimes little warning. He thought he'd already surrendered his desire for control on a hilltop in Beverly Hills, but it seemed his fingers still grasped for it. But . . .

He watched Adanne breathe deep, watching him back, sensing his mood beneath the surface as she seemed to do so well.

"I don't understand how you can go through so much and still hold on to faith."

Adanne was silent for so long, John wondered if she had even heard him. She glanced back at him, her eyes luminescent with the sheen of tears.

"It's not me doing the holding," she whispered.

John swallowed, her tender and rich words filling his heart with needed strength. She had labored through some storms and probably still struggled now, but her simple statement revealed how anchored she remained.

He could take refuge there. In that place with her.

Adanne shifted back to the makeup table, but then reversed her movement, her eyes sparkling with mischief. "Since you're off today—and I almost quit—you feel like going for a drive?"

19

John inhaled the cool air flowing in through the open window of Adanne's truck. The streets Adanne drove through faded gently from newer businesses and subdivisions to older, carpenter-style homes with mature trees, and stores that had peeling paint and seemed to hold bits and pieces of Hope Springs nostalgia.

The scenery gave him the strangest sense of home, childhood memories of running from house to house, darting through backyards and alleys, stirring up trouble and then helping friends get out of it. That had always been his favorite part. Stepping in for the ones who needed it most.

John leaned back against the passenger seat to watch her wind through the roads that led to what she called the heart of Hope Springs. The way felt familiar, but he hadn't driven these routes enough to know where they were headed. Some tension lingered in the truck between them. But it wasn't as sharp as it had been at the beginning of the shoot. Remorse and vulnerability were good ways to soften the edges. They stirred up more of a longing for home, for a steady place to lean on. And maybe for him to be that place for someone else in return. Solid enough for them to stay.

On the outside, Adanne appeared to need nothing and no one. A woman who loved God, served with tender care, and was deeply loyal. Yet the pain that presented itself called out to him. The tightness of her shoulders or the way she held her hands, her fingers, the slightest change in the flick of her wrist . . . *Stop*. But his eyes refused, roaming over the face so intent on the road and their destination.

Adanne's cheekbones carried a kiss of the fading sun, the golden light of late afternoon that turned her rich brown eyes into an alluring dark amber. Her full lips lay bare and inviting, poking and twisting here and there as she wrestled with whatever thoughts she wanted to say. Golden hoops gleamed and swayed to the rhythm of the drive. She was beautiful. A poetic flow. Altogether a mystery and a masterpiece laid open.

His mother was right.

Bellissima.

Did Adanne know it? Down deep in the place that motivated her every move? Did she know how much she moved *him*?

John turned back to the road. Who was he to tell her?

His eyes flitted back to the change in scenery, the smaller houses, older apartment buildings, and restaurants that spoke of a time passed over. A note of disappointment washed over him.

"You're unusually quiet."

John broke free from his thoughts and turned to Adanne, her eyes still golden in the sun. He gulped.

"Just taking everything in. Nice town. Probably full of stories."

Adanne tilted her head, turning her attention back to the

road. The truck slowed to match the decreasing speed limit. "Especially in this area."

She swept a hand in front of her. "This is where Mama grew up. She lived here for most of her childhood and teenage years." Adanne leaned toward the wheel, motioning with her head toward another building.

"My granddaddy owned that restaurant over there." She pointed to an aged edifice that probably served delicious food on paper plates dripping with grease. But the back was new with industrial elements.

"Does someone in your family still run it?"

She clicked her signal to turn left. "It's been out of our family for a few years now. Sold it to help Mama get her graduate degree and finish paying off her house."

Adanne came to a stop in front of another older, but cared for, brick building. It stood three stories high, about the size of a small elementary school. "And this . . . this is where my parents met."

They got out of the truck and John stepped up to the building, seeing it more clearly than he had when Pastor Ben brought him here. He'd never ventured inside during the community meal since the tables had been set up on the wide concrete patio of the entrance. His head tilted back to take it all in. It could use a paint job, and some foliage had taken shelter along the right wall, no longer content to grow along the ground. The well-trimmed lawn, clean windows, and newly repainted display that read Hope Springs Community Center were signs that the building had not fallen out of use.

"What did your dad do?"

John waited for Adanne as she locked her truck, slinging her purse over her shoulder. She hopped over the curb and walked with sure steps to the front door, keys in hand. He noticed the shift in her posture. Pride over her family's history seeped from her. His heart swelled at the honor of being shown this, especially after she wanted to keep a portion of it away just a few days ago.

"My daddy was a teacher at the school down the street. He ate regularly at Granddaddy's restaurant. When he mentioned having trouble with a few students, Granddaddy suggested he stop by here to talk to Mama, who had a degree in social work even though she did hair on the side."

Adanne turned the key and opened the door wide, letting the sun stream into the dark foyer. With a few clicks and switches, the opening flooded with more light. A small reception booth stood off to the right with pens, wristbands, and name tags on the counter. To the left were couches and small tables. Various board games and books were stacked neatly on a shelf.

A set of double doors stood in the middle, leading farther inside. Adanne set her purse in a small drawer behind the booth and locked it up.

"Please continue." John looked at Adanne expectantly.

"So, Daddy comes here to get some input. When he took one look at Mama, he met for more advice beyond the office hours. One thing led to the other, and the rest is Stewart family history." Her eyes twinkled. "Daddy would never admit if there really were things he needed help with, or if he was just looking for a reason to ask her out."

Adanne laughed, her smooth chords plucking at him in places that had long lay buried by disappointment. This glimpse of Adanne unfettered stirred and sobered him—in the best way.

John attempted a chuckle in response. "We always need a reason to get closer." He winked but felt the weight on his heart lift as he contemplated his own motives. In its place, the whispers of an idea took shape.

Adanne nodded, releasing her amusement with a satisfied

sigh. If she sensed anything underlying John's words, she didn't let on. "Let me show you my favorite place."

Adanne opened the double doors and led him into a dark room, the echo of their steps on the floor familiar. She ran an experienced hand along the wall and flipped on the lights.

Section by section, the room lit up, revealing a court with stacked chairs in the corner and a goal stationed on each wall. Positioned in the left corner of the court stood a cage of basketballs. Adanne walked over to it with confident strides, grabbed a ball, and threw it to John with unexpected precision.

"Oof!" He caught it with a claw-like grip before it knocked the wind out of him. "You've been holding out on me, Adanne."

She grinned, resting another ball comfortably on her hip. Her eyes danced with fire, melting away the last of the tension.

John held the basketball toward her with one hand. He grinned, sparks lighting at her expression.

Adanne slammed the ball she held to the floor, catching it between her hands with a powerful slap. "Well then. Let's see what you're working with."

John walked backwards to the center of the court. In an instant, he took his sweatshirt off, revealing a fitted T-shirt.

Adanne's mouth worked to suppress her amusement. "I won't get hit with a lawsuit when I crush your pride, will I?"

John liked this bit of trash talk. "Just don't cry when you get whiplash from my moves and you can't apply my makeup anymore."

Adanne paused, but in a blink, she shook off whatever held her back. She pushed her sleeves up, pocketed her earrings, and tucked her necklace into her shirt. She walked confidently toward the middle of the floor, her hips swinging with the strength of muscular curves.

The makeup artist met him in the middle, challenge and invitation on her face.

"Come on, then."

•　•　•　•

"The director is going to kill me."

"So dramatic, Mr. Pope. Nothing happened."

"Yeah, but it's the *possibility* of an injury happening. But I would blame you anyway, so it shouldn't matter for me." He chuckled, moving out of the way of her playful swat.

"You're just saying that because I beat you!"

"Oh no, Ms. Stewart, we decided it was a tie."

"Only because we forgot to take score at the beginning. But you know I made seventy-five percent of my shots." Adanne sniffed.

"Beginner's luck!"

Adanne tried to swat at John again, but it was difficult from her place sprawled on the floor. She needed to get back in shape.

"Beginner?! You keep talking smack, John Pope, and I'll really give the insurance company something to cry about."

John cackled, rolling over from his own bodily heap to lie on his side, propped up by his right elbow. In this moment, Adanne was grateful for the makers of deodorant. Otherwise, John would run for the hills from her sweaty funk. She closed her eyes, detesting the fact that she didn't want him to run anywhere, anytime soon.

"Speaking of insurance and contracts and films, what's your favorite?"

"My what?" Her eyebrow lifted.

"You're favorite movie."

"That was a horrible transition, by the way."

He waited for her answer, amusement lighting his expression.

Her eyes darted away. "Don't laugh, but besides the obvious answer of *Love & Basketball*, I really like *Pride and Prejudice*."

"Why would I laugh?" A fit of coughing said otherwise.

"You are! So much for vulnerability."

"It just doesn't seem very Adanne-ish."

"And you know what is?"

"I'm trying to find out. Hence, the reason I asked."

"Hence, that seems very Jane Austen of you." She gave him a playful smirk, flustered by his desire to know her, even in this ridiculous way. She shut her eyes to the longing she saw mirrored in his. "But yeah, I like the movie. Who wouldn't want to have their own version of Mr. Darcy meeting them in the morning fog?" She chuckled.

Instead of responding in kind, he seemed to sober, his eyes focused on her. Her fingers itched to brush the sweaty locks from his face.

"What happened to your dad, Adanne?"

She placed her hands on her stomach and breathed in deep. "Killed. Accidentally."

Another shaky breath. "It happened in this area. He visited a student at home one day and walked up to a domestic violence situation. The dad had a gun, but said it wasn't loaded as he swung it around."

Adanne swallowed, trying to push down the pain again. But finding it harder to do lately. "I was nine. Daniel eleven. Mama took it hard. We all did. That's when she decided to use the last of her inheritance to get even more involved in the community." A soft chuckle released from her chest. "I remember her saying, 'Baby, I'mma let hope spring up in all this pain.'"

John moved into a squat, his gaze on the floor. "I get it.

You're not only trying to save your family but this place in the community that your mom, and dad, gave everything to."

"Mm-hmm." Adanne fixed her eyes on the ceiling of the small court. "Rather lose me than all of this."

She got quiet. Silence preferable to the story that got heavier with each breath. So many unshed tears. She glanced at the man next to her. But maybe there was a chance for hope to spring up for her too.

• • • •

"Guess I should head back to set. I need a shower." John held the door of the center open as they walked out. Adanne loosened her ponytail, flipping the braids over one shoulder.

"You're on hold all day, right?" She peered at him, shielding her eyes from the dipping sun.

"Yeah, but since I need to pick up my car, I figured I'd run lines in the trailer. Helps me focus."

"You're focused enough, Mr. Pope." The way her eyes squinted when she said his name made him laugh. "Why don't you come play tourist with me? No one would ever guess you're you, looking like a high school basketball coach."

"Haha, is that what I look like now?"

"Let's test it out. I'd be remiss to not show you one of the best parts of the Huntsville metro area." She tossed his sweatshirt to him. "Come on, see for yourself why this place is not as sleepy as you think."

After the thirty-minute drive to Huntsville, John's mouth dropped when he saw where they were headed. Even though the U.S. Space & Rocket Center was closed, Adanne parked, led him straight to a side entrance, and then began to sweet-talk the woman at the door of an exhibit hall.

"Can we just take a quick look around? My friend is from out of town." She spoke in a disarming tone.

"I don't know, we're setting up for an event." The woman shot a glance at John, unsure. He grinned in return, his eyes shadowed by his ball cap.

"But . . . maybe for just a few minutes. As long as you don't touch anything."

"That's all we need. I promise we'll be in and out." Adanne tossed her a grin of thanks. John followed her lead, his eyes widening as they stepped into the Davidson Center. Adanne laughed at his audible gasp.

"Wow!" He looked up, taking in the length and breadth of the Saturn V rocket.

She handed him his ball cap, which had fallen when he tipped his head back. "What do you think?"

He blinked and looked down at her, cheesing like a kid. "This is one of the coolest things I've ever done."

She crossed her arms. "I'll have to take your word for it. I'm sure you've seen more extravagant places than this."

He walked around the room, avoiding the round tables set up in the middle. His eyes bounced from the Saturn V suspended above the entire length of the exhibit hall to the various displays lining the walls. "I've always wanted to come. That time-travel movie was the closest I've been."

He glanced at her. "I was a jerk then. On edge all the time. You're not the only one I burned."

Adanne nodded with a sigh. "The industry can be wonderful and hard. I was naive, thinking that somehow the job would pause at the same time my life did."

"I shouldn't have let Katrina record live on set. Should have asked what happened. Fought for you."

"John, you didn't *know* me. Just another crew member behind a mask. Inconsequential."

He glanced up at the looming rocket. "Not in my book."

If she heard him, she didn't acknowledge it. Instead, she ran her fingers along a metal railing. "This is Jason's favorite place. Thought I'd bring you here as a way to say thanks. Again."

"Maybe we'll come here with him, when he's better."

Adanne smiled, the fluorescent lights glinting against her necklace. The hope in her eyes more captivating than the rocket above. "Yes. *When.*"

20

*Y*ou look nice today."

Adanne glanced down at her blouse, hoping John didn't notice her cheeks warming at his compliment. Her typical work wear had been replaced with a delicate knit merlot blouse, the gathered shoulders giving her a particularly feminine feel. Her braids were pulled into a bun and she had sparkling rose-gold studs in her ears.

"Thank you." That was unexpected. Sweet. But she couldn't blame him. He didn't exactly see her most glamorous side during early morning call times.

When the director scheduled reshoots for Saturday afternoon, she'd almost forgotten about the performance at the Plantain and Pies venue. Trying to convince Kenya to give the tickets to someone else hadn't worked. Still . . . she peeked at herself in the mirror. It would be good to go. Even if she only caught one song.

Adanne rolled up her sleeves and wrapped a black apron around her waist. At least for one day she looked somewhat like the professional makeup artist she was supposed to be.

"You have some big plans this evening?" John leaned back, closing his eyes as she prepped his face.

"Nothing big. Just needed."

John grinned, his eyes flashing when he opened them. "That doesn't sound the least bit mysterious."

Her laugh felt light, easy. "Promise I'm not intentionally holding out. An old friend is performing in town tonight. My cousin Kenya convinced me to stop by. Plus, after our basketball game . . . which I won"—she eyed John's reflection—"I realized it would be a cool way to remember my dad."

"How so?"

Adanne tipped her head to the side. "I remember the drives we took when I was younger. Blasting Mama's eardrums with my high-pitched squeals as I tried to sing along." She could see her mama now, holding her ears as Adanne tried to follow the vocal runs of her favorite singers.

She chuckled at the memory, pleased to hear John join her. "On rainy Saturdays, Daddy brought out his old records. I'd play with my dolls, giving them makeovers. Luther, Smokey, and Stevie playing in the background.

"And when Daddy had a really hard day, Mama welcomed him home with a glass of peach tea and one of those records. Instrumental. Some jazz or gospel. He'd stand and listen, sipping from that glass as he looked out the window. And when a record played out, he'd sit in his favorite chair, sometimes praying. Sometimes just letting the silence soothe his soul before dinner."

Despite the warm glow of memories, Adanne swallowed the sorrow rising in her throat. Some things were without explanation. Her dad gone so suddenly. So soon.

"I love these stories, tell me more." John settled in with a shimmy, as if he sat in his own well-worn recliner.

"Listen, we need to hurry. We're losing light. Golden hour is on the way." Adanne patted the back of the chair as was her custom. "But . . . if you're that curious, and don't have

183

late night plans, you can tag along. If you behave. I happen to have an extra ticket, unclaimed."

"So, I guess I should keep the fan club away."

"That *would* be helpful, yes, but I'm pretty sure that the people you encounter tonight won't be that concerned about you."

John sat back with a satisfied smile. She turned her head, holding back her dimples.

The way he settled into her chair with contentment gave her a delicious sense of satisfaction.

The little movements and nuances she noticed were undoing her. It was the nature of her role to be more aware of any physical variances so she could adjust them with her palette and color wheel. But what tool could she use to balance out whatever this was before she fell deeper into the comfortable rhythm they seemed to be settling into?

The dissipating tension was a relief. But without her lingering distrust, how would she handle the attraction that grew the more she was with him?

• • • •

"Are you ready for this?" Adanne tilted her head, her gaze assessing, as John held the door open to Plantain and Pies later that night.

The distinct scent of roasted coffee and buttery sweetness drifted toward him as he followed Adanne into the dimly lit venue. She pulled out her phone to show the ticket barcodes to the host up front. John had been in his fair share of seedy places and had honestly expected this small Southern locale to be along the same lines. But stepping in took him by surprise and into a whole other world.

Plantain and Pies was bigger than he anticipated, yet with furnishings strategically placed to create a cozy environment.

Bookshelves lined the wall to their left, potted plants dispersed among the books, some fronds hanging down a shelf or two. The walls bore pieces of African art interspersed with framed Southern landscapes.

Persian rugs lay in various positions on the floor with round tables, tufted couches, and sofas mixed in. Guests sat flipping through books over glasses of jewel-toned wine, while others sipped specialty coffee, sampling scratch-made appetizers and desserts. The centerpiece was a small stage set up with vintage instruments and a mic stand.

John's shoulders relaxed, the room wrapping him in comfort, almost as deeply as the church pew had. This was a place where cultures met and thrived, nurturing connection within the dimly lit room.

His eyes drifted to Adanne, who shrugged off her jacket and laid it over an arm. With one move she swept her loosened hair to the side, exposing part of her neck to the warm, fragrant air. She turned to the side, taking in the room, the glow of a nearby pendant light illuminating her profile. The lines around her full lips smoothed and her cheek bone rose with the lift of a contented smile. Her eyes glistened as if she'd come back home.

Gratitude spilled into his chest for being here with her, and peace filtered into his soul. Hope Springs sure did have its secrets.

Adanne glanced back at him, tilting her head toward a table in the far-right corner. Her eyes sparkling gems.

Secrets *and* treasures.

"I'm going to order an appetizer of fried plantain. I may share." She grinned when they sat down. "You'll want to get the pie." Adanne slid a laminated menu toward him. "But you can decide for yourself."

"Oh, can I?" he teased, picking up the menu. How could he choose? Everything looked incredibly delicious and not the best combination for his eating plan. Plantain was an obvious restaurant favorite, with various menu options featuring it. The dishes seemed to be a blend of West African, Caribbean, and American Southern cuisine. "Out of all these, you would pick pie."

"Always." Her hands crossed over the menu she hadn't even glanced at. "Savory, tarte, cobbler, crisp—doesn't matter. I'll choose it first." She lifted her shoulder. "And why not?"

John's mouth watered. He was a fan of chocolatey, coffee-infused desserts, or anything his mother made, but the confidence saturating Adanne's tone stirred his taste buds.

He put down his menu, grinning as he settled into the leather chair. "Tell me what I should pick, then."

Adanne leaned forward, quietly assessing him in her usual way. But tonight, the eyes that roamed his face held a different glow. Warmth, thick and sticky, pooled in his belly.

She licked her lips and tapped the bottom one in thought.

"Didn't know dessert choices were this serious." He cleared his throat, yearning akin to hunger rumbling in his core, but not something even a delicious dessert could fill. Was it the scent of fermented drink close by? Or the intoxicating presence of the woman sitting across from him, tap, tap, tapping her lip as she thought?

Either way, he wouldn't come from this evening unscathed without a little assistance.

Lord, I may need some backup here.

Finally, she pulled his menu to her and lifted it slightly to signal that they were ready to order. "For the pie, I'm getting apple with some warm mango-sauce drizzle. You look like you're in need of a Southern staple, some peach cobbler. Maybe with homemade vanilla ice cream."

"That sounds like a good plan." John held her gaze for a moment, then chided himself for even that. He came here to relax, unwind, not to work himself into something he had no business finishing.

Adanne leaned back in the soft leather of her chair, the shift in music from the stage drawing her attention. Recognition flitted across her eyes as the platform filled with musicians. A lone singer stepped up to the mic.

He glanced around the room, his tight curls clipped and faded at the sides. "Are we ready for more? Always a pleasure to be in my hometown. Ain't no place like Hope Springs, Alabama."

A few cheers of agreement lifted from the tables, along with glasses and mugs, some bottles of sweet Nigerian malt in the mix. John chuckled at the enthusiasm, pricked with the need to feel the same kind of belonging.

The singer plucked a few chords on the guitar he held. "Yes sir, ain't no place like *home*. I even see some familiar faces here tonight." He held the guitar in place, pointing at a few in the dim room. "Even one that I still can't believe showed up."

He turned to the left and his eyes focused on their table. Oh no, had he been recognized? Did this singer know who he was? John gulped, not wanting this to be a repeat of his first outing with Adanne. She stiffened, the tension in her body spreading to him. He closed his eyes. This was a mistake. Would she ever get relief when she was with him?

"Yeah, I'm talking about you, Dee. Miss Adanne Denise Stewart!"

John's eyes flew open, his shock drowned out by relief that he wasn't about to ruin this night for her. *But now this guy is the one to blame.*

Adanne's eyes rounded, one hand gripping her necklace and the other crumpling the napkin on the table.

The singer grinned, charisma dripping from every part of his posture. "Y'all may not know this, but Miss Adanne Stewart over there was my middle school crush."

"Ty!" Too bad he couldn't hear her fierce whisper, but he threw his head back and laughed anyway.

"Mm-hmm. But as a sixth grader I didn't stand a chance with her older, eighth-grade self. Y'all know how that goes. But it was really because of her song at our talent show. Nobody could sing old-school soul like her old soul."

Adanne put her head down, shaking it, but John didn't miss the smile tugging at her lips.

"Come on up and show us what you got, Dee. No better way to open my second set."

Adanne put her hands up, but it was too late. The audience was already clapping their encouragement, some of them had no doubt been in the audience of that talent show so long ago.

Adanne turned to give John an almost pleading look, but he was too intrigued to attempt any kind of rescue.

She dropped her head again. John wondered if she would use that moment to walk out. When she lifted her head, she shook it and mouthed, "I'm so sorry."

Maybe she didn't want to repeat that embarrassing karaoke moment he caught her in before. John prepared to push his chair back but instead of gathering her things, she picked up her glass, took an extralong swig of water, and rolled her shoulders. "He's not gonna leave me alone until I go up there."

And with that, John's mouth unhinged as she made her way to the small stage, the most confident sway in her approach. Adanne stepped up, covering the mic handed to her to share a few teasing words with her classmate. Then they both glanced back at the musicians, nodding their heads in time to the song they chose.

After a moment, the singer, Ty, faced the crowd, his dark eyes gleaming. "What a treat we have *tonight*. Welcome to the stage my first crush, who really is too good for any of us."

He chuckled and weaved before Adanne could elbow him in the side. "Adanne Stewart, singing a classic by Deborah Cox."

As the first notes flowed from her mouth, John gripped the sides of his chair. That voice had been hidden in his MUA all this time? Her singing in the trailer that one morning had been overly loud and playful. When he'd stood next to her at church, her voice had blended with the congregation's. Even straining his ears, he couldn't pick it up.

Now, the richest, most authentic chords spilled out, telling the story of love unexpected, unwanted, yet surprisingly longed for. Every bit of her shyness and reticence seemed to slip away as her vocals pulsed with strength and vulnerability, holding his attention captive.

If he didn't need a drink earlier, he may need one now. His heart quickened, his swallow a sorry attempt to calm its pace. When he could finally pull his eyes off her, he peered around the room. The other patrons were locked in, some nodding their heads to the rhythm, familiar with the chords and lyrics, moving their lips in time.

Some closed their eyes, swaying with the melody, smiling at others in the overflow of the waves of unfettered soul coming from the single spotlight in the room.

John set his gaze on Adanne again, feeling all the air suck out of him, when for a moment, her eyes traveled in his direction. She gifted him with a lift of her lips, the dip in her cheek appearing even as she sang, pulling him in. His restraint was almost toppled by the longing to kiss her amid this caramel-scented room. But in a blink, she adjusted her focus, finishing out the song with a melodic run.

As the applause swelled and slowly died down, John watched Adanne give her school friend a demure smile and hug before making her way back to the table as if she hadn't just wrecked him.

The music shifted, and before he could form another

thought, he was on his feet to meet her, her eyes soft in the dim light. Did Ty call for couples to approach as the music shifted? John wasn't sure if it was his thoughts or the microphone, but the question came out anyway.

"You wanna dance?"

She glanced around, and for a moment fear of her rejecting him slipped in. Maybe she was tired of getting pulled into the spotlight.

But worry fled as her eyes flickered back, a tender smile lighting up her face.

"Come on, then." Her words were breathless. From the song probably. Probably not from the way she stepped into the middle of the floor, letting him wrap one arm around her waist and hold her hand to his chest with the other. She was probably just being nice as she placed her arm on his shoulder, her eyes set on him.

It was just a few moments. A dance within the span of a three-minute song. But it was enough to make him cup her face at the end. She placed her hands on his wrist, letting her forehead touch his for a moment. Halting the kiss she probably didn't want as badly as he did.

"Plantain is on the table," she whispered, releasing her hands. He nodded and reluctantly led them back to where their food waited.

When he bit into a piece of the sweet-smelling dish, he paused midchew to stare at the morsel that left a sheen of oil on his fingers.

"This is so good!"

"Mm-hmm. You haven't truly lived without experiencing fried plantain with a bowl of rice and stew. My grandmother used to make it all the time."

She happily bit into a slice.

"Where was your grandmother born?"

Adanne beamed across from him, her nose scrunched up

in the cutest way. "In Nigeria. She moved to the States when she was young. I'm actually named after her."

"Ah-dah-neh." John pronounced her name slowly, savoring each syllable. "What does it mean?"

"Maybe you'll find out one day," she teased, her expression sweeter than those caramelized edges of plantain.

"But your voice. You're so talented," John sputtered. Her nearness was as arresting as her song. "Why didn't you pursue music as a career?"

She shrugged, her cheeks lifting in their subtle way. "Just because you're good at something doesn't mean it has to be your dream. Or your hustle."

She took a sip from her glass, then wiped the condensation off her hands with her crumpled napkin.

"This was something special between me and my dad. Singing along with all the greats. And then afterwards, Mom and Daniel and I would sing together, think of him. Nothing I've ever wanted to put on display—unless forced." She grinned, leaning back as their desserts arrived.

Even the steaming cobbler and tantalizing scent of spices couldn't deter him from his astonishment. John didn't understand how she could be so nonchalant about what almost took his breath away. It pulled him more than he cared to admit and bothered him more than he thought possible.

Another woman not that long ago had wrapped him up with her voice and charisma. Her combined singing, modeling, and acting chops made her an industry triple threat and dangerous to his heart. Him and his romantic Italian soul.

That woman had broken his heart.

And this woman—he could still hear her voice serenading his thoughts. He couldn't let a beautiful voice fool him again, no matter how rich, how lovely.

Adanne glanced at him, her mouth tilted in pleasure as she took a bite of her pie.

Despite those eyes like melted chocolate, he had to stay focused and finish this shoot well. His career couldn't afford the least bit of distraction or wrong speculation.

She was right all those weeks ago. He needed to stop following her around, put distance between them, and focus on his manager's strategy.

That would ensure everything stayed purely business, transactional, without the threat of something too personal that would push him back over the edge.

21

*J*ohn woke from his nap on Sunday afternoon with the ringing of his cell phone.

His dreams had held glimpses of a face with sparkling brown eyes and thick, black lashes and, to his chagrin, a lingering melody. That pleasant mood dispelled quickly when he answered the phone.

"Why is it so hard to get in touch with my not-so-favorite client lately?"

"Mike. What have I done to fall from your favor?"

"Absolutely nothing, which is the point. You're lying too low. There's an awards show coming up in a little over two weeks, in case you forgot."

No one could forget the special type of March madness in Hollywood called awards season. John shifted himself to a sitting position. "I'm working on it."

"And I am too. We need to connect as soon as you're available. Say tonight? Got a new opportunity for you."

Mike was ever hunting those opportunities. But maybe his agent, Peter, had some auditions lined up. He hadn't heard from him since their roundtable in LA.

"Fine. You sound desperate."

"Good. Make sure you look halfway like the movie star you are. Nora found one restaurant in your little town that will work. She'll send you the details. Meet there."

John grunted and hung up. He stared at his phone, considering Mike's words. He probably *should* put more effort into this plan. But if he had to choose . . .

Seeing where Adanne's family originated stirred a longing in his heart. As much as he tried to dismiss the connection he felt, his dreams laid out a different script. The pull to her and this not-so-sleepy town triggered an acute longing he'd been afraid to admit. Her simple words from that plantain-and-pie-ladened table playing in the background. *"Just because you're good at something doesn't mean it has to be your dream."*

When he left college to pursue acting, he was ready to escape. He ran away from the actions of his father and the life he feared would imprison him.

His natural charm, mild acclaim in high school theater, and side modeling gigs in college turned into a moderately successful career. Now he had money, the slow uptick of marketable roles, a string of high-profile relationships, and yet . . .

He thought back to Adanne's smile and the light in her eyes as she drove through the streets. The pride she had in her roots. No matter the painful memories. She was willing to give up all the things she loved to take care of that place, to be there for her people. He longed to go home to a place like that. Somewhere that anchored despite the storms.

"I guess that's you, Lord, isn't it?" He blew out a breath. "My anchor and home."

All that time he'd been running from everything else, the one he really ran from was God. He sensed it when he gave his life back to Jesus on that overlook off Mulholland Drive.

But that wasn't the end of his journey. Just an invitation to a beginning still unfolding.

"So, what's next? I think I'm good at what I do. But is that your dream for me?"

He didn't have straightforward answers to what was around the corner. But what he could do was just be faithful to the next moment in front of him. For now, that meant meeting his manager tonight and seeing what happened from there.

●　●　●　●

Adanne took one last bite of the shrimp and grits from the patterned bowl in front of her. "Alonzo, you outdid yourself with this."

Her throat rumbled with satisfaction as the last bits of butter, cheese, and polenta melted in her mouth.

When she got the call earlier in the day to pick up a box of pastries, she jumped at the chance even though she hadn't planned to stay long. Some would get dropped off to her brother and then the rest she'd add to the monthly buffet at the community center.

Alonzo's Bakery and Bistro had earned quite a reputation for soulful, Southern cuisine. Several media outlets featured the magnetic chef and his menu over the last year. A rare example of good publicity. Because of that, the restaurant in downtown Hope Springs had become a popular spot. Adanne couldn't afford to eat there, but thankfully she had an in with the chef and owner himself. He never failed to give her something to help with their monthly neighborhood meals, whether it was food, drinks, or decor.

She forgot her excitement over the pastries as she took another bite.

"Alonzo, why is this so good?"

Her friend laughed, his voice rich and smoky. He pulled his chef's hat down over his thick hair.

"A little smacking of the lips never hurt no one."

She tugged lightly at his chef's jacket. "I know I need to go. You're about to have a busy night."

"Not as busy as you think. One of my sections was bought out by someone based in LA, of all places."

"I'm assuming you're not talking about Lower Alabama."

Alonzo chuckled. "Nope, the other. He wanted to use the space to set up a meeting."

"Must have really wanted some privacy."

Alonzo shrugged. "As long as the money comes in to pay my staff and I don't have to close completely, I'm cool. Plus, he'll recommend me to some of his other clients."

Adanne leaned over the counter to peer through the kitchen door's window. "So, he's hosting his client here?"

"Not exactly. He set up a meeting between *two* of his clients. One of them looked familiar when she arrived. Way too done up for my taste, but very attractive. Not from around here, though."

"Hmm. Well, I'm proud of you, Lonzo. You know that. And I'm thankful that we only have the community meals once a month 'cause if you keep giving me free food during my pickups, I'm gonna cut you off."

He laughed out loud. "That you would never do."

She smiled and followed him as he carried the box of frozen pastries to the kitchen door. "You sure it's cool for me to go this way?"

"I won't have you walk all the way 'round the back at this hour. Like I said, we ain't full. No one in this section but those two in the back corner." He propped open the door with his foot and handed the box of frozen pastries to her, ready for her to warm in the oven before next Saturday's brunch. Before he handed it over, he leaned down to look her in the eye.

"Dee, you know I love y'all. If you need anything, like meals for your brother's family, call me. Matter fact, let me know a good time to drop by and I'll bring food personally."

Gratitude filled her chest. How had she convinced herself that no one else cared? *Thank you, God.* She shifted the box to the side and leaned forward to give Alonzo a kiss on the cheek.

· · · ·

The lamps on the table added mood lighting to the dim restaurant. John admired the design immediately when he walked in. The atmosphere was similar in feel to Plantain and Pies a few streets over. But instead of a stage in the corner, there were black-and-white pictures of singers and musicians.

Textured chairs gave off a relaxed, cultured vibe with the green velvet upholstery. Honey-rimmed picture frames and charcoal accents finished off the look. The design transitioned tastefully into the dining area, where chairs of the same velvety material hugged the thick butcher-block tables. It was called a bakery and bistro but was far from an afternoon stop. Instrumentals rolled out of hidden speakers in rhythmic waves, setting John at ease. As did the chef, who greeted him at the door and led him to where he planned to meet Mike.

But that calm disintegrated when, instead of Mike, a familiar, strikingly beautiful face greeted him. Her dark-auburn hair hung in waves down her back and over her shoulder. Barely hiding her low-cut, fitted top. A slow smile curved on her lips and brown eyes flashed with open interest.

Mike set him up with one of his former co-stars. The woman fans said years ago had the best on-screen chemistry with him. What was she doing here in Hope Springs if not to be an option as his awards-show date?

Now after small talk and with their food ordered and delivered, John glanced at her as she sipped a soda water. She'd only picked at her Caesar salad, while he'd gone for shrimp and grits, one of the best dishes he'd eaten in a long time. He would thank Mike for sending him to this place, right after he wrung his neck for setting him up.

John turned his thoughts from possibly pummeling his manager to the conversation with the woman in front of him. Their connection on film had been easy, and had almost cost him his developing relationship with Katrina. But now that he was single, he felt unease in Harley's presence.

"So, John, what do you think?"

"About what, Mike's suggestion?"

"Of course."

Her laugh tinkled, revealing the expression that made her fans weak. "It's been a few years since a big hit for me as well. When my manager got wind of what Mike was thinking, he said this could be a great way to get us both out there."

It wasn't a bad idea. Harley was beautiful on-screen and off, a great actress, and usually a pleasant person to be around. He didn't want to stir up the gossip mills, but he also didn't need Mike planting too many other women next to him as they approached the awards night.

"No, not so bad of—"

The bang of the kitchen door against the wall distracted him, piercing the relatively quiet restaurant. He turned his head toward the sound before he could finish his agreement.

Adanne stood in the kitchen doorway, smiling a little too

easily with the muscular chef. He handed her a large pastry box, and after a few more words, she leaned over to plant a chaste but affectionate kiss on the man's cheek.

His chest constricted as she glanced at the chef again, who pointed in their direction. Adanne paused, uncertainty playing across her features as she took in the scene of John and his date.

John gulped. He wished she'd seen him alone, even though he had nothing to hide. He lifted his hand. Following the lead of the chef, she shifted her shoulders as she walked toward the table.

"Hello, Mr. Pope and Ms. . . . . Carlisle, right? I wanted to introduce you to my friend if that's okay."

Harley flashed her three-thousand-watt smile. "Yes, of course. Were you wanting a picture?"

John cringed, clamping down the urge to smack his hand against his forehead.

Adanne cleared her throat. "No, that's all right. And I'm already acquainted with Mr. Pope." Harley arched an eyebrow but said nothing else. John stared at Adanne, at a loss for words. All he could see was how well she seemed to fit next to the handsome chef, that kiss on his cheek refusing to stop replaying in his mind.

"If you'll excuse me. I'll talk to you later, Adanne." Alonzo nodded at them all and made his way back to the kitchen.

Adanne gave them a tight smile. "It was nice to see you both. I better be off as well."

Her eyes grazed over John, expression blank.

She turned toward the entrance, the hanging light bulbs appearing to swing in rhythm to her departure, their glow overshadowed by the illumination of her.

After a couple strides, Adanne's steps slowed as she glanced over her shoulder.

She didn't say the words now and he wouldn't have heard

them if she did, but the echoes of her "come on, then" lingered like an invitation, beckoning John.

The soundtrack playing in his ears an echo of the melody she sang over last night's swaying crowd.

An image of her kissing Chef Alonzo on the cheek, fresh on the surface of his no-longer-conflicted thoughts.

Was her song the other night centered on this friend of hers? A relationship John had not been aware of until this moment? But Chef Alonzo only called her his friend. Only a friend?

Was that what she was to *him*, nothing more than a friendly film-crew member? Was that all he was to her?

Something flowed over John, hot and thick. Something suffocating and spinning.

"Adanne! Wait."

He burst from the table.

"John?" Harley reared her head back in surprise.

"Excuse me, Harley. Be right back."

He didn't have a clear thought when his feet moved him from the table toward the front. But what pounded in his heart were her words a couple weeks into her job. *"Maybe someone down-to-earth will be less likely to make you fall . . . and break your heart."* They surrounded him like a cyclone, propelling him forward, reminding him of the idea in his head that he hadn't fully considered until now.

Adanne turned to him just outside the restaurant door. Eyes rounded over the large box she carried.

John stared at her for a moment, breath stolen not by the physical exertion but from what he wanted to say. No, not yet. Her expression held questions and something else. Something akin to disappointment?

"Yes? John?"

He gulped. "I uh—can I carry that box for you to your car?"

Her mouth tipped. "Nah, I'm good. It's just right there." She pointed with her chin over her right shoulder, where John saw her car parked under a lamplight.

"If that is all you needed . . ." Adanne lifted the box. "I've got to get these to my freezer."

John hesitated, warring with his words and a bit of fear. "Yes, okay. Good night."

He shifted back, but the pull that had propelled him from his chair remained. "Wait. I wanted to check. Will you be on set tomorrow morning?"

Adanne tilted her head, looking at him like he'd grown a second set of ears. "Of course I will." She dipped her head. "I'll see you then."

· · · ·

After Harley's driver picked her up, John sat in his car for a few minutes, thinking about the evening. Despite his initial surprise at the restaurant, it turned out better than he thought.

He knew exactly what to do next. It may cost him, but he had to take a risk.

A ping came from his phone.

MIKE
How did it go? Did you like my surprise?

JOHN
You could say that.

You wanted to punch me initially.

Correct.

It's a plan then? All set for the awards?

Almost. But I'm taking care of it. It will be a nice surprise.

Finally! I'm flying out to NYC in a couple hours,
so Nora and team can work out the details.

👍

John closed the chat and tapped his phone on his chin.
He *would* take care of it. Now he prayed that every detail
would fall smoothly into place.

22

The brushes banged down louder than usual.

When one skittered across the floor, Adanne ground her teeth at the fifth clumsy drop of the morning. She kept her eyes focused on her work, intentional movements to keep her emotions in check.

Glancing up, she caught John eyeing her in the mirror. His expression was one she had never seen before. Nervousness, amusement, and . . . longing?

"Are you good, Adanne?"

"Yes."

"I don't think that palette is."

"What?" She checked the tray she'd been using and noticed one shade crumbling in the corners. "Mercy."

"Why so uptight?" He continued gazing at her through the mirror with an amused smile.

"Why all the questions?" Adanne huffed, accidentally grazing his shoulder. She shook out her arm to release the charges traveling up to her neck and hit a container of cotton swabs. John caught it in one hand with the skill of an athlete, *or* a highly trained actor.

"Adanne?"

"*John*. It's the last day before hiatus and set change. Just want to get this right."

She drummed her short nails on the counter, took a deep breath, and turned back to her client, friend—whatever he was, that should not matter. At least it didn't at the beginning.

Probably a good time to find another job anyway. Like yesterday. Doris would likely be back in a couple weeks, and filming would wrap shortly after. She'd gotten distracted from the real reason she was here. And it didn't—shouldn't—have anything to do with Mr. Pope.

"Yeah. So. The other night?" John raised his eyebrows. Adanne perked one of her own. She wouldn't admit what seeing him with that woman did to her insides.

"The chef. You two close?" An odd note came across in his normally confident tone.

Adanne reared back. "You mean Alonzo?"

John looked at her with hooded eyes. "Is that a friend? Boyfr—?"

Adanne cackled so loudly it surprised her. If she'd had food in her mouth, it would have flown across the room.

"Please. Alonzo? I've known him since middle school. Along with Ty. Alonzo begged my granddaddy to give him a job in the kitchen. He worked there until he graduated. Granddaddy helped him get into culinary school. That man's like a cousin to me."

John's expression changed. Curiosity shifting to relief. He wouldn't get off the hook so easily. She had some questions of her own.

"What about you? How was your date?" She averted her eyes before he caught her gaze in the mirror. She checked the call sheet for the fiftieth time.

John grunted. "My manager's skills never cease to amaze me. I thought I was meeting *him* instead of her."

"I assume you've met her before?" Adanne forced her voice to remain even. Just simple information, a bit of a chat while she finished up. Nothing to be moved by either way.

"Harley and I worked together on a movie years ago."

"Your manager wants her to be with you at the awards?"

"Yes, he does." John paused, looking at her with barely veiled amusement. "It seems I have entered an interrogation."

She shrugged. "You started it. Are you really nominated?"

"Do you not pay attention to anything that goes on in the film industry?"

"Not everything." Adanne smirked. "Look who's asking the questions now."

"Not even just a little social media stalking?"

"Please, why should I be looking you up on my off time when I'm in your face now?"

John laughed out loud. "Touché. I'm not *personally* nominated, but my last film is up for Best Picture."

John shook out his palms under his cape. Adanne made a sound of disapproval when his movement affected her application.

"So, she was someone from your list, then?" She had never been this candid with him. "You finally made your decision on who to take."

· · · ·

"I guess you could assume something along those lines." John spoke through tight lips, while Adanne corrected a stray mark on his chin. Her fingers fumbled with her brush. He tracked her jumpy movements as she rushed before the AD called for an ETA.

"Congratulations, then. I can call off the list of ladies I had in line for you."

A slow grin spread across his face. "It was a productive night, although you have piqued my interest with the mention of *your* list."

"Pshh." She flicked a towel.

He laughed, resisting the urge to pull this feisty woman close. See if he could hold her fire tightly in his arms. Let it melt deep into his skin.

"It worked out so well, in fact, that I have a favor to ask you."

Adanne unsnapped the cape from John's neck, her curiosity diminishing her earlier frustration. But the movement irked him. Even though Adanne would remain on the shoot, she wouldn't still be assigned to him if Doris returned before wrap. This may be the last time he sat in Adanne's chair. The last time he watched her shake out and fold the cape with slender fingers as he left for that day's scenes. The last time he felt her enveloping warmth and inhaled the scent he associated with her. But he hoped to change that. And soon.

"I'm listening, Mr. Pomponio."

John's ears perked at the way his real surname rolled off her tongue. He shifted against the armrest to get a better look at her, trying to keep his cheesy grin to a minimum. "I'm in need of some additions to my team. What would you say to coming to California for the awards in two weeks?"

Adanne leaned against the counter, visibly taken aback by this offer. John guessed she hadn't been out of Hope Springs for a while. Maybe since before her mother passed away.

"I don't know if what I do will help." Her face shifted from bewilderment to her usual poker expression.

John swallowed a smile as she continued.

"That red-carpet spotlight. That's above my expertise."

He shifted around to look her in the eye. "You underestimate yourself, Ms. Stewart."

"Seriously, John. I need to pray about this. I've got—"

"There will always be something going on. But yes, pray about it. I want you to be at peace. But I think it'll be fun."

John brushed off his hands and sprang from the chair. But instead of heading for the door, he turned toward Adanne, stopping her in her pacing tracks.

"Just don't let worry stop you. If you say yes, I'll take care of everything. Trust me."

• • • •

Adanne inhaled the fresh air, savoring the small window of time before pollen saturated every surface. Spring was on the way. That was something to be grateful for.

Most of the trees stood in defiance to the budding of their leaves, although some had gotten an early start on their blooms. Soon all would display rich greens and overflow with blossoms of dogwood, redbuds, and even cherry. But none of them could fight the emergence of spring for too long. Neither could she.

She'd been ready to let go of the possibility of *him*, to lead her wrestling thoughts in a new direction. But yesterday's invitation to travel west had stirred something to life.

The feelings she tried to hold at bay moved in her like a whirlwind.

Setting her on the path to her parents.

Granted, they weren't here. They were fully alive with the Lord—their ways remembered in the mark they made in town. But this place, this bittersweet garden, still held a sacred peace she couldn't avoid for too long.

Fresh flowers lay on both graves. It never failed, someone had always just been by, paying their respects, giving their thanks. Adanne had no idea how many people her parents impacted.

She sat down on the bench cemented between the head-stones and brushed away a few blossoms that had found their own rest here. Stretching out her legs, she gripped the seat.

"I am afraid to go," she whispered. "Afraid of what that means."

She looked over the rolling hills of the memory gardens.

"Daddy, you would be so proud of me. I've been learning to hold my tongue."

Settling back, she exhaled a small laugh. "It's not been easy, let me tell you. But I think you would like him. I didn't at first. And to be honest, I don't know what to think of him now. And how to feel about going back."

There were so many emotional layers attached to the place where her dreams had died. She could blame John all she wanted, and she did for a while, but she'd made a choice. One that she'd make a thousand times over, no matter the consequence. To be there for her mom, taking care of her that last year of her life. To sit by her side, breathe in the lavender scent that permeated her lotion and "calmed her nerves," as she'd said. Driving her to and from dialysis and learning how to run all the errands in between.

Even now, guilt snuck its way in. A niggling thought hovered as she considered her nephew and other responsibilities—that something devastating could happen again if she went back. Even for a moment.

Although a cool breeze flowed over her cheeks, Adanne felt heat spreading in her like deepening embers, the kind that pressed heavy on her chest.

She didn't have the capacity to consider another heart-break. Who did? But if she took this step, even for a few days, she would be thousands of miles away from the ones who needed her. Who would take on her pickups? Check the food pantry?

The pressing heat inched up her neck, tightening her throat. *Breathe.*

And as much as she wanted to be in this place, to sit and imagine that her parents sat on either side of her, they weren't here. Their caskets, their remains, their memory even, but her living, breathing parents were not.

With sudden clarity, she knew where she needed to go.

An hour later, Adanne glanced around the kitchen she hardly visited. She'd forgotten how much she loved it here. Justine Stewart kept the heart of her home fragrant and full of food. The neutral-toned walls were accented by scattered greenery and stainless-steel kitchen appliances. Her father's brother and his extroverted wife hosted lively family gatherings, continually inviting others to be a part of them. But over the years, Adanne had declined invitations more than she'd said yes. She justified her absence with her need to work to earn more money. Carry out tasks that no one else could do but her.

After all, she had a brother to support and a community center in jeopardy. But there were deeper reasons at play that she didn't want to acknowledge. Being at this house with all of them still felt strange, and very hard.

"I'm glad you're here, Dee, it's been too long." Justine came around the corner to squeeze her niece's neck.

"Mm-hmm, *too* long. You been avoiding us or something?" Uncle Albert popped his head into the kitchen to sniff. He sent a wink Adanne's way. "Y'all almost done with the food? I don't think we've eaten on time *one day* in this house."

"Oh, get on out of here. I don't go messing with you and your grill." Justine flapped her hand as her husband ducked back out snickering. Adanne watched as her aunt moved her shoulders to the music wafting in from the living room. How could she so easily forget that these people were her family too?

"He's not wrong, though." Adanne sighed, propping her chin up with her hand.

"About dinner? Girl, you know there is nothing done on time in this family."

Adanne attempted a laugh, the sound hollow. "Not that. About me. Avoiding."

Justine turned to her, placing a bowl of steamed broccoli on the large island. Adanne reached to position it next to the basket of rolls from her perch on a padded barstool.

The older woman assessed her niece, her relaxed hair brushing her shoulders in textured curls. She curved her lips in a soft smirk. "I noticed."

"I hoped you wouldn't. Or at least that it would make sense."

Justine sat on the stool next to her. "Why wouldn't we notice when a part of our family is not here? Everything that hurts you affects us too."

Adanne hung her head, letting her twists graze the sleeves of her blouse. She was tired. Bone weary.

Her aunt placed her hand on her back, patting it gently. "I know it's been hard, baby, to come here. To see your daddy in Albert's face. Thinking of your mama always bustling around the kitchen, helping me get the food out on time for our monthly dinners." She paused, poking out her lips. "Yeah, I admit it. She kept me on task."

Justine let out a laugh, and as if on cue, they both sighed deeply. Justine's words came on the end of a hum, low and contemplative. "I wish it got easier. It doesn't really. But I think it should get *lighter*. Especially when you let the people who love you help carry the load."

She continued patting Adanne's back. The soothing motions of a mother.

"That's what we're here for, sweetheart. To help you carry

all this. We love you, Daniel—*all* of you. We just never want to force you to let us help without your consent."

Adanne leaned into her aunt's shoulder, giving herself permission to receive the embrace her heart craved.

Moments later, the family gathered around the dining table, joined by Salome, the quieter of the Stewart sisters who still lived at home. Kenya burst through the front door in her usual flurry, apologizing for being late. The only one missing was Adanne's cousin Celise, the middle child, who was off on an editorial shoot.

After Uncle Albert blessed the food, platters and bowls were passed around. Food flowed in and out of animated conversation.

"I think you should do it." Kenya pointed her fork at Adanne. "John wants you to be there for a week, which means you'll have time to shop and sightsee." Kenya sat next to her father, spouting off her opinions as she wielded her fork like a pointer. Salome sat in between her mother and Adanne.

"I don't have money for anything extra," Adanne mumbled, savoring the roasted bite of broccoli. Her aunt knew how to season her veggies.

"Girl, stop worrying. Enjoy some downtime for once in your life." Kenya let the end of her utensil dangle for emphasis.

"Being part of an awards-show prep team does not feel like downtime." Adanne pushed her plate to the side, her appetite diminishing along with her control of the conversation.

Kenya leaned in. "Maybe not, but it will be fun. Something new."

"Would you stop with the new?"

"Huh?"

"Never mind."

Salome's neck rotated back and forth as if she was at a tennis match.

Justine made a tsking sound, shaking her head.

Albert cleared his throat. "Kenya, leave Dee alone now. Let the woman make her own decisions."

Adanne gave her uncle a look of gratitude, pushing down a lump as she took in his eyes, so like her father's. Just like hers.

"John must really want you there." Kenya remained unmoved by her father's reprimand. She grabbed a roll, using it as her new mode of communication before she devoured it. "Who knows what part you'll play in the whole evening."

"All I know right now is that I'm supposed to fly to Los Angeles in two weeks and meet John's assistant."

He was already on a plane to the West Coast for pre–awards show luncheons and meetings. As the conversation shifted to another topic, she started back on her chicken, thinking about her last conversation with him. All the nuance she would probably replay over and over from what could have been her last day as his main MUA. John's laugh, his nearness, the warm and masculine scent that lingered on his cape.

No need to make this invitation complicated by wondering about his motives or the feelings stirring in her own heart. If there was one thing she was good at, it was pushing aside how she felt in order to do what needed to be done.

Adanne dropped her fork into her bowl, the clattering stopping her family in midconversation. "I'll do it. I'm gonna go."

● ● ● ●

The days leading up to Adanne's trip to the West Coast passed in a blur. To her surprise, community members were enthusiastic and some even grateful to help cover her various roles. After she called Pastor Ben's assistant, volunteers from church filled the remaining shifts at the community center. Ms. Bernice's daughter, who worked at a nearby restaurant, volunteered to do pickups so she could give back to the place that had given her family so much.

Justine completely took over the meals for Daniel's family, saying, "Baby, I've been waiting for the chance to do more. You know I cook for an army anyway."

And now, as Adanne sat in her nephew's hospital room, she felt the weight she'd been carrying for so long begin to lift.

Almost. Jason would complete his last round of chemo in a few weeks, and if his reactions stabilized, he could go home.

Home.

Adanne rested her head on her clasped hands and gazed at his body as he napped, imagining the curly, dark hair that would grow again and the dimples in his infectious smile. She would make sure he always had a home to go to. Whatever it took.

"So, flying out this Wednesday, huh?"

Adanne blinked. "Yep. Day after tomorrow."

Instead of turning to her brother as he entered the room, she scooted closer to her sweet nephew, envisioning his face as he'd interacted with John. That memory filled her with warmth from the top of her head to her toes.

"You know we're going to be good, right?" Daniel placed a kiss on top of his son's head. They would be all right, but would she?

"I'm happy you're going to Cali, sis." Daniel sat down on the stiff hospital room sofa. He placed an arm around her shoulders. "There's no auntie that loves Jason more than you."

Adanne smirked, poking him in the side with her elbow. "I'm his *only* aunt. At least first aunt."

He grunted with a chuckle. "True."

They both leaned back, settling against each other. Daniel rubbed his goateed chin against her hair. "But doesn't make the love matter any less."

23

*T*he plane to the West Coast glided smoothly above the clouds, paying no mind to the turbulence in Adanne's stomach. Three years had passed since she'd crossed the skies from California to Alabama to care for her mother.

Becoming a professional makeup artist had been a dream come true, working with all kinds of clients as they prepared for their special moments. Mama was her biggest cheerleader when she earned a more specialized certification for special effects makeup. But her first job in that role ended up being her last when she made the decision to leave.

Adanne leaned against the window, the skies before her suddenly preferable to the first-class seat she occupied. Maybe this was a mistake. There were too many emotions to wade through, but with increasing awareness she noticed that the primary one wasn't grief. That would always remain, a melancholy that overflowed from the heart of a daughter missing her parents.

It also wasn't worry for her family. She'd even held off on putting her house on the market, hoping her meager savings could be a buffer for the center before she was forced to decide.

What she felt now was the anticipation of a schoolgirl passing her crush in the hallway. The excitement that bubbled up when she'd prepped for her senior prom and waited for her date to pick her up. The hope she had when the football player she'd liked during her brief time in college had remembered her name.

All those feelings flared up and overwhelmed her as she focused her attention on the next day when she would see John.

• • • •

"So." Adanne turned from her perusal of the trendy restaurant, her fingers absently running over her parents' rings. "Where's the rest of the team?"

John gulped when she caught him staring. He couldn't help getting drawn in by her innate beauty, the authenticity she carried. The way she hummed when she thought he wasn't paying attention. Not so interested in fitting in anywhere, it seemed, yet always looking like she belonged.

"What team?" He took a swig of water, hoping to wash away the nerves piling on thicker than aging makeup. After they'd ordered and commented on the decor of the eatery, they'd settled into a timid banter.

"Your prep team." Adanne raised one of her thick eyebrows, her lightly glossed lips poking out in their adorable way.

"About that . . ." John grinned, pulling off his sunglasses.

Before he could say more, the server arrived with their plates of steaming food. He licked his lips with appreciation at his open-faced sandwich piled high with fried eggs, bacon, cheese, and chipotle mayo. Adanne had ordered an omelet with too many vegetables for his taste, and some turkey sausage on the side.

"May I?"

Adanne looked at his hand in surprise as he offered it to her. She tucked back a smile—and probably a sarcastic comment—and took his hand, her touch light. Warmth crept up his arm from the feel of her fingertips.

"Lord, thank you for this food and the hands that made it. Thank you for Adanne being here this week. What she means to me—er, my team. Ah, also, I pray specifically for her meal and the dishonor she did to that omelet with the kale, spinach, and cilantro she added, with a dash of hot sauce. Hot sauce? In Jesus's name, a—"

"Ah, excuse me, sir."

John laughed, pulling his hand away, but to his surprise and boyish pleasure, Adanne held on.

"I know you did *not* just call me out in prayer over my omelet choice."

John grinned. "I did." He tugged, but Adanne's grip was stronger than he gave her credit for. "You going to give me back my hand, Ms. Stewart, before you pull it off? It would not be becoming of a future movie ensemble award winner."

"Tuh." Adanne released it and crossed her arms. "You're not a winner in my book if you can't see the delicious complexity in putting these together. And you failed to mention the mushrooms and peppers I added. If my granddaddy heard you, he'd swat you."

She gave him a teasing pout, but his heart leaped when he saw her eyes dancing. He would call her out in prayer any day to see her light up like that.

●   ●   ●   ●

After eating in silence for a few minutes, Adanne put her fork down—although the tasty meal made it hard to do. "This team of yours . . ."

"Well . . ." John's smile still teased, but she hadn't flown across the country to flirt with him. When she didn't return his humor, he cleared his throat. "My team is a little smaller than I let on."

She crossed her arms, abs tensing against creeping worry. She had a sinking feeling there was a lot more he wasn't sharing.

"Just a couple of people, and honestly, I don't really like all the fuss before a show."

Mild panic expanded from Adanne's chest and crept up her neck. But John's expression set off something entirely different in her belly. His eyes were tender with a dash of nerves and a certain type of look that could melt away her building apprehension. The expression of a man who looked to be in—

"What am I doing here, John?"

John moved his water glass to the side of the table, along with the succulents and other table accoutrements in between them. He reached into the pocket of his jacket, pulling out a shimmery cream envelope, and slid it across the table to her.

"Open it. Please."

She eyed him but did as he said. Her surging curiosity almost distracted her from the current that had flowed through their fingertips when they touched.

"I don't understand." She pulled out a certificate to a spa. Then a preloaded gift card. She gasped when she saw the amount written on a slip of paper taped to the back.

"John. What is this?" Words barely above a whisper.

"I wasn't entirely transparent with you, Adanne, though I tried to say it right so that I wouldn't lie."

John's lopsided smile gave his handsome face the look of a nervous schoolboy. It dumbfounded Adanne that she had that effect on him. He reached across the table and took her hand, carefully honoring her space while stewarding her touch. She closed her eyes as heat spread from his grasp.

When she opened them, his gaze was still on her, as warm as the center of his palm. "I want you here, Adanne." He cleared his throat, shifting in his seat. "As my date. Honestly, I don't know how to say this in a way that makes sense. But I'm tired of trying to play an inauthentic role in my personal life. Even for something as trivial as choosing an awards-show plus-one." Adanne watched his chest expand, air exhale out of his mouth. Gathering more wind to speak. Her, speechless. "When I saw you that day at the restaurant . . . I wanted . . . I—everything came crashing together for me. I knew you were the one that I wanted—no, needed—to stand with me."

He chuckled, running a shaky hand through his thick hair.

"I feel like I'm asking you to prom. But even if you say no—and please know that you are free to do so—I want you to enjoy all these things. To be pampered and taken care of like you've done for me these past few months. Like you do for so many."

Adanne's heart beat erratically, her fingers trembled. She glanced back at the items in her hand, unable to look him in the eye. "I don't know what to say. I—"

"Say yes, girl!"

Adanne looked up at the sound of a familiar voice. Kenya and Celise stood a few feet away, grins stretching across their faces.

"Wait—what?!"

Pleasure oozed from John's voice. "I wanted you to have family with you this week, whatever you decide."

Adanne gaped at the gifts and then at the dear faces of her cousins. She shook her head in shocked disbelief.

"How can I say no?"

John stood, extending a hand to help Adanne rise. The

pull between them magnetic. When he dropped his hand, he stepped forward as if to say more, but he replaced that uncertainty with a tender resolve that warmed her down to her toes. "I'll see you in a few days, then, Ms. Stewart. The ladies know what to do."

With that, he left, cap and sunglasses on, whisked into a car that had pulled up out of nowhere and then headed out of sight.

Adanne stood, wobbly from John's invitation and declaration. She was attending the awards. As John's date? Wait. He had feelings for her?

But the processing had to be put on pause as her cousins hurried forward to embrace her in a cloud of pressed hair and perfume. They paid no attention to the other patrons, who were distracted by their exuberance.

"Kenya, Celise? What's happening?"

The women stepped back, their grins as wide as the Los Angeles freeway. Kenya blinked back tears.

"Adanne, you've done so much for us all these years. When Auntie died, you took on her roles with passion. But it's time you let others take care of you."

Celise nodded. "You deserve to be spoiled and play the part of the queen you already are."

"John's assistant got in touch with me right after you talked to us," Kenya continued. "She told us he wanted to know if I would come along and if I knew of someone else that could help round out *your* team."

Adanne's bottom lip quivered. John had been attentive to every detail. As if he . . .

No. Don't go there yet.

Adanne shook her head again. *Yet.* Hope unraveled from that single thought and wound itself around her shoulders, warming her like a cherished blanket. She squeezed her eyes shut before she lost her control in this lavish restaurant.

Kenya, still holding Adanne's shoulder, grinned in her face. "I'm going to make sure that we stay on schedule and don't miss a detail."

Celise shrugged in her usual nonchalant way. "And I guess I'm here as your pseudo stylist to make sure you don't look terrible. Lucky for you, I'm between gigs." She gave Adanne a sly look. "And thankfully, I already hired a real stylist to pick out some pieces to choose from."

"You both dropped everything to be here with me. How can I ever repay you?" Adanne put her arms around them both as they walked out the door and into the blinding sunlight.

Kenya dabbed at her eyes and then gave her cousin one of her crazed looks. "Let's be real, this may be mostly about you, but I would not miss out on being around one of the biggest parties of the year, okay?"

• • • •

"I can't believe I'm sitting at this spa in LA with my cousins, sipping on sparkling water that probably cost more than my light bill."

"Don't be ridiculous." Celise wiggled in her cushioned recliner to find a more comfortable position. "Well, maybe half of it."

The women giggled. They'd spent the rest of Thursday afternoon sightseeing and then shopping the next morning. Kenya, of course, took the lead with her ideas of what Adanne should buy. Celise brought her expertise on the right shades of nail polish and on facial creams, making sure she received the best treatments at the spa.

With all the shopping and pampering, there was one enormous detail left.

"What about the dress?" Adanne played with her necklace, running the gold bands along the silver strand.

Kenya and Celise smiled at each other, a secret passing between the sisters. They had forbidden their older cousin from trying on gowns or even looking at them. She tried not to let her anticipation turn to worry so she could fully immerse herself in each experience.

Most of all, she determined not to dwell too much on the fact that she would soon attend one of the biggest awards shows of the year *with John*. It felt so strange to have shifted roles like this. To go from being a makeup artist who disliked her client to getting invited to be the date of said client, who'd become her *friend*. The friend who also made it clear that he saw her as more than that.

The thought was terrifying, in the most delightful way.

"You good, girl?" Kenya gazed at her with half-closed eyes as she succumbed to the vibrations of her massage chair. A technician massaged her feet before starting the pedicure.

Laughter bubbled in Adanne's throat. "I should ask you that, but it looks pretty obvious that you are feeling *real* good."

Celise glanced up from her magazine. "Seriously, Dee, this *is* a lot. You've gone from Hope Springs, Alabama, to the Oscars in Hollywood, California. Eyes will be all over you. Cameras flashing, rumors churning, headlines popping."

Adanne hadn't thought about those implications at all. More than a date, this was the culmination of John's manager's matchmaking efforts. Except she wasn't supposed to be the winner. Yet, here she was, feeling like Cinderella and Queen Esther all rolled into one. Picked for a ball she didn't feel qualified for.

24

*T*he morning of the awards, the girls sat in fluffy, white robes, enjoying brunch after another round at the hotel spa. Adanne wasn't sure if it was the massage and facial or being a few days removed from home, but the stress seemed to be leaking from her bones. The intriguing dilemma with John didn't even feel overwhelming. She would enjoy what he had set up for her and not take it any further in her mind. To do so would reveal more than she was ready for. This was just another part of the job.

But a job she still needed a uniform for.

"Okay, girls. The anticipation is killing me. What about the dress? I don't think my tennis shoes and sweatshirt are gonna cut it. How does this stylist know what looks good on me?" She took a bite of the sliced watermelon in her hand, the liquid a welcome addition to her parched throat.

"The answer is in the name, Dee." Kenya slid off the headband she'd been using to hold her straight hair back. "It hasn't been *that* long since you were immersed in the industry."

Celise took a sip of her orange juice, setting it down like the refined fashion model she appeared to be. "You worry too much. It's taken care of. Besides, I sent pictures." Her eyes darted to her phone. "We should have what we are waiting for by three, two . . ."

Kenya hopped up to answer the sudden knock at the door. Adanne gaped at her younger cousin. Celise shrugged, lashes fluttering. "Your open mouth will not be a good look when the cameras are flashing later."

Adanne shook her head for what felt like the thousandth time over the last couple of days. She didn't know whether to be impressed or a bit concerned. "You terrify me sometimes, Celise."

Celise raised her perfectly arched eyebrow and took another long sip of juice. "So say all my photographers." She placed her glass down gently, running a hand over her sleek cut. "And maybe a few ex-boyfriends." Her eyes lit up as she took in the parade coming through the door.

"Ah, Lina, you never disappoint."

Kenya caught Adanne's eye and mouthed, "What in the world?" as a train of dress-filled racks streamed in.

Celise stood at the door for a few long moments, waiting for all the carts to be pulled in by hotel staff. The last person who walked in was a petite woman with close-cropped red hair framing her pale, freckled face.

Celise squealed, giving an unusual display of emotion, and rushed to her stylist friend. She stopped just short of an embrace, giving Lina an air-kiss on each cheek.

The gowns flowed in complementing colors, ranging from traditional black to peach, gold, honey, rust, cream, and rose gold. Shades, she realized with delight, that would be perfect with her skin tone. She felt the urge to run her fingers across the various fabrics and textures but didn't trust that she wouldn't leave a smudge somewhere.

On another rack hung an assortment of cocktail dresses, skirts, and tops. The shades stayed in the same family, but some pieces bore pops of color that worked well with the shoes laid across the bottom.

The last rack revealed velvet-lined boxes of different sizes containing necklaces, earrings, bracelets, bangles, and even brooches. The largest boxes held clutches intended to match the final outfit selection. Extravagance spread out in the sitting area of their suite. Heady and overwhelming.

Adanne placed her arm around her cousin, sagging in disbelief. Kenya laughed and laid her head against her taller cousin's shoulder.

"Is all this for me?"

Lina turned from chatting with Celise and gave her a sweet, plum-stained grin.

"Of course it is. I don't travel light." She ran her small hands against the spectacular pieces. "I called in a few favors to some designers that owed me. Especially since *your* date might end up on the stage if the movie wins. We'll make sure you're wearing the perfect dress."

"Oh, this is not about me."

Lina pursed her lips and gave Celise a knowing look. Kenya just smiled as she took in the dazzling display. Their subtle reactions set off flutters in her belly. One of these amazing gowns would drape her body as she walked down the red carpet with John. As his date. For the world to see.

Adanne stepped back, clutching her necklace, and fell with unusually dramatic flair onto the plush gray sofa.

This wasn't the work trip she had expected at all.

●　●　●　●

John glanced at his Montblanc for the tenth time as the Lincoln rolled smoothly down Santa Monica Boulevard. Two years ago, he would have already downed a couple beverages to calm his nerves. But lots of prayer and the citrus-infused water bottles stocked in the limo would have to be enough. Thank God for that change.

John ran a hand through the hair his stylist would kill him for touching. If it wasn't for his movie's nomination, he would have avoided this night. The glitz and glamour captivated some, but John had seen part of the underbelly. It wasn't for him. Not anymore.

He took a deep breath. He *would* enjoy this evening. Because for the first time in a long time, he would walk down the carpet with someone whose company he cherished more than he thought possible. Even when he'd dated Katrina, their affection fractured in the flurry of activity. Their worst fights happened before appearances on red carpets. The spotlight revealing what they tried to ignore.

He smoothed nonexistent wrinkles from his pants as his car pulled up to the hotel entrance. A camera light popped outside the window. A reminder to smile instead of grimace. He'd forgotten how voracious the photographers and journalists could be, even before they hit the red carpet. He hoped that being surrounded by family for as long as possible had increased Adanne's comfort level and would allow her to descend in peace.

If Kenya stayed on schedule, Adanne should come down in just a few minutes. David, his stylist, sat across from him, a lint brush and mini sewing kit tucked into an inner pocket of his own blazer for emergencies. Seated next to him, Nora kept her eyes glued to her tablet, checking for any missed details for the night. He gave them a grateful grin and waited for the door to open.

They stepped out of the limo behind him, going over a few details as he waited for Adanne.

Even though this hotel didn't host a large number of awards guests, they'd still set up barriers on either side of their walkway, allowing for the easy exit of industry professionals. A wise decision considering the number of paparazzi, journalists, and curious onlookers that had gathered. When John stepped closer to a barrier, he heard a spectator gasp. "Who is that? She's gorgeous."

His breath caught as he took in the most captivating image. Between the heads of the guests lingering at the front entrance, he saw her step away from the door, emerging through the growing crowd. Her skin glowed in the flash of camera lights, and with the light of the setting sun, the elegant figure made her way tentatively down the barricade-lined entrance of the hotel.

He dodged a few photographers and potted plants to get a better view, ignoring his name being called by others in the distance. Her approach drew him like a magnet. The dress glided over her form in a cascade of warm copper and gold, accenting her curves and toned arms. Her dark hair shone and was shaped into a style that looped and fell over a bare shoulder. A flowing sleeve covered the other, and as she turned to glance at her cousins, John's mouth grew dry at the way the dress dipped to reveal the lithe muscles of her back.

Adanne turned to look where Kenya gestured. John snapped his mouth shut as her eyes locked with his, her cheekbones lifting with the hint of a smile. Time slowed as he gathered his senses, his heart beating an intense rhythm.

David caught up to him, serving as stylist and security.

"Wow." He said little but spoke when it counted.

"How's your wife? Kids?" John tugged at the collar of his dress shirt.

"Stop that." David readjusted the collar. "And don't change the subject." He gave what resembled a smirk. "Or get ahead of yourself."

John adjusted his bow tie. "Too late."

He'd never had his breath taken so completely. She stood only a few steps away, absolutely captivating. A star that caused everything else to fade. The crowds blurred. John swallowed and savored the vision of her. He didn't care what Mike would say. Or what the papers would write. Or if his nominated movie won a blasted statue. He knew her heart to be gold already. And now she looked every bit of that and more. The stylist Celise had selected did an amazing job highlighting all the parts that made Adanne dazzling. But no expertly applied makeup or designer gown or expensive jewel could speak to how stunning she was.

He clenched and unclenched his hands not knowing what he should do with them. Should he hug her, give her an air-kiss on the cheek, an *actual* kiss on the cheek? How did he do this when her appearance here was beyond what he imagined?

Her eyes shone with more appreciation the closer she came. Among enough aromas to make anyone's head spin, her familiar coconut and lavender scent was a welcome addition.

John looked down at the newly manicured hand she placed on his arm. The heat of her touch seeped through his sleeve, setting his heart once again off rhythm. She released the fullness of her smile, eyes flickering with gold flecks. A more dazzling display he had never seen.

"Thank you, John. For this. The last few days meant the world to me."

John lifted her hand, soaking her in. He let the light touch from his lips to the top of her hand say the words his mouth momentarily could not.

Adanne drew in a breath, smiling on the exhale. The softening of her eyes made it all worth it. Made him want to change every plan and spend the next few hours out of the spotlight. Instead, he led her to the open door of the limo, cradled her hand as she carefully stepped inside. He lifted the edge of her dress away from the street, tucking it around her satin shoes as she settled in.

• • • •

Adanne considered herself to be a woman of few words, but never without them. But here she was, speechless and overflowing with the giddiness of a girl who had been pampered beyond belief, and she felt like she was being cradled by a dream.

The absolute appeal flowing off the man next to her couldn't be denied. No pinching would wake her up from the reality of him. *Oh God, what do I do with him?*

They kept their eyes forward. A padded row and tinted privacy glass separated them from the other members of John's team.

Adanne thought of her own glam squad, the one John had intentionally picked for her. Her cousins had hurried her down the stairs like little fairy godmothers, primping, checking, tweezing, and tucking her to their satisfaction.

She released a giggle from her throat. John looked at her, his attentive gaze beckoning her to continue.

She leaned toward him. "Just thinking of my cousins. My glamorous, lavish-lifestyle-living cousins who are going to eat and then watch a movie. *A movie?*"

Her laugh bubbled out, melodic and light to her own ears. "On the biggest night of the year they will skip the parties and sit in the dark to watch actors on-screen that they could have met on the street."

John joined in on her amusement, his laughter dissolving more quickly than hers. He cleared his throat, his eyes flickering over her face. With piercing clarity, she realized she wanted him to taste her joy. To press his lips against hers. Hold her face. Pull her close to him.

"I'm probably laughing because I'm so nervous."

Adanne placed her hands against her stomach after touching

a different, more jeweled necklace around her neck. She liked this one, but surely missed the other.

She wanted to say more, but her words got trapped in a swallow. And in another.

"I have a confession too." John shifted.

"What?" She turned, hands still clenched, her lips rounded over her husky word.

"I—uh—I'm always nervous in these moments. Every gathering, festival, audition, fan meeting." He smirked.

"No! You seem so at ease." She gasped, shaking her head. "And it irritated me so much."

"It's very true. That's why I jump in so energetically sometimes. Helps me work out the nerves. Without guzzling them away." Adanne smiled in understanding.

He leaned back, his eyelids heavy. "When I was a kid, especially when nerves got to me, my mom would hold my hand, pat it, and say, 'Anchor, gioia mio. Find that solid ground and you won't have to worry.'"

"Your mom is a good advice giver."

"She is. And she almost came with me tonight."

"Oh. Well, I'm sorry I took her place."

John held her gaze. "I'm not."

Adanne blinked, the fingers at her belly trembling as she unwrapped them from her core.

"My mom used to sing," she whispered with a tentative smile, feeling vulnerable. "On Christ the solid Rock I stand . . ."

It came out no louder than a hum, a weighty hush, filling their private space. More intimate than singing on the mic that night at Plantain and Pies, when he couldn't have known how much the strum of her heart yearned for him.

He gripped the seat as the lyrics poured out of her mouth.

"All other ground is sinking sand . . ." Adanne sang, inwardly stepping over her own tripping doubts to find her footing. Strength seeped from the lyrics. Settling her with peace.

"All other ground is sinking sand."

Her fingers stopped their fluttering. She reached over, tugging John's arm, uncurling his fingers, holding his right hand in both of hers. His eyes glistened like the jewels around her neck.

"Here. To anchor us both."

25

The car couldn't be their hiding place any longer. John hoped some of the bigger names had already passed by so that he and Adanne could walk in with fewer distractions. He didn't want to scare her off before she had a chance to enjoy the night.

John's team had been sworn to secrecy about his date's identity, ensuring Mike that the surprise would be worth the wait. Hopefully watching from a swanky viewing party across the city would cushion his probable shock.

Snaps and pops of cameras greeted them first as they approached the intersection of Hollywood and Highland. Adanne leaned over to get a glimpse of the spectacle beyond his shoulder. Her grip grew tighter. With his free hand, John lowered the window. The initial hum that had filtered in turned into a steady roar. The fans standing behind barricades waited with giddy anticipation to get a photo of or even a wave from their favorite celebrities.

The limousine slowed, pulling to a stop at the covered arrivals area. It was almost time for their entrance. An attendant with a red jacket and black bow tie stepped to the door, pulling it open. Adanne gave John's hand one more squeeze. Before he stepped out, he turned to her, her lovely face at the center of his gaze.

"You asked me that day if I was good."

She smiled at his words, her eyes twinkling in remembrance.

"I didn't know how to answer because I wasn't sure anymore. But over the past few months I've felt what that could mean, by being next to you." He stepped out of the limo, extending his hand to pull her to himself.

"Anchor, Mr. Pomponio," she whispered, stepping out like a dream.

"Rock solid, Ms. Stewart," he answered, drawing her close.

They breezed through last checks with David and Nora and through the security screening. Thankfully, Mike hadn't sent his publicist to greet them first. Nothing he could say would matter now anyway, but for Adanne's sake, John was thankful.

He tucked Adanne's arm into his as they stepped onto the red carpet, media personnel from around the world already positioned for interviews and photos.

At her intake of breath, John tossed her a grin, inclining his head. "They won't bite." She squeezed his arm in response. He quite liked this feeling of Adanne Stewart being tethered to him.

"John Pope, over here! John! This way." He pasted on his signature smile, buttoning his jacket with the skill of red-carpet experience. He turned his attention to the group of people gathered behind the barriers, widening his grin, and then shifted to give a more jovial smirk to the cameras.

He was happy to oblige the ones who'd had a part in building his career, but there was still a chord that felt out of place. After months on set in a smaller town, away from these settings, he'd gotten out of rhythm with this sort of stardom. However, he would push those strange nerves aside, if only for this night.

John nodded at the industry professionals he knew and shook hands with the actors he'd worked with on previous projects. He introduced Adanne simply by name, keeping their movements steady along the carpet, her arm tucked tenderly into his.

Adanne remained a picture of elegant poise watching him engage in interviews at various spots along the way. He did his best to ease around photographers and minimize the number of pictures taken or media members squinting at her with curiosity. It wouldn't be long before Mike started calling. He could feel it. But he would soak up every moment and not lose the wonder of being here with her.

● ● ● ●

Everything felt like a whirlwind, the spinning of a merry-go-round. But instead of nausea, she felt the flutters of a thousand butterflies. Her skin tingled with the whirring of their wings, tremors at the core of her that could move mountains.

The past few weeks had been frustrating at times when it seemed like she was getting pulled into a spotlight she hadn't asked for just by being with John.

He flashed a smile at a journalist from Denmark. The relaxed banter setting everyone at ease increased the quiver in her belly. He drew others in with his charm, but over the weeks he'd been unwrapping himself to her. Inviting her to share this moment with him.

While thousands of uninvited academy members placed their names in lotteries to win the chance to attend, here she stood, joining him in snapshots for photographers from South Africa, Sweden, and India. Standing next to him in a gown that probably cost more than the community center's debt.

No, Adanne, keep your eyes on the dream. John stepped away from his interview. She needed to soak this in while it lasted. Bask in the glow of his attention on her, as if she were the only one in the room. She savored the feel of John's arm as it circled her waist, leading her across the exposed sliver of the avenue of stars and into the grand entrance of the Dolby Theatre.

Her breath hitched as the grand staircase came into view. The nominees around her would travel up those stairs, hoping to leave with a new title attached to their name. What would hers be after this? When the night carried on and away, how would John see her?

Before they reached the steps, she paused to gather her flowing skirt with one hand. John helped, making sure the hem stayed away from her feet. Satisfied she wouldn't fall on her face, she looked up, ready to ascend. John smiled down at her from the step above. The activity on either side of them melted into the edge of her vision, the two of them caught in a shaft of rippling light.

"How does it feel?" His voice wrapped her in lustrous warmth.

"How does *what* feel?" Could he hear her whisper? Her voice too heavy to hold any other weight.

He inclined his head, eyes on the cameras flashing, but his voice intimate and low. Just for her. "How does it feel to be the most beautiful woman in the room?"

Her parents had raised her to see her own value, first through God's eyes and then through theirs. As John's eyes flickered back to her, what she would have written off as a tease was revealed by his intense expression to be authentic. His words as true as he could say them.

He offered his hand, securing her against his side. As they

ascended the staircase toward the theater, she decided that she could happily endure being found beautiful by him.

• • • •

John didn't realize how much he'd longed for Adanne's nearness until he finally sat by her as the preshow started. Her presence had branded him deeper than the strokes of her makeup tools. Every day in her chair, a gift unfolding.

Even now, her eyes glowed, roaming the theater. He could sense her cataloging every color, texture, and shade. Sometimes she recognized an actor and leaned into him to ask a question. But what sent his heart skittering out of his chest was when he caught her at certain moments glancing at him with tangible awareness, her high cheekbones warmed and highlighted by the subtle, dimpled smile he'd grown to love.

Love? Wait.

"John, this is it. Prayers." Adanne's voice drew him from his jolting realization, her breath warm against his ear and spiced with cinnamon from the mints hiding in her satin clutch.

The countdown began for the Movie of the Year segment. John barely registered the nominees, even after the name of his movie reverberated around the theater.

He couldn't be at that point already. Could he?

It wasn't a confession of love. Just an observation of her on this night. But that was why he brought her here, wasn't it? He couldn't imagine anyone else. Being here. With him.

"John! John!" The object of his affection grasped his arm, her delight rolling over him. His eyes moved from the view of her lovely brown skin against his suit to the soft texture of her lips. Her smile, and then the flicker in her dewy eyes.

"Dude! We won!" The magnetic pull broke with a slap on his back. On his left, other members of the cast and crew made their way to the stage to join the director and producers. Before everything fully registered, he stood up in the wave of victory and found himself on the stage. They'd won.

Their independent film, which was the only project he'd been hired for two years ago, *won*. But as the words of the director carried over the audience and the award trophy was passed around, there was only one object that drew his eyes. The woman in the sunset gown and the subtle smile he loved.

• • • •

Adanne burst into applause with the rest of the audience as the group of cast and crew from the winning movie gathered onstage. The fervent clapping of her hands had nothing on the rapid beat of her heart. Or the warmth pooling in the depths of her core.

The days leading up to this moment had been some of the most refreshing of her life. She hadn't realized how much she'd needed this time away until the pent-up tension slipped from her body. Indulging in the spa treatments and carefree talks with her cousins . . . it had been so long since she'd let herself go enough to enjoy her surroundings and the people who filled them.

Then the preparation for this night—*mercy*. Choosing the perfect dress to walk the red carpet—all so surreal. Her job was to enhance the looks of her clients, but for the first time, she stood at the receiving end. It was a dream. Something she'd envisioned for fun but never in a million years thought she would experience.

Yet, that wasn't the best part. Her heart felt like it would gallop out of her chest, not because of the jewels adorning her neck that had momentarily taken the place of her usual wedding-band chain or the gown that fit her perfectly with its chiffon waves.

As the clapping died down, her eyes narrowed in on the

source. John's gaze roamed the crowd for a few seconds, appreciation on his handsome face. But as everyone else looked toward the director or at each other, his focus zeroed in on her. His green eyes were shimmering jewels, his hair trimmed and styled back. Instead of the constant five o'clock shadow he usually had for work, his face was clean-shaven, adding another level of charm to his classy form. The tux he wore had a timeless fit, with black satin-striped pants and a white dress shirt, the jacket an appealing shade of dark emerald, soft and velvety.

A speech boomed from the microphone, but something else entirely passed from John's steady gaze to hers.

All those weeks, while she'd tended to the details of his role through her makeup brush, he'd been tending her heart, pushing down barriers and hindrances, wanting to get closer even when she tried to push him away. And now?

She thought of his words right before they'd sat down. When he'd once again caught her off guard with his level of attention.

"How does it feel to be the most beautiful woman in the room?"

Adanne had never been so compelled to kiss a man as she had in that moment, her shyness melting into a rightness she couldn't shake.

She'd done her best to swallow down a response that would reveal too much of her affection, but before she could say something witty back, he'd offered his elbow and then tucked her arm into his side, his touch tender. Protective.

She pulled air into her lungs, her breath shuddering, doing little to settle the heart that seemed to be a butterfly with new wings. She could not contain the implications of that gaze. It spilled out into warmth that lifted and filled her cheeks. She was undone. Anything else was likely to tip her over.

26

The elevator door opened to a gentle rush of cool, scented air. Adanne stepped out wearing a slender satin skirt that hit right below the knees with a gentle flare. Cream wasn't a usual color of choice for any article of clothing she owned, but she had to keep reminding herself that she wasn't rushing off to a kitchen or makeup application. Tonight, she would attend one of the many after-parties of one of the biggest awards shows of the year. Plus, her cousins wouldn't take no for an answer, and the color paired beautifully with a fitted rose-gold top that shimmered in a hue similar to the gown she'd worn to the awards.

Her shoes were a bit more dramatic than she liked, but the girls had insisted. As the usually stubborn one, she didn't know what to do with being bossed around. When Kenya and Celise stepped off the elevator behind her to wave her on before their movie, love for them overwhelmed her. Adanne turned back to wrap her arms around their necks.

"Love you both so much," she whispered. They stood in that embrace for a moment until Celise unhooked Adanne's arm.

"You are cramping my aloof style." She sniffed.

"And messing up her makeup." Kenya laughed, flicking a tear off her mascara-coated eyelash. Adanne gave them a trembling smile, blew out a breath to get herself together, and then turned toward the handsome man waiting for her in the lobby.

At the click-clack of her heels on the marble tile, John turned from two young women enamored with his presence. His polite expression melted into a slow, appreciative grin that crinkled up the lines around his eyes.

His look made Adanne value her age and maturity. Confidence oozed through her as she took in John's intense awareness.

"Once again, you are breathtaking."

Even with all her womanly realization, his words took her back to middle school. She bit her bottom lip to keep from giggling. "You don't look so bad yourself."

He had on different slacks and a casual top under a designer sport jacket. Nope. He didn't look bad at all. Adanne nodded at the girls, who blinked at her in surprise. She tilted her head toward the revolving doors of the entrance.

"Mr. Pomponio, shall we?"

His mouth tipped and he slid a hand into his pocket on his pivot, offering her his other to hold. "We shall."

After a few moments, Adanne settled into the comfortable leather seat of a black Mercedes instead of the limo she and John had ridden in to the awards. She leaned against the cool glass of the tinted window, watching the streets blur by. The palm trees, drier landscape, and even pastel skies were so different from the setting of Hope Springs.

These streets were where John spent most of his time when he wasn't filming. So far removed from her crepe myrtle–rimmed parks and dated buildings with creeping greens. Her chest rose and fell. She adjusted her skirt and then fluffed the blouse toward her neck.

"Thinking hard?"

Adanne turned toward John. She picked up her clutch to use as a makeshift fan.

"You could say that." She shook that pseudo fan harder as he scooted closer. His arm lifted from its place at his side. But instead of placing it around her, he reached past her face to point out the window.

"That area is where I attended acting school. I met Mike but didn't connect with him again until years later when he started his talent agency." He tapped his chin and then pointed again, his arm brushing the silk of Adanne's blouse. She gripped her arm, following his gaze. "And that's the building where I booked my first gig."

They sat in silence for a few minutes. But John didn't increase his distance. Instead, with every bump or turn, he shifted closer. Until there were mere millimeters between them.

"And that home," he said, his breath warm and minty against her ear, "is where I made the decision to start over."

Adanne hadn't even noticed their turn up a hill into a more residential area. The car passed a multitude of large, extravagant houses until it finally pulled to a stop at a clearing that held several walking paths, park benches, and rocky outcrops. She turned to John in surprise.

He held up his hand before she could say a word.

"Before we go off to this party and try our best to mingle while avoiding the ones that will have way too much to drink, I want to show you a place that is special to me."

His face beckoned, stirring a flutter in her core that she couldn't contain. All the questions that mingled with the memories of the night finding their landing place here. She gripped her clutch tighter. *I need some air.*

"You plan on seducing me, Mr. Pomponio? I have standards. And rules."

241

"And walls." John smirked. "But I would never, Ms. Stewart. Just, thank you. For being here." He placed a hand on top of hers, his head tilted toward her with unmasked vulnerability. "With me."

She smiled, weak from his sincerity.

"I wanted to stop here because I've been thinking a lot about new beginnings and what that means for me. I don't have all the answers. I just know that here on this hill, two years ago, God met me. Reminded me of who I was and helped me let go of every weight of the past."

Adanne's eyes roamed over the face of the man who'd become more dear to her than she could imagine. "Will you tell me the story?"

He took a breath. "I ended up in circles and relationships that weren't always healthy. I was a bitter, cynical man with high expectations, ready to lash out when they were crushed.

"One day I didn't show up to a meeting with Peter, my agent. Instead of rescheduling, he showed up at my condo."

A wry smile crossed his face. "He found me still in bed, hungover, the worst I'd ever been. Instead of Mike's usual remedy of coffee and an aspirin, Peter gave me a glass of water and asked me if I really wanted to fall over the edge into a full-blown addiction. With my head on fire, I told him I didn't. So, instead of meeting about future movie roles, he drove me to his mentor's house, a guy named Garth Tracey. A business exec running numbers by day and hosting Bible studies for industry members at night."

John turned to Adanne. "After a few weeks, I drove to this spot. Threw my sins over the edge . . . instead of myself." He placed his left hand on his chest. "Jesus transformed me, made me brand-new."

Adanne swiped away the moisture on her lashes as he shifted his gaze toward the scenery outside the window. "I want to remember *that* and this place as I figure out what new things I'm supposed to do. And the type of man God wants me to be."

Adanne's heart swelled at his words. They were his, but they felt like they were from the heart of God for her too. What new thing was God doing in her life? And how much did it have to do with the man whose arms she wanted to wrap herself in?

"Thank you for sharing this with me, John. All of it. I'm honored to see a place that means so much to you."

His smile held gratitude and a tinge of relief. Bringing her here had cost him. She hoped it was worth whatever the risk.

John pressed a button to speak to the driver, then opened his door. Before Adanne could make sense of what was happening, he stood at her side, opening the door for her, offering his hand to help her out.

The fashionable heels that her cousins insisted on just about made her lose it on a thatch of pebbled ground.

"What I wouldn't give for my tennis shoes right about now." She spoke into the gentle breeze flowing against her face and hair. She rubbed her arms against the cool draft.

John slipped something from the limo and shut the door. He approached her with an enigmatic expression on his face. Without words, he draped a small, soft blanket over her shoulders.

"You planned for everything." She smiled, still trembling. "Don't we need to hurry to your party?"

"No one gets there on time. Most will have gone to several others before this one." John's lips tilted in a sheepish smile. "I would rather be here."

Adanne pulled the blanket tighter around her neck. It wasn't as cold as her actions warranted. But since he insisted on dismantling her distance, she intended to hold on to something.

Somehow.

That movement didn't deter John from taking one of her hands again. He extended her arm and twirled her in a slow semicircle. Her satin skirt brushed against her legs in the approaching twilight.

Then he pulled her close, their noses touching.

"I've got a song for you." He hummed against her ear. Her laugh came out throaty as she tipped her head back.

"John, you don't have to sing."

"What? You don't think I can?"

"I'm not sure, but . . . I'd rather you do something else."

His eyes flicked to her mouth.

Tugging at the blanket Adanne still grasped with one hand, he pulled it around the two of them. Adanne's hands pressed against his chest, but she relaxed until her arms wrapped around his waist, her head against his shoulder. The feel of his arms around her back was better than words. Strength seeped through her tight muscles and flowed to the place in her heart she never thought could be reached.

John looked at her with the most tender expression she'd ever seen on his face. She knew every line, every nuance and shade. The sparks and flickers, the small moles and age lines. But she'd never seen this.

Without taking his eyes off her, he slowly lowered his head, making sure she really did want this too. She turned her head to the right, escaping the intensity of his gaze for a moment.

"Is this okay?" he breathed.

"I think so." *Yes, of course it is!* "Won't the driver see us?"

"No, but do you care?"

Adanne met his eyes again. Seeing herself reflected there. Cared for. Who was she kidding?

"Not anymore."

Their lips met, the contact gentle, searching. The meeting of two hearts, searching for home. A new thing among the ashes of past mistakes and regret. Invitation and permission to enter, to take up room in places that had otherwise been closed off.

As their kiss deepened, Adanne realized John fit here. He felt like home and fit here, in the groove etched out in her heart. The one she filled to overflowing with her running so she wouldn't notice her loneliness. Wouldn't notice her gr ef. She'd forgotten Jesus's promises. That life wouldn't always be this way. But she hadn't believed him and, in all actuality, didn't think part of the package would be in the form of the one who stood before her, kissing her like he'd finally found home too.

Adanne pulled back, releasing John's waist. He smiled against her lips.

She shouldn't feel this way about him. The differences between them might be too complicated to conquer. But the look in his eyes told her a different story. His heart had been hers to hold tight for longer than she probably realized.

Shivers ran up and down her arms, making the hair there stand up.

The past few months of tension had led to this. A moment that felt like a beautiful beginning. Someone willing to carry her heart safely too.

She leaned in to press her lips against his one more time, soft and light, before stepping away.

"What's wrong?" John looked dreamy and disheveled. His dark, wavy hair shifting with the gentle wind.

"Nothing." She smiled, savoring his eyes, relishing this moment. Hoping that it would last beyond the dread curling in the pit of her stomach. "We should get back. You have people waiting."

27

*J*ohn, such a surprise! Didn't see that coming! All thanks to your performance, I'm sure."

John lurched forward as a producer slapped his back. Thankfully, he recovered quickly enough not to spill the sparkling water he held. He raised his drink to the jovial man. "Gotta keep everyone guessing."

John took a sip as the balding, older man made his way to other circles. Same networking, flirtation, unofficially made deals, invitations for coffee and tea and dinners and trips on yachts and so on, some that would turn into empty promises. It was all the same, yet he wasn't.

For many, that was evidenced by his movie's surprise win. But for him—and maybe the one who stood not too far from him—the evidence was much deeper and more eternal than a gold-plated figurine.

Adanne stood engrossed in conversation with his assistant, Nora, who'd met them there to ensure that Adanne wouldn't feel left out or out of place if there were discussions and congratulations he needed to engage in. Especially since the host of this party was a major Hollywood producer who had specifically invited him. But John would rather have been with Adanne, back up on that overlook. Or even better, walking through downtown Hope Springs, bannered by budding trees, her soft eyes glowing in the waning light.

As if sensing his gaze, Adanne glanced up, a smile in her cocoa eyes. Her braids remained in the same style as earlier, but those combined with her evening outfit made her look like she belonged on a stage, singing with her rich tones. She carried herself with poise, the same posture he'd noticed every day at his makeup chair. Made even clearer in comparison to some of the people milling about this rooftop event. Industry insiders and colleagues driven by ambition and agenda. Or others whose insecurities led them to pursue approval by any means necessary. Usually more visible than their more authentic peers. Adanne's humble confidence was one of those lights shining in a dark place.

Even though she seemed more tense here than she had on the way to the hill, her presence still soothed.

And her kiss still lingered on his lips.

John tilted his head in a wry smile. He hadn't necessarily intended for that to happen, although he couldn't say that he hadn't hoped something like that would. But he'd promised her that she could trust him before she knew what he had planned for this night. Plus, the moment felt special, almost sacred. He wasn't about to incur God's displeasure by messing with one of his daughters. He moved toward Adanne, ready to leave early to spend more time with her.

"Oh, there's that grin we all love. Was that meant for me, Johnny?"

John's stomach tightened at the familiar cadence of a sultry voice. He'd been so engrossed in his thoughts that he hadn't noticed the woman approaching him. He blinked to make sure he was not seeing a mirage. Of all places, why here? She'd been nowhere on the red carpet and had no reason to be, with her fiancé supposedly working a European tour.

Katrina stood before him, her petite form elevated by stilettos. Chestnut hair fell in thick, smooth waves down her back. Her black cocktail dress fringed in a length of lace that barely concealed her legs. John swallowed, keeping his eyes on her face. Her ice-blue eyes rimmed with the lashes that helped her book multiple makeup and fragrance deals.

"Katrina. Long time."

"It has been." Her lips curved into a wry smile, but her eyes were tense, tired, pleading. Why had he never realized before how weary she seemed?

"Have you been okay?" He looked at her with genuine concern but refrained from embracing her.

"Never been better. Why do you ask? Do I not look the part?"

Katrina appeared as striking as ever. But she represented the past for him. She'd been a big part of his life before, but that changed. Not just because she broke up with him but, he realized, because of Jesus *in* him. Transforming his desires along with his heart. And that heart did not beat for her anymore.

"You are stunning. As always. I just—"

"You're just being your usual, overly concerned self. But you have no reason to worry about me. I came here to talk about *you.*"

Katrina clapped her hands together a few times while moving closer to him. "First, congrats on your movie's win." John instinctively moved his head to get a better view of Adanne. Unfortunately, her braided crown disappeared in the crowd that had multiplied in the past few moments.

"Second, I have some news you may be interested in."

"Katrina, I need to check on my—my friend."

"Wait. Can we talk?" Katrina stepped forward, but he placed a hand on her arm to step past her.

"There he is! You found him!" A large hand clasped his shoulder, pulling him into a sort of embrace, the newcomer's arm slung across his chest. He shifted to find the party host right behind him.

"Rick, hey. Good to see you."

John glanced to his left, but still couldn't see Adanne. He hoped his assistant was taking good care of her until he could get back to her side.

He forced himself to face the host. "Great party."

"Yes, yes." Rick Dawson waved John's comments away. "I've got some exciting news for you. Your movie pulled out quite the upset. They should have nominated you for best supporting actor but for whatever it's worth, it looks like your career is back on the rise." John managed a smile that hopefully didn't resemble a cringe. Rick leaned in. "I'll cut to the chase. A movie is in the works, and we want you. Mike told me this would be the best time to catch you."

He did, did he? Before John could try again to signal Adanne or his assistant, he found himself guided to a corner of the rooftop.

The crowd parted as they made their way through. John nodded and shook hands as he passed by. Katrina walked possessively beside him. He wondered if she was uncomfortable too, but a smug smile graced her lips as she walked through with ease.

Before they made it to the plush sofa in a darker corner of the rooftop, Katrina took his arm. "This is what I wanted to talk to you about."

Her breath fanned warm in his ear, her nails grasping his upper arm. "This might be an amazing opportunity for both of us. I thought we could work out a way to not make it awkward."

John pulled back. Was this the woman he thought he was in love with all those years ago? What happened to her fiancé? Or did she not even care?

"God help me. Give me wisdom," he breathed out as he sat down to hear about the opportunity that could change his life.

● ● ● ●

When Nora left to take a phone call, Adanne hoped she could join John during a break in conversation. He appeared nonplussed by the attention surrounding him and kept seeking her out when they were separated. A wave, warm and inviting, washed over her whenever she saw his eyes searching for her. In a crowd of beautiful, wealthy, and important people, his gaze parted waters and met hers, unspoken words lingering from their moments together on the overlook. More promises waiting in the wings.

But after another person took his attention away, the surrounding crowds seemed to increase until she lost her moment to move toward him. Adanne stepped forward, not wanting to leave the safety of this wall near the rooftop exit. She smiled and nodded as several people passed her, some she even remembered from current films, but after a few moments, her unease rose when she noticed other looks being thrown her way. She wandered around a few groups and the deejay and picked up an appetizer from a roaming server.

As she walked, she noticed Nora in a corner, off the phone and talking to two others.

"Sorry to interrupt, but have you seen John?"

Adanne ignored the guilt in the assistant's eyes. She didn't need a babysitter. What she needed was the man who'd flown her across the country. Maybe they could call it a night and find something more than appetizers to eat.

"I'm sorry, Adanne, I'm not sure where he is."

"But I know who was looking for him." Nora's friend spoke up, a gleam in his eye. The other group member smirked.

"Knowing her, you may need to search in one of those dark corners."

John's petite assistant silenced her friends with her eyes. "Don't listen to them, Adanne. John shouldn't be far. Is there anything *I* can help you with?"

"No, it's okay. Just going to go grab a bite."

Adanne turned, unease continuing to rise in her belly, stirring close to frustration.

Why would he leave her for so long? He knew this wasn't her scene.

Adanne walked toward another attendant to grab an appetizer and a cup of cucumber sparkling water. As she reached for the smoked-salmon bite sitting on top of thin crackers, something caught her attention beyond the server.

In a secluded spot past the lit pool in the middle of the roof sat John and two others. One, a large man who filled the space with his presence, and the other, a striking brunette who draped herself over John. To his credit, he looked engrossed in what the other man was saying and not like he was paying attention to her.

But it didn't keep Adanne's stomach from flipping. She set the cup back on the tray, eyes locked on the scene.

"Miss. Are you finished?" Adanne blinked at the man dressed in all black and nodded. "Uh, yes, yes, I'm good. Thank you."

Adanne took one step forward but thought better of it. What would she do or even say? Who was she to John, really?

Makeup artist? Community representative? Temporary plus-one? Hilltop kisser?

Someone to finally be at home with? Here?

Adanne took a deep breath and stepped toward them. At the very least, he was her ride.

In the same moment, John reached out to shake the hand of the man in front of him. As he turned to say something to the clingy woman, she gave him a passionate kiss on the lips and threw her arms around his neck.

Recognition of who that woman was stopped Adanne in her tracks. She pivoted on her stiletto heels and did everything but run toward the door that led to the exit.

There was no need to define this thing between her and John when whatever they were obviously didn't matter. These were not her people. This was not her scene and never would be.

Never again.

Adanne rushed through the exit, punching the elevator button as her chest heaved.

"Lord, if you were to ever come to my rescue, now would be the time."

She needed a ride to come as quickly as her next breath. Her cousins were still out somewhere in the city, but they'd worked so hard to give her the experience of a lifetime. They deserved to watch a movie and enjoy some precious moments of sisterly bonding.

For now, Adanne was alone. In the same place where her dream had been dashed those years ago, destroyed by the same hand. The same man!

She lightly stomped her foot in an uncharacteristic gesture, then tried to steady herself as the elevator made the final stop on the bottom floor.

That action bothered her further. Proof that she'd become so vulnerable, she couldn't even tamp down her emotions anymore. John had taken her to a tipping point—right over the edge—and she was grasping for some semblance of her former composure. Longing for the safety of familiar walls.

Adanne crossed her arms as she stepped outside, patting away the chill, a feeling so bereft lingering that a thousand blankets wouldn't diminish it.

Lord, please, don't make me have to wait any longer. She opened her phone to find her rideshare app. It was a busy night, with parties happening all over the sprawling city. But to her relief, an available car popped up on the screen, only five minutes away.

It couldn't have come sooner. Who knew when John would notice that she was missing, or if he even cared? She didn't want to see him . . . couldn't. Not when she'd finally believed her feelings and his weren't just fleeting.

Adanne gritted her teeth against the image seared into her brain. John locked in an embrace with his ex, not too long after tenderly pulling Adanne into his arms on that overlook off Mulholland Drive.

How could she be so foolish? She never should have come. Never should have done a lot of things. But every small step had led her here. She hadn't been rash. Just deeply falling for him.

This felt like loss, swift and sudden. Hope dashed to pieces.

When a car pulled up in front of her, she had to blink several times to recognize that it was the same one from her app. Releasing the grip on her arms, she cringed, reminded of how tightly she'd been holding on to herself, her nails biting into bare skin.

Everything from her manicure to her outfit reminded her of him. She wanted to tear the clothes off and forget that she'd even thought for a moment this could be the sweetest surprise—a new beginning of epic proportions.

Adanne stepped into the black Toyota, offering a wobbly grimace to the driver as he adjusted his phone and put the car in drive.

The city streamed by in luminescent lights until the streets melted into a watery haze. Adanne dashed away a traitorous drop. How she missed her mama. There was no one else she wanted to run to, curl up on the couch and eat homemade cobbler with. Anchor herself from this storm of rejection within her mother's embrace.

There is space in my arms for you.

Adanne had barely registered the whisper that whooshed in when a ping drew her attention to her phone.

Grateful for something to distract her, she tapped open the notification from her social media feed. That hadn't happened in a while. After barely checking it over the years, she'd almost forgotten there was still one in her name.

She flipped open her app to a punch in the gut. In the top right corner of the main news feed was a picture that would have sent warmth through her just an hour ago.

A snap of a television screen, someone from Hope Springs delighted to see their hometown girl on the red carpet in Hollywood. That woman's skin glowed with wonder, her shimmery dress reflecting the flash of camera lights. And the man who draped his arm around her waist appeared besotted, his face turned toward her, mouth tipped in admiration.

But that had to have been nothing more than an act.

Because in the shadow of rooftop corners, John revealed his true nature. No matter what he said, his heart still belonged to Katrina. And now his rejection of Adanne would be on display for all the world to see.

28

The weight of her arms used to be so right. But not anymore. Now they were chains. It wasn't Katrina necessarily, he thought, as he gently lifted her limbs from around his neck. It was the realization that he had moved on from that season and somehow, in the last few months, freed himself of what linked them together. The fullness of that release was evident in the aftermath of the unprovoked kiss.

Rick jumped up to find his next opportunity. John peered at Katrina, her hands in his for a moment. "I have a lot of things to think about. But I know that something happening between us again is not one of them."

Katrina blinked. The smile didn't leave her face but tightened. Lost its luster.

"I'm not engaged to Victor anymore."

John weighed her words. But that bit of news didn't change what he already knew to be true.

"I admit, I wasn't always the best to you. We weren't to each other. And yes, when you left, it broke my heart." His smile was rueful. "But it needed to be broken. I needed to let God put it back together again."

Katrina rolled her eyes to the ceiling. "Here we go."

"Listen." He held her hands tighter, waiting for her to look back at him. "I do care about you, and I want you to know the freedom I've found. Through Jesus. For you to know how loved you are, regardless of who you are with. But it's not with me anymore."

John's thoughts shifted to the one whose presence lingered with him for most of the evening. The one he hadn't seen in twenty minutes.

Oh no. Adanne!

John released Katrina's hands. He moved to leave but paused. Turning back, he embraced her one last time.

"What was that for?"

"For reminding me of what really matters."

John hoped his smile showed how genuine he was. He needed to pray over what they'd discussed with Rick, to think through all the possibilities. But the one person he didn't have to think about was nowhere to be found.

"Nora, where is Adanne?" His assistant was in a lively conversation with a group standing at the opposite corner of the brightly lit pool.

Her eyes rounded. "I'm sorry, John, she went in search of you, and I haven't seen her since then. Here, I'll look with you."

Nora hurried among the guests as John tried to call Adanne's phone. After several attempts, he met back up with Nora.

"I'm going to take the car and see if she went back to her hotel." John bounded down the rooftop stairs, too impatient to wait for the elevator.

Thirty minutes later, he made it to her hotel room door. He hoped she was there since she hadn't answered any of his calls. He hadn't been able to reach Kenya or Celise either.

He shouldn't have left her side or, better yet, should have pulled her along with him.

John released a breath and pressed his finger to the suite's doorbell. After a few moments with no response, he lifted his hand to knock.

And almost knocked Adanne in the face as she whipped open the door.

She shifted her head with the deft moves of an athlete, returning to her position with a slight scowl on her otherwise impassive face.

John should have been overly apologetic. Groveling at her feet for being inconsiderate. But fuzzy slippers with puppy ears on the front covered those feet. She'd exchanged the alluring outfit from the party for West African–print leggings and a long T-shirt with "Coffee is my love language" scripted on the front. Her hair was piled on top of her head, wrapped in a colorful scarf.

She looked adorable. And furious.

John's lips tilted into a grin he couldn't resist. "You didn't say goodbye."

Fire flashed in her eyes. John didn't take her as a woman who said certain words, but she seemed like she could send some choice ones his way.

Unfortunately, it further enamored him.

"Is it true?" John's thoughts slipped out before he could stop them.

The emotions that flitted across her face were almost comical. "Are you being for real right now?" she finally spat out. Her eyes narrowed like laser beams.

He pointed to the text on her shirt. "I just would have given you a lifetime supply of lattes if I knew—"

"You've got a lot of nerve, John. Is this some game to you? Another ploy to manipulate the headlines in your favor?"

Before he could say a word, Adanne's phone flashed in front of his face. He blinked and stepped back.

This was why he hated social media. Somehow, a picture of him and Katrina slipped through the cracks of the supposedly iron-tight publicity team. He was surprised that Mike hadn't been the first to contact him. As he saw the evidence of Katrina's kiss, his eyes lifted to Adanne's.

"I'm so sorry. I know how it looks, but . . . it's not how it looks."

"I saw it with my own eyes."

John tried to step forward again. To do something with his hands instead of holding on to the doorjamb.

"Katrina is my past, Adanne. I promise that what you saw was not something I caused, or even wanted."

Adanne crossed her arms, gripping her phone mercilessly.

"I don't know what game you're playing, John. But I'm not a part or a project. The people of Hope Springs are not your charity case."

"Believe me, Adanne, I know."

She put her hand up. "I'm not quite sure you do." She scrolled up and showed him another post. "Who took that photo at the center?"

He squinted at the caption. "John Pope serving the poor and needy of Hope Spri—" His eyes shot up. "Adanne, that was never my intention. I—"

She raised her hand. "Believe *me*, I'm thankful for all you did for me, *and* my cousins. It was the best week. And to-night . . ."

Her head turned away. John took a chance. Touched her face, turning her eyes back toward him. In that moment, her gaze met his with genuine hurt instead of fury. The look of a woman whose expectations were dashed to pieces. In that instant, more hope stirred in his heart than it had when his lips met hers on the overlook.

"Adanne, this night was one I will never forget. I need to tell you . . ."

The sounds of women chatting wafted down the hall, silencing his confession. Adanne stiffened, shifting away from his touch as her cousins came around the corner, laughing and still eating movie candy.

John watched Adanne's face return to its usual mask. A shield pushing him away.

She moved back, out of his reach.

"Well, hello, John. Congrats on your movie's win. And Adanne, I thought you two would be out celebrating until much later." Kenya stepped up, grinning.

Adanne kept her eyes on him, her voice level. "It was time to go home."

The finality of her words hit him in the gut. She might as well have slammed the door in his face.

Celise made a sound with her throat. She sent a casual wave John's way and practically pushed her older sister through the door of the suite as Adanne made room for them to enter.

When John felt like they were out of earshot, he put his hands out. Hoping it would give off the sense of his humble surrender. "Please believe me. I would never intentionally hurt you. Can we talk more? Over coffee? Dinner? A walk in the park?"

She let out a mirthless laugh. Her sigh at the tail end of it squeezed John's heart. She didn't trust him. Maybe she never had.

"That won't be possible. Or necessary. I already changed my flight to leave early tomorrow morning."

It was John's turn to struggle with his response.

"What you saw doesn't compare to what is between us, Adanne. I—I don't know what else to say."

Adanne held the door, waiting, maybe expecting him to

say more. But what could he do? If she didn't want to stay, how could he force her? It wouldn't be the first time he'd unsuccessfully tried to keep someone from leaving.

"You have to let go." With an exhale she stepped back into the suite, the door closing as she did. "And maybe that means letting go of me too. I'm more than a publicity stunt. Goodbye, John."

John stared at the door for a few moments longer. Unable to reconcile the elation of a couple of hours ago to now. Once again being the one to cause Adanne pain, and in the process, he'd sent shards into his own heart.

He made his way toward the elevator with slow, defeated steps, wrestling with the urge to knock down Adanne's door and do whatever it took to make it up to her.

His phone vibrated in his jacket pocket. A message from Nora asking if he'd found Adanne, and then a link to a headline, revealing the same picture Adanne showed him.

Is John Pope Getting Back with Katrina Daline?
Sources tell us that the former couple of the year have something in the works, especially after the songstress's recent breakup with record executive . . .

John gripped the phone, ready to throw it against the wall. Instead, he clicked the name of the first person he could think of who could make this go away.

"Mike, get these posts deleted!"

"What are you talking about, John?"

He let out a sharp laugh, running his hands through his hair and then clenching his hand into a fist. He climbed into the back seat of the black Mercedes waiting for him.

"'Sources,' Mike? God help me . . . did you do this? Put this out there? Let all of this get out?"

Silence. Then after clearing his throat, "I can't control

what people post. It goes to show how important it is to be intentional about these things."

"Intentional? This was about me and who *I* wanted to go to the awards with."

"Maybe if you thought more about her—*if* you really cared—you wouldn't have dragged her across the country."

John pushed back into the leather of the sedan, frustrated at his manager's words but also at the nudge of guilt poking his middle. "Mike, what did you do?"

"Covered my client."

"How is getting me involved in more drama covering me?"

"Rick has you on a short list for an upcoming biopic. I did what I had to do to make sure the attention you get benefits your future." Mike's voice rose, speaking over the crowd at whatever party he was at. "This is the best of both worlds. The possibility of getting back with Katrina *and* a big-budget movie almost in the bag."

"This is so far removed from what I wanted, Mike!"

"You weren't open with me. Did you not think about the implications?"

"What? That I might genuinely care for someone outside of this shallow industry?"

Mike's voice shifted into a fierce whisper. "Sounds like judgment, John."

"Not so different than your assessment of the people in my film location. You had them pegged as incompetent from the beginning. Only a means for me to step up in my career, not as *actual* people that matter more than a photo op or publicity stunt. Before you say anything else, I need to say this. For the first time in a long time I want to do what is right by God and others, not because of how it will elevate my status or—or advance my career. And if you can't understand that, maybe this is where our friendship ends."

"I did what I did because we *are* friends, John!"

John wished he could run instead of being stuck in this car in the middle of the freeway. "Mike, I can't do this right now. Have a good night and enjoy the fact that you got exactly what you wanted."

29

adanne fumbled with her keys, fingers heavy. If she could just unlock the front door, she'd be okay. Ensconce herself within the safety of the walls that represented the little bit of stability she had left. Everything else seemed to be slipping between her fingers as easily as these keys were. Everything she held dear. Including the necklace she never should have taken off.

She'd forgotten to retrieve it from the closet as she prepared for the awards last night. And her cousins couldn't find it anywhere. Caught up in the wonder of the day, she'd let her anticipation override everything else. She *never* forgot that necklace. Why did that place, and that night, have to be where she left what meant the most to her? That loss deepened the rejection to a tangible ache in her chest. How could a beautiful night turn so quickly into acute betrayal?

After finally unlocking the door, she threw the keys onto the kitchen counter. Her stomach rumbled with unmet hunger, her appetite just returning after a day of air travel. It was enough to try to contain her emotions on the flight over the country, fighting back the urge to weep in the middle of strangers. Because of her last-minute change, she'd opted for coach instead of returning in first class.

The fairy tale was over anyhow. Initially she'd convinced herself that perhaps the dreamy weekend would unfold into something meant to be. But now it served as a reminder that everything else she thought she held securely in her grasp would eventually fall away too.

Adanne leaned her head against the refrigerator door. There would be no satisfaction found in there either. She'd given all her perishables to Daniel before she left because she was supposed to be gone longer. She could order delivery but wasn't interested in eating the type of food available at this hour.

The longing for her parents rose. So strong, her throat ached for release. Who could she call to lift her now? When she felt like her legs were too weak to carry her into her bed, much less the next day and the day after that? She'd convinced her cousins to stay in Los Angeles to enjoy the rest of their trip. And it was too late to bother her brother. For all she knew, he was at the hospital dealing with his own monumental burdens. How much did a broken heart matter in the grand scheme of things?

Out of habit she opened the fridge door. Instead of the glass of juice she thought would alleviate her craving, she found two Tupperware containers that she hadn't put there. Her fingers grasped the first one that had a note taped to the top. Adanne put it on the counter, placing the paper aside to lift the lid. Her mouth watered at the sight of the grilled chicken, sautéed greens, and glazed carrots resting inside. She turned back to the fridge and pulled out the smaller container. Peering through the clear package, she saw specks of cinnamon swirled around caramelized slices of fruit. Homemade peach cobbler. Her fingers trembled as she set the lid down and opened the folded piece of paper.

Hey, baby girl. I hope you don't mind me calling you that. It just felt right considering. The girls told me what happened. I wanted to call you, but . . . I know how these things can go. I didn't know exactly what time you'd arrive today so I thought at least you could come home to a home-cooked meal. It's not much but it's with all my love. I'm praying for you. And you better believe you can call me when you need me. When you're ready. Love, Aunt Justine.

Adanne grabbed a paper towel to sop up the liquid leaking from her eyes before she read the last part.

PS. I don't want to tell you how to live your life. But if I were you, I would tell that actor man a thing or two. You make your peace, even if that means you give him a piece of your mind.

"Thank you for that last part, Auntie." Imagining her saying those very words brought a chuckle to her lips that distracted her from melting into a puddle of tears. She would cry later.

Maybe later the courage would come to do exactly as her auntie said. But right now, she would warm up the contents of these containers, curl up in her bed, and dine on the meal made with the nurture she craved.

* * * *

"Hi, Mamma."

John held his phone to his ear as he walked toward the large windows of a private lounge overlooking a portion of the busy LAX airport.

After a week of meetings, interviews, and weighty regret,

he had just a couple more places to go before he made it back to Hope Springs to wrap filming. A few more flights before he could figure out how to face Adanne.

"Hello, gioia mio. It's been a few days. Still glowing after your movie's big win?"

"You could say that."

"Okay, wrong response. Spit it out. What's got you in the pits after such a career highlight?"

John laughed. "Mamma, you do know that the award was really about the producers, not the actors."

"Hold on. Let me get settled in my prayer chair. Now, tell me what's going on."

John envisioned her sitting in the recliner in the corner of her bedroom. Large enough to swallow her petite frame, covered in crocheted blankets passed down from his Nonna. He recalled the mornings he would wake up and see her there. Especially as the drama between his parents intensified. When his father finally left, the chair sat empty for a time. But she slowly made her way back.

John knew for certain it was her prayers that kept bringing him back to his senses. Talking to her now as she sat in her place of devotion encouraged his troubled heart.

"I'm thankful for the win and the opportunities coming my way. But—"

"Yesss?"

"I think I may have let one get away."

"Ah, problem in paradise. Would this *one* happen to be the beautiful woman who sat next to you? I saw glimpses of her as the camera panned during the show."

"You know who that was, right?"

"I wasn't born yesterday, son, although I tend to look it."

John chuckled, grateful for his spunky mother.

"What went wrong? If I saw correctly, she positively glowed that evening. And not just from her impeccable skin and beautiful makeup. It may have had to do with the handsome man sitting beside her."

"Mamma, you're biased."

"Bah. I'm not obligated to say anything nice. I only say what I know to be true. I saw something sparkle between the two of you, but I noticed it at the hospital first. I've been praying ever since."

The sheen that spread over his eyes surprised him. So, he wasn't fooling himself. What he'd been feeling these months wasn't just movie magic.

"I'm struggling with what to say. I need a script to memorize or something."

His mother chuckled. "Maybe it's because you're not supposed to just *say* it. Maybe you need to show her. For some people it's not about words, but love displayed in actions. In loyalty. Through sacrifice."

John paced in front of a cushioned seat as her words washed over him. She was right.

"John, what did you need from your father at a certain point?" His mother continued before he could respond. "Was it more words? He'd always been good at that."

John cleared his throat, choking on the change of direction. It came out of nowhere, but he felt the impact deep in his belly.

No, John realized. After a while, Dad's words became white noise. The picture he'd presented to the public was not how he lived his personal life. Growing up, all John wanted was his dad's presence, not just talk.

"Think about *her*." His mom's voice softened, sensing what he couldn't seem to vocalize. "What does this lovely woman know of you? Does she need practiced lines that speak more to your skill, or is she the one that is worthy of the vulnerability of your heart?"

John let those words sink in. Reminding him of the boy

who longed for his father to come home from one-night stands and gambling sprees. The teenager who'd watched his mom suffer in silence while his father had multiple affairs, parading a new woman down the aisle of the church to join with her in so-called holy matrimony. He hadn't entered a church since, until . . . until Adanne.

"Mamma. It's her." He paused, the confession settling in his chest, anchoring him in what he knew to be true the day he caught her singing her heart out in the makeup trailer. And in all the songs since then. "And you're right. She needs to know that she can trust me. With her pain, her dreams. With her heart. I want to be the one she feels safe with. Because I already feel that way with her."

He couldn't believe he was saying the words out loud. And to his mother, of all people. But there they were, laid out in his mind like the scripts he recited. However, they were deeper and more nuanced than any prose he'd ever had to memorize. She was more than memory, more than lines to spout out. There was no one else who mattered like she did.

"I know, son. Now show her."

John heard the smile in his mother's voice. Felt the emotion rippling its way through her words.

"You know better than I the best plot points of a good love story. There's always a twist. Some sort of—"

"Grand gesture." John finished her words.

"Correct."

"So, this is a love story, then. You think I'm in love with her?" He bit the inside of his cheek against the boyish smile trying to take over.

She laughed, the sound lifting a heavy weight from his shoulders.

John grinned along with her, purpose and resolve running through him. Who was he kidding? "Of course I am."

"Of course you are. Now, hurry and hang up so you can get to work."

"Love you, Mamma."

She smacked a kiss into the phone and ended the call.

He stashed his phone, sensing the shift toward something new.

Change was inevitable in the movie industry. Spotlights came and went, relationships at times felt relegated to call sheets, but when it was a wrap, people moved on.

Yet, in her subtle way, Adanne had wrapped herself around his life. Even when given the opportunity, she hadn't let go. Inviting him deeper into her world, opening herself up to the possibility of something more.

Until he crushed it with that kiss. Not because he wanted that from Katrina. But because he hadn't made the choice to fully let go himself. He'd let every rejection linger, leaving baggage that he and other people kept stumbling over.

The new wasn't about his career, he could see that now. It was about him making the choice to shake off those old things, his old ways of doing, and let God lead him into the full life he was meant to live. One where he broke off the expectations he placed on others. Opened himself to love rooted enough to last.

Adanne deserved all of that. Not pieces of him. She was worth him being whole before God.

30

nxiety curled in Adanne's stomach, wrapping around her middle until it was a heavy weight she couldn't dislodge. Her hands gripped the steering wheel of her truck, which had been in park for twenty minutes. According to her call sheet, she was expected at base camp early Thursday morning, and now she was at risk of being late.

It should be easier than this. It shouldn't matter so much. But each moment she'd spent with John had pulled her out of her comfort zone, closer to the edge, until a dreamy night in a beautiful gown tipped her right on over.

She could still see the way John's mouth spread into the most delicious smile when he was waiting for her at the hotel entrance. His pleasure was undeniable. The way he looked at her made her feel like she was the only one who mattered.

The brush of his tuxedo's velvet sleeve against her bare skin was ingrained in her muscle memory. Warm, welcoming, easing her nerves yet increasing her awareness with every passing minute.

Adanne raised her fist in frustration but landed it softly on the wheel. She should have known better. Should have kept the walls up with him, kept him distant from her heart.

But then what?

What do you mean, Lord? "Then I wouldn't be here," she whispered back. "Feeling helpless and confused and—"

In love.

She groaned. She didn't want to hear that. Especially from the One who knew her better than anyone else. It felt too full of faith, of hope, and to her chagrin, full of love.

She loved John. Somehow, during these months of being wedged between the makeup chair and mirror, of their long talks and long walks into each other's stories, she had more than fallen over the edge.

Adanne took a deep breath at the revelation, clutching her unzipped jacket together. She'd been avoiding this for so long, and now that it was here, it looked like John hadn't been serious at all. But of course, he'd offered nothing. Not really. He never made her any promises.

He just showed surprising attention and interest in daily conversation. He gave her a glimpse of his faith journey as he accompanied her to church. He displayed his generosity and compassion in multiple ways. And then surprising her in LA. Providing all that she and her cousins needed to have an amazing time, whether or not she said yes to being his date for the awards. The kiss and cool breeze on that hilltop reminding her he would rather be with her than anywhere else. All that *had* to mean something. But it seemed to fizzle away when he was back in his usual element, among his people and his ex-girlfriend.

Was it all for nothing?

Adanne squared her shoulders. She had to find out. Not over the phone in any of his calls she kept ignoring. Face-to-face she would say the words she hadn't been able to at the

271

hotel door, and maybe, just maybe, the glimmer of hope that flickered in her heart would remain. At least she'd know.

She turned off her car and headed to the makeup office to check in.

"Hey, Adanne." A production assistant greeted her after scanning the badge hanging from the lanyard around her neck. "Sorry, Alex is out, but I know she needed to talk with you."

"How long will she be away?"

The sandy-haired man checked his watch. "I'm not sure, but shouldn't be long. She left to take a phone call."

Adanne tapped her finger on her chin. Her nails still colored with the evidence of her time in California. "Well, I'll head to the makeup unit to wait. Be back in a few."

As Adanne walked, worry continued to tighten her stomach. She shook her arms out, balancing her tote bag on her shoulder, reminding herself that she could do this. She could face John if he was in there. Lay everything out, and deal with the consequences. This issue wouldn't keep her from finishing her job well.

After breathing out a silent prayer, Adanne pushed open the door to the trailer that had felt like a pseudo home over the past few months. But instead of John in the chair, she saw another man. Someone shorter and better dressed. He wore gray slacks, a pale-blue button-down shirt, and an earbud in one ear. On his wrist was an expensive-looking watch. At the sound of the door, he turned his head toward the front, his dark-red hair gleaming from the lights of the mirror.

Recognition registered in his pale-blue eyes.

"You must be Adanne," he said, jumping up with surprising speed. "Did I say it right?" Before she could register his approach, he stuck his hand out to her. She shook it with hesitance, overcome by the feeling of familiarity, although she'd never seen his face.

"How do you know me?" She stepped to the side to put her purse on the couch.

He gave her a tight grin, continuing to make her feel like she was under a microscope. "Who doesn't know you?"

The lithe man walked backwards to the makeup desk, making himself at home in the synthetic leather–lined chair. "You made quite an impression at the awards show. Everyone wondered about the mystery woman at John's side."

Adanne assessed him with a cool gaze. "You don't seem to approve. But I'm still not putting the pieces together of who you are."

He laughed and clapped his hands together. The sound reverberated in her mind, setting off a tone of foreboding. "I'm Mike, John's manager. The one responsible for making sure his career continues to succeed."

The dread that Adanne felt several moments ago in her truck spread into her chest, squeezing tight. She swallowed, forcing herself to smile, not liking the one coming from Mike.

"What can I do for you?" She made her way to the mirror, hoping that John or someone else would come soon and relieve her of this man's presence.

"Actually nothing. And *that* won't be necessary." Mike swiveled to her as she reached for the drawer under the table. Adanne looked at him with an eyebrow raised.

Mike continued to grin. "I thought Alex would tell you to save you a trip, but since you're here, it looks like that hasn't happened yet. There's been a change in plans and your services are no longer needed."

• • • •

273

Later that afternoon, Adanne sat at the island counter in her aunt and uncle's house for the second time in three weeks. Thankful for the reminder that she had a place to be beyond what she could create for herself. The countertop she rested her arms on was the kind of solid she needed.

It had taken her too long to realize the foundation she had. Here. She needed to make this her rhythm again. If everything from the past few months had led her to this point, it was more than worth it. And with the payment deadline approaching for the community center, and her house still the only viable option, she may need more support than she realized.

"What will you do?" Kenya sat across from Adanne, her pretty face squished from resting her chin in her hands.

"About what?" Celise sauntered into the kitchen, followed by Salome, who seemed to have been the victim of another makeover attempt by her older sister.

"About the job that she just lost from the film set."

"I'm so sorry, Dee." Salome sat down across from Adanne. Celise gave her cousin a sympathetic pout before grabbing a pink lady from the fruit basket. She started rummaging around every kitchen drawer for a knife after washing the apple.

Adanne snickered at the look on Kenya's face as she waited for her sister.

"Ahem. Did you hear what I said, sis?" Kenya poked out her lips.

Celise continued to bang open a few more drawers until she found what she was looking for. "Anyone want a slice?" She looked over her shoulder, waving her knife around. "I feel like I'm forgetting something. And I can't think through solutions when I'm hungry."

Salome giggled. Kenya rolled her eyes as her sister proceeded with her snack but couldn't help raising her lips in an amused smile.

"What options do you have now?" Kenya asked Adanne.

"None really. At least not yet. The community center barely brings in donations anymore, so there's not much coming from that besides what pays Daniel's salary."

Adanne grabbed the apple slice Celise offered as she slid onto the empty bar stool. She'd spent too much of the last two years trying to do everything herself. To be the rock of the family like her parents had been, but not letting anyone else be that for her. But that was beginning to change. And somehow John had a little to do with that.

The lump in her throat was hard to swallow.

Salome slid a hand over and placed it on top of Adanne's. She bowed her head, willing the ache in her neck to go away, before she spoke.

"I feel like my only option is to sell my house." Adanne kept her head down, the gasps from around the table almost too much for her tender emotions. "I've been weighing it for a long time. The community center is more important to the people in the neighborhood. I can live anywhere. But I can't lose what my parents built together."

Salome squeezed her cousin's hand. Kenya sighed, drawing Adanne's face up. "I get it, cousin. I do. But there has got to be another way. Because ultimately God built that. If it's supposed to continue, he will sustain it, right?"

Salome nodded. "Right."

Adanne leaned into the back of the stool. "If I had half your confidence and positivity, Kenya . . ."

It was Adanne's turn to be on the receiving end of Kenya's pursed lips and raised eyebrows.

"Gurl, what you talking 'bout? Did you not get a good look at yourself in California? The clips of you walking down the red carpet?"

"Or the way *he* couldn't take his eyes off you?" Salome's soft voice broke in. Her gaze knowing, tapping on the core of Adanne's distress.

Kenya shook her head, not noticing her sister and cousin's quiet exchange. "You put us all to shame. Working your tail off. Sacrificing so that your brother and his family have what they need. You carry heavy burdens yet walk through life like a queen. Honey. It's you we need to learn from."

Celise put down an apple slice and leaned over the table to look Adanne in the face. "And it's you we love and want to help. Not because of all the things you do, but because of who you are."

Adanne choked down a sob. Everything she'd pushed down for so long rose to the surface. Why did she consider herself so far removed from nurturing love? It was all around her, here in this kitchen. Poured out on her from the Lord through so many people. A reminder that she'd been too blind and stubborn to see.

"Well, look at you, little sis, coming through with the words." Kenya's face held genuine shock.

Celise shrugged, chewing thoughtfully on her apple slice.

Salome smiled. "Let's do more than talk. Let's take this to God now. I know he's got a solution. And more than we can even hope for." She turned her sweet expression to Adanne. "Is that okay with you?"

"Yes!" A wail and shudder releasing her of every barrier. The loving words of her cousins had unraveled her to the point of no return. Gratitude bubbled up and out, making a path for her tears.

The sisters surrounded her, hands on her back and shoulders, tucking arms around her waist, rubbing her back, weeping with her, drying the tears as fast as they came. They lent her strength that had been there all along. Scents of perfume and paint and lingering fruit wafting over her in their embrace. She let loose the burdens she'd held so tightly to. Reminding her that the new thing is sometimes the old truths that need to be unearthed. *I perceive it, Lord. I see it, Jesus*, her heart cried out.

And surrendered.

She squeezed the arms surrounding her tighter.

Then wept and surrendered again.

She relinquished her grip, opening her hands to release everything she'd been afraid to let go of. Dismissing the worry and doubts and fear that had plagued her every move. With God's help and the love of her family, she would keep those hands open and only carry what she was supposed to. Or even better, trust God to carry it all for her.

Amid her cousins' heartfelt prayers, Adanne let the tears of grief and release flow until she felt totally spent.

After those precious moments, and using half a roll of paper towels, the women deposited themselves back on their seats, a weighty, restful silence hanging between them. Salome sighed. Kenya cleared her throat. Adanne smiled at the lightness in her heart.

Celise slapped both hands flat on the counter.

"That's what I couldn't remember! I just heard about this yesterday, but it didn't register with me then because there wasn't a need."

"What are you saying, CeeCee?" Salome coaxed, using the name she'd given her sister when she couldn't pronounce "Celise" as a toddler.

"After my shoot in Georgia yesterday, a friend of mine told me that a film studio just outside of Atlanta is hiring more crew. Among them, full-time makeup artists with full benefits."

Adanne's eyes widened. Celise grinned. "This could be your opportunity. What perfect timing since you find yourself conveniently free. And if you're thinking of selling your house, maybe it will be easier to do that and move to a new place. I'm sure they'll love to interview you, considering your expanded portfolio."

Something new. It was a great opportunity, even though she still didn't have complete peace about letting go of her house. Or her place here in Hope Springs. But maybe this was just the step of faith she needed to take.

31

John smelled her before he saw her. Doris always lit apple-cinnamon scented candles while she worked. He had to admit that coming into his trailer each morning and smelling that aroma brought a little comfort to the start of his days on set. Especially when his nights were more than crazy.

But that was before that cinnamon candle had steadily been replaced by the pleasant fragrance of coconut and lavender. Rising from the warm skin of the woman who'd taken up space behind his chair and made a place in his heart.

Apprehension tightened his chest as he crossed the threshold of the trailer. He would have taken Adanne's disappointment, even her ferocity. He didn't know how to take her unexpected absence when he saw Doris standing next to her overflowing makeup kit. Grinning like a grandmother who had just come into town.

Before he knew it, he found himself in her generous embrace. He flinched as her extra-long nails bit into his shoulders. "Happy Tuesday, darling, I missed you. So good to see you."

He gave her another squeeze in response. "How is—it was your sister, right?"

Doris nodded, assessing him with her eyes even as she spoke. "Yes, honey, she's getting better now. One day at a time. But look at you."

She stepped back, more intense with her perusal. "Still looking like your handsome self, but what's with those sad eyes?"

The older woman sashayed back to her spot by the mirror. "Not happy to see me?" John's heart constricted, picturing Adanne there.

He was thankful for Doris's return, but he felt Adanne's absence like a vacuum—sucking out the words he'd prepared to say since she wasn't answering her phone.

"I guess you could say a lot happened while you were gone."

Doris peered at him over her purple-rimmed glasses. "So it seems. My replacement treated you well, I hope."

John placed his bag on the couch. The routine he'd gotten used to no longer the same without his attempts to talk and flirt with Adanne at the end.

"An absolute professional," he responded, sitting down on the chair.

The older woman patted his shoulders and gave them a squeeze. "I have no doubt, but seeing that she was your date at the awards, I wondered if she'd broken your heart in the week between then and now."

John shifted in his chair to look at her. "You know about that?"

The glasses slipped down her nose again. "Baby, you know social media is a thing, right?"

He huffed and turned back. Boy, did he.

Doris shook out a black cape and placed it carefully around his shoulders. "I keep up with my favorite client. Plus, Mike filled me in before I got here this morning."

John turned his chair.

"You gonna sit still today?" Doris protested, both hands on her generous hips.

"What does Mike have to do with this?"

Doris raised her eyes in surprise at the expression on John's face, but to her credit, she plowed through. "He's the one who invited me back if I was ready. Said it was time for a staff change and you needed me."

Heat spread up John's neck.

Doris turned to glance at the call sheet for the day. "I'd actually been thinking about retiring. Stick around for my sister's recovery, but since she's doing better, I thought, why not?"

John turned his chair back around, his feet dragging across the floor. It wasn't out of the range of possibility for Mike, as his manager, to hire or fire staff members. He'd done it before, multiple times. But why now, when filming was about to wrap?

His anger simmered. Mike had no right to meddle in his personal life.

Because it *was* personal, wasn't it? More than a professional need or bias. He wanted Adanne to remain close to every part of his life.

John fumed as Doris worked, but as the news settled in him, hope rose again. Adanne hadn't chosen to leave. Maybe there was a chance for the both of them after all.

• • • •

During the lunch break, John grabbed a bagel with smoked salmon from craft services and headed to his personal trailer to find his phone. After debating whether to dial Adanne's number again, he pulled up Kenya's instead.

"Kenya? Hey, John Pope here. Have you seen Adanne lately? I can't get in touch with her."

"No. Haven't." Huffs came through the line.

"Getting in a midafternoon run?"

Kenya chuckled on the other end. "No movie magic here to keep me in shape."

John took a bite of his bagel, chewed, and swallowed quickly. He leaned back against the soft suede couch where he practiced his lines and took naps.

"But I know where she is." The jumping stopped, and Kenya sounded like she was panting.

John sat up, lunch forgotten. "Tell me. Please."

"Celise told her about a job opportunity in Atlanta. She's been there for a couple days interviewing."

John choked. This wasn't going according to his plan. "Is she seriously considering it?"

"Well, she *did* talk to one of my Realtor friends about putting her house on the market."

John felt the earlier hope drain out of him. He could have kicked himself and his pride for not finding her sooner. For not flying back earlier. For letting Katrina get so close to him.

"John?" He sat in his thoughts so long, he almost forgot Kenya was still on the other end.

"Kenya, sorry. Just thinking."

"Well, I don't know if I can speak into this. But Adanne isn't gone yet. Maybe she just needs a reminder of all the reasons she should stay."

John took in her words. Chewed on the promise there.

"Thank you, Kenya. Now tell me, what's going on with her house again?"

● ● ● ●

John raked his hand through his hair as he walked through Hope Springs' small downtown. A rumble in his middle reminded him of the small bagel bite he'd had during lunch. His appetite had slipped away after the conversation with Kenya. But now that his day on set was over, it was a good time to fix that.

He glanced around, getting a better sense of his surroundings. The blue bridge of the park appeared far off in the distance. He stood across the street from Plantain and Pies, and if he remembered his location well enough, that was not too far off from Alonzo's restaurant. Shrimp and grits may not be on the menu anymore, but his mouth watered at the memory. Even though it was too early for dinner, he would grab a bite to eat and make some plans from there.

"Hey, man. Welcome. Again." Chef Alonzo greeted John with a big grin. He stood behind the podium, making some notes on a tablet.

John gave a wry smile. "You wouldn't happen to have grits on the menu, would you?"

Alonzo's eyes lit up, his dreadlocks pulled into a ponytail. The chef's jacket he wore gleamed white and fresh, which probably would not be the case after the dinner crowd.

"You liked those, huh? It's a Hope Springs favorite."

John slipped off his ball cap.

"The best thing I've tasted in a long time."

"Then you should come more often. That meal rotates, but I'm sure we can find something to fill you up for now."

Alonzo grabbed a menu and directed John toward a table in the corner with sunrays filtering through the window. The top held an amber glass bottle, a simple sprig of greenery, and old-fashioned salt-and-pepper shakers.

Alonzo placed the menu in front of John as he sat down. "Take your time and let me know what we can get started for you."

John glanced over it and handed the menu back. "Everything looks great. I'm good with whatever you think."

"I knew I liked you." Alonzo gave him a thumbs-up. John nodded his thanks in time for his phone to buzz. Mike. He drummed his fingers on the table a few seconds and then reached for it before his manager hung up. He needed to get this over with.

"John! How was your day back?" Mike's exuberance belied the tension John sensed underneath his tone. The same rolling off him in heated waves.

"Is it that Tuesday?"

"It is. Our monthly meeting day."

"Well, consider this your Tuesday off."

"Wait, John. We need to talk, and I would rather do it now than later."

John needed to process how he was going to approach Adanne. He had little tolerance for the one who had stirred all this up in the first place. Yet it was his choices that had caused the ripple. He had no right to blame anyone but himself.

"You have fifteen minutes, Mike." Or less if his food arrived before.

"I just need five seconds. I'm sorry."

John caught his phone before it slipped. "Come again?"

"Don't act so surprised. I'm not heartless."

John scoffed. "No, but you usually don't apologize."

"People change. You're adamant about that taking place in your own life."

"Yesss . . ." John didn't want to raise his hopes, but this shift in their usual Tuesday conversation piqued his curiosity. Especially after blowing up over the phone last week.

"What exactly is this sorry for, and to what do I owe this shocking declaration?"

"Enough with the theatrics. You're gonna make me spell it out? I'm sorry for disrespecting your decision and exposing your friend to the public eye. Although, one of the biggest awards shows of the year is not exactly private. Rethink your strategy next time."

"Ah, now there is the Mike I know." John shook his head. "Why did you have her let go?"

"You mean take care of my client by handling a staffing issue? Getting Doris back to the makeup chair where she belongs?"

"She's ready to retire."

"Doesn't matter. She would do anything for you."

John gritted his teeth. "That's not the point. I care for Doris, and despite your plans, I care for Adanne too. A lot."

John felt Mike's attitude shift. "Don't you think my concerns matter? I've been with you through thick and thin, every up and down of your career. Helping steer this ship to make you as successful as you can be. Can't throw away our hard work because you get a soft spot for a crew member. One that could get you distracted on set, blasted on social media, or worse—in a lawsuit. Did you even think about the potential legal implications of a workplace romance?"

John sat back in his chair. He hadn't. He had never crossed any lines with Adanne, but he could see Mike's point.

"Yeah, I didn't think so," Mike huffed into the phone.

Lord, forgive me if I took any wrong steps in my desire to do right.

He didn't regret taking Adanne to the awards or the friendship they'd developed, but maybe he'd worked too hard trying to squeeze her into his world, so desperate to be near her and the sense of home he felt with her.

The heat of his frustration cooled. "You've always had the best interest of my career in mind."

Mike sighed. "I'm not your enemy, John. Just didn't want to see you tank again like you did after Katrina."

John nodded as the picture became clearer. Mike had seen

him at his worst. This hadn't just been about raising his celebrity status. For Mike, this was his attempt to keep John successful *and* sober.

"Mike, I get it. And thank you." Mike was an experienced Hollywood manager, making moves with cool calculation. He may never understand John's faith, but he was passionate about his career.

"Tell me, John. Is this Jesus thing for real? You would change everything, just like that?"

"I don't plan to throw my entire career away haphazardly. But someone special once told me that just because I'm good at something doesn't mean it has to be my dream, my whole life. That's what I'm trying to figure out. I got into acting because I was running away from what I couldn't control. Controlling it in my own way unsuccessfully. I've decided to live my life centered on Christ instead of me. I don't know what will come from that, but I know that I'm going to run *toward* him, and not away."

Mike's silence was so long, John pulled the phone away from his ear to make sure they were still connected. After another moment, he heard a shaky exhale, not as polished as Mike's usual responses.

"Am I going to have to brush off my grandma's Bible to understand you?"

"That's up to you, but if you do, try to stay away from applying the book of Esther, or any other matchmaking strategy, to my life."

John laughed along with Mike, something tight and unfamiliar in his throat. He was glad his relationship with Mike didn't have to end over disagreements and disappointment. That it could continue and maybe even evolve into something more solid than before.

"Noted. Speaking of making a match. Seems like that makeup artist lit one in you."

It wasn't the most enthusiastic statement, but John would take it. And run. "You could say that, Mike."

"So, what are we going to do?"

"We?"

"You're my client, John, and my friend. My goal is for you to be established in the industry and personally. Contrary to what you may believe, I take a lot of pride in who I represent. It reflects on me. I admit that you've been different the past year and a half. I didn't want to trust it, thought you couldn't handle it. But I see the change. And I'm going to choose to believe that your choice in this current state is a benefit on all levels."

John cleared his throat. That was a blessing if he ever heard one. And even though these words hadn't come from someone like his father and probably never would, they were sincere and specific enough to ring a bell of redemption. What response did he give to that besides his honest longing? "Just praying that choice is still mine to make. It got a little complicated, as you know."

"Meh." John could see Mike's casual shrug in his mind's eye. "I'm good with complicated. I may be able to help."

After John hung up with Mike a few minutes later, Alonzo brought his meal out himself. The steam from the blackened-fish sandwich waved in front of John's face. The ripened plantain slices on the side beckoned an image of Adanne, singing under pendant lights to a soulful melody.

"This looks good."

Alonzo beamed, tossing a towel over his shoulder.

"Can't even take credit for half these dishes. They are recipes adapted from the restaurant I worked in as a kid."

John nodded. "Adanne's grandfather."

Alonzo smiled, surprise on his face. "That's right. She tell you?"

John nodded. "She did. And if you don't mind and have

a few minutes, I would like to talk with you about an idea. A way to help our mutual friend."

Alonzo gave John a knowing look, as if he didn't believe for a second that he and Adanne were just friends.

"Should I ask what's up with the two of you? Or should I let the photo in the entertainment section of our local paper speak for itself?"

John winced and took a bite of the fish. How many times did she get hit with reminders of that night?

Alonzo pulled out a chair and sat across from him with a chuckle. "I won't pry into that side of your business, you go on and enjoy your food. But honestly, I've been praying about a way to help more. And I'm not the only one. Adanne doesn't realize how valued she is. By all of us. We wouldn't be who we are without her."

32

The trip to Atlanta was everything Adanne had hoped for and more. She would have the opportunity to sharpen her skills while helping the head MUA run a growing department. Even more perfect that the job was close to home.

She needed to talk this over with someone she trusted. As she pulled up to her brother's house on Thursday afternoon, she was pleasantly surprised to see that both Daniel's and Monica's cars were in the driveway. Who was with Jason at the hospital?

Her delight gave way to creeping guilt. If they both needed to be home, it should have been her sitting with Jason.

I said I would let you carry it, Lord. Please help me trust you for my family.

A blanket of warmth settled on her shoulders, like the hands of her cousins when they prayed over her. The weight that tried to press her down dissipated. Peace.

A small smile tugged at Adanne's lips as she raised her hand to knock. She could get used to the feeling of relinquishing control.

And Lord, I choose to trust you with John. You know how I feel. But he belongs to you. Not me.

Before she raised her fist to knock again, the door swung open.

"Sis! I thought I heard a car. Back already?"

Adanne frowned, unable to reconcile Daniel's question with the look of pure joy on his face. "Is this a bad time?"

Daniel shook his head with a grin, pulling her into his foyer and shutting the door behind her with fluid motion. "I just thought you were still out of town."

Adanne entered with measured steps, unable to shake the feeling that something was off. "Just got back." She tilted her head to look her brother directly in the face. "Is everything okay?"

Daniel released a laugh, one so light that she felt her own heart lift. The lines of worry that had occupied his face for so long more smoothed out.

Daniel opened his mouth to respond but was interrupted by Monica's voice.

"Adanne? Is that you?" Her sister-in-law rushed to her, a bright scarf covering her dark curls. Her skin shone as if bathed in light. Monica wrapped her arms around Adanne, the gesture tugging on her heart even more.

What is going on here?

"How is Jason?" She looked back and forth between them.

The couple exchanged looks, tears welling in their eyes even as their grins widened.

Daniel placed his hand on Adanne's arm.

"We had a bit of a shock today. Two, in fact." Monica's chest expanded. "Before Daniel tells you about the second, why don't you come and see the first surprise for yourself?"

Monica led her down the hall into the open living area. At the dining table, sitting in front of his favorite fast-food meal, was her nephew.

"Jason?!" She hurried to his side, kneeling so she could lean her head against his thin shoulder. She felt him tilt his bald head toward hers, a smile puffing his cheek out against her hair.

Adanne stilled, letting his presence soak her soul with wonder. After a few minutes, she cleared her throat and looked up. Monica stood swiping at tears while Daniel beamed down at them both.

"What happened? I thought he still had a few more treatments before they reassessed him."

Daniel laughed. "Sis. All I can do is thank God because when the doctor came in this morning, I thought he was bringing me bad news. His look was so serious. But he said that his reaction had minimized and that he could finally go home between treatments. The cancer cells are decreasing, and his other counts are leveling out. He said we could wait a little longer if we wanted but he was confident that Jason could come home. He's on his way to remission."

Adanne stood up on shaky feet. She looked down at her nephew again, who grinned, his mouth stuffed with a grilled chicken nugget. Just seeing him with half his former appetite was miracle enough.

"I'm so happy to see you, Jason."

"I know." Her nephew kicked his feet happily. "I'm happy too. Jesus told me I would get better." Adanne ran her hand over her nephew's smooth scalp, lifting her head in gratitude.

After she hugged Monica again, Daniel motioned for her to join him.

Adanne sat down on the couch, her eyes still rounded. She sunk into the rust-colored leather sofa.

Daniel chuckled. "God is good, huh? So, ready for that next surprise?"

Adanne placed her hand on her stomach. "I don't even know."

Her brother leaned forward but then stopped. "Wait. How was Atlanta? You get the job?"

Adanne waved that away with a flick of her hand. "Doesn't even matter right now. What else do you need to tell me?"

Daniel grinned. "That's why I made you come sit down. You may have more serious thoughts about Atlanta when you find out what happened."

Daniel continued his forward movement to reach for a manila envelope on the coffee table. He handed it to his sister.

It was addressed to Daniel from the bank. The bank that would be calling soon to collect on the payment for the center. Adanne released a heavy breath. "I don't know if this is a surprise I can handle. It may be one I already know, Daniel."

He raised an eyebrow. Guilt made a pass at her again. She should have been more open with her brother, but she didn't want him to be burdened with anything other than the care of his son.

"I'm sorry I didn't tell you before now. I thought I could save enough to handle it and, at the very least, sell the house."

She covered her face with her hands. "And now after you've gotten such good news, you have to deal with this."

When Adanne lowered her hands, her brother's eyes narrowed in confusion. "I don't know what you're talking about, Dee. If you open this letter and read it, you'll see that it's all been paid. Well, almost."

She stared at her brother in disbelief. "Wait, what?"

"You heard me."

"No, I don't think I did. Tell me again."

Daniel opened the envelope, pulling out two sheets of notarized paper.

He handed them to his sister, making sure she had a good grip before he released his hands.

"One's from the bank." He pointed to the letterhead. "And the other . . ."

Adanne blinked at it, trying to push away the tears coating her eyes.

Daniel leaned close to his sister, placing his head against hers so they could take in the second document together.

"Adanne," he whispered, his voice overflowing with relief and tender compassion. "This letter was in the mailbox today when we brought Jason home. About the center. An investment group wants to meet Saturday morning to discuss paying the bill in full. And they want you to be there too."

33

The shock still hadn't worn off. The community center would remain in the community, so it seemed, serving in the way God intended. Her parents' legacy living on.

Thanks to an investment group who wanted to meet at the hotel across from the park. Daniel offered to come along even though Adanne told him to stay and soak up time with his son. But here he was, walking with her in comfortable silence to attend at least part of this meeting before he went back home to his miracle.

Thank God for them. And for her?

Adanne's hand moved to her chest out of habit but dropped back to her side as the memory of her lost necklace resurfaced. She'd called the hotel as soon as she'd landed and realized what she'd forgotten. And then texted her cousins when the hotel had no answers. But Kenya and Celise had no success finding it either.

That loss almost overshadowed the purpose of today's meeting and hopefully the better news that would follow. Only God knew where that cherished piece was. Maybe it was time to let go, in more ways than one.

"Gotta love this town." Her brother lifted his chin in pride, adjusting the sleeves of his button-down. She couldn't agree more.

They continued their stroll around the edge of the downtown pond, retracing the steps she'd walked with John months ago. She still hadn't returned any of his calls and had no clue if he remained in Hope Springs since filming should have been wrapping soon. Her feelings hadn't abated, but she didn't think she could take the risk. As a working actor, John made his home around Hollywood. Did she really want that?

Did something new have to be away from Hope Springs?

For the moment, she and her brother would meet with these mysterious benefactors, talk through the details. She'd decide the next step for her future from there.

"Give me a moment, Daniel." Adanne paused at a red bench facing the water's smooth surface.

Daniel stopped, glancing at her with concern.

"I'm good, I promise. Just need to sit in this for a few minutes."

He nodded, understanding filling his gaze. "I should call and check on the fam anyway." He smiled to himself. "Feels so good to say that and know my son is home."

Yeah, there was so much to soak in.

Daniel walked closer to the pond, holding his cell to his ear. Adanne carefully avoided the remnants of dried bird waste and sat down on the cold bench.

With the possibility of being alleviated of their bills, there was no pressure to stay.

But she belonged here. Not because she was forced to be. Hope Springs was home. She hadn't let it feel like that the last few years because the implications brought so much pain.

Yet . . .

Adanne set her eyes on the fountain in the middle of the

pond, her brother's gentle pace in her peripheral vision. Hope still rose, bubbling up despite every obstacle. Redeeming the past. Pointing to what could come.

Like something new. She smiled to herself. That first time John came with her to church, she hadn't known what to think about it all. But little did she know that message would continue to resonate.

She inhaled her struggle and breathed out a decision that brought tangible peace. For now, that new thing still looked a lot like her beloved town of Hope Springs, Alabama. And perhaps it was because she finally saw it through eyes not tinged with hope deferred. Rather, she could see it through the lens of a dream developing—in the way God intended.

When Daniel finished his call, Adanne took one last look across the water before joining him on the path toward their meeting at the hotel.

She unbuttoned her blazer, the air growing warmer. The leaves shimmered green among blooming flowers, Alabama shedding the last vestiges of winter.

As they continued, she noticed two figures walking toward the small blue bridge. After a few steps, she stopped in her tracks. These weren't strangers about to pass by.

"Hey, that looks like Alonzo and . . . is that who I think it is?"

She sucked in her breath, barely hearing her brother's words, her stomach in waves. John stood on the opposite side, a short distance away from stepping onto the bridge. The desire to scurry past him flitted through her mind, but his expression kept her firmly planted. And she couldn't go on without greeting their family friend. But why in the world were they walking in the park—together—this early?

"Man, it's been a long time!" Daniel took the first step. He walked onto the bridge, reaching out to shake Alonzo's hand, pulling him into a hug.

"It has, it has." Alonzo beamed, pounding her brother on the back. "Sorry I missed you when I dropped off food the other day."

"All good, brother. We really appreciated it. Thank you." Daniel tossed another grin at the taller chef and then turned his attention to John, who pulled his focus away from Adanne to face him.

Alonzo put a hand on John's shoulder. "This is John Pope. I take it y'all haven't met."

Daniel reached out a hand and, when John did the same, placed his other on top. "We haven't, but I assume it's you I need to thank for what you did for the kids at the hospital. For my son."

John nodded. "It was a group effort. And an amazing time." His eyes shifted from Daniel to Adanne, who was still planted on the path, unable to do anything but watch this meeting unfold.

Our meeting.

"Um, Daniel. We're going to be late."

Alonzo looked from John to Adanne and back. "I—uh— don't think you need to worry about *that*, Adanne." He made eye contact with Daniel, who leaned back as if a light bulb had sprung up over his head. Daniel gave a slow nod, shifting his attention back to her.

"You know what, sis? I think you can handle it."

Adanne blinked at her brother, snapping herself out of what felt like the strangest reverie. "Wait, what? You came all this way to leave me?"

Daniel stepped off the bridge, placing his hands on her shoulders as soon as he was close enough. "You got this, sis. And you are worthy of *this*. Daddy and Mama would be proud."

He gave her an affectionate kiss on the forehead, ignoring her confused look, and turned to walk back onto the bridge.

After giving John a knowing smile, he slapped Alonzo on the back.

"You still serving brunch on weekends?"

Alonzo chuckled, rubbing his hands together. "I think I can whip something up."

Adanne gaped in disbelief at the two men crossing over to the other side, talking about french toast and fried apples, maple-coated bacon, and other foods that she would apparently not be eating with them.

Instead, she remained here, with him.

John took a tentative step forward, handsome in a denim jacket over a green shirt. He placed a hand on the railing and propelled himself forward with gradual ease, until he stood just a few steps away. His fingers drummed a light rhythm on the bridge railing.

Adanne grasped her purse strap, her knuckles pointed. John's gaze didn't leave her face. In his silent perusal, she felt his eyes caress her cheek, her nose, her chin, her forehead. Taking in every part as if he beheld a masterpiece. In that exchange and in her brother and Alonzo's odd departure, she saw the truth.

"It was you."

"It was me. Kind of."

His lips spread into a smile that warmed her from the inside out, despite the morning chill.

Adanne bit her lip to keep it from twitching.

"And I'm so sorry for what you saw. For not explaining myself well. For letting the past shadow this." He waved his hand in the space between them.

"I am too." Her words caught in her aching throat. John took her hesitation as encouragement to step closer.

She crossed her arms, throat burning. "So, my meeting is canceled, then?"

"If you don't mind." John took another step forward.

"And if you will forgive me? For letting my baggage get in the way. For what happened and how it hurt you. That is the last thing I ever want to do."

Adanne wanted to keep the walls up. But there was nothing else to build those on. There was no logical reason she could come up with to keep this man from her life.

"Yes, Mr. Pomponio. I forgive you." His sigh of relief sent currents through her. She turned away so she wouldn't wilt under the intense look in his eyes. "But you didn't have to do all of this, John. It's too much."

"I didn't. Well, maybe not like you think I did."

"What do you mean?"

"This is not to buy your affection, Adanne. Although, as King Xerxes said in the Bible, I would give you half of everything I own and more. Because . . ." He placed a tender hand on her cheek. "You're more than worthy of it."

The pull of his affection was heady. Breath whooshed out of her lungs, a feeble attempt to curb the emotions overflowing.

"How's everything paid for?"

"Semantics." John grinned. "And lots of community involvement. After hearing the need and talking to Alonzo, it didn't take much to get others involved. People who love this town like you do." His eyes glowed with purpose. "Many didn't even realize the center was struggling."

That part was on her. She hadn't been open about what kind of financial situation they were in. But thankfully the precious time with her cousins had reminded her of the beautiful strength of community. God helping her, she'd do her best not to forget.

"So, without your permission, which I hope you will forgive us for as well, we formed a pseudo committee. Each of us pledged to be faithful contributors to HSCC. We hope this inspires others to join in and help more consistently. With this type of backing and the funds that have already poured in, we wanted to give your family this."

With shaking hands, Adanne took the envelope he offered. When she pulled out the check, she staggered, the amount almost a physical weight. A miraculous, joyous, comforting weight. This was more than she could comprehend. Enough to cover their debt and Daniel's salary for two years. But more than the amount was the realization that they didn't have to do this on their own.

She grasped her neck when she saw the names printed at the bottom of the letter. Pastor Ben Southerland, Alonzo Majors, Blessing Chukwu of Plantain and Pies, Ty Anderson, Albert and Justine Stewart, Giovanni Pomponio . . . and other names that represented different areas of Hope Springs.

"Your real name is Giovanni?" she squeaked, her throat aching, hands trembling.

John's mouth tipped in a boyish grin as he took a tentative step closer.

"Adanne, I remember you saying you didn't mind losing yourself if you didn't lose what mattered to your family. The thing is, I realized I don't want to lose you. Not from the set. Not from this town. Not from my life."

Adanne opened her mouth and closed it again. A fish out of water. Unable to comprehend this level of care.

"But more on that later. I want to talk to you about something else first."

"O-okay?"

"You ever hear the story of this bridge?"

"A time or two." She took a step toward him, a small smile pulling at her mouth, her eyes damp. "But I'll humor you."

John made a show of clearing his throat. "It's a universal story. One that would make a great movie. The history of hope springing up in a Southern American town."

She released a giggle. "You sure you're on the right side of the camera?"

John held both his hands up, thumbs pointing to each other, parallel to the ground.

"In this story we see the ripples of that history through the life of a beautiful woman who has carried her parents' legacy on her shoulders. Several scenes later, in walks a man—not so bad looking himself."

Adanne scoffed, blinking away the tears that seemed so close to the surface lately.

"Ahem. A man enamored with this lead woman."

His hands lingered up, framing her face before he gradually lowered them.

"They come from two different worlds, so it seems, but the more they get to know each other, they realize they want the same thing."

John stepped closer. Adanne followed suit, her left hand on the railing.

"And what is that?" she whispered, not taking her eyes from him.

John broke his storytelling demeanor to let a playful smirk cross his lips.

"Really good food. Like barbecue and pies and plantain and shrimp and grits and—"

"John!"

Adanne's insides continued to melt as he tossed his head back, his laughter opening her heart even wider. He settled his intense gaze back on her.

The man once obscured by the filters she'd seen him through now stood out in raw clarity. His jaw was determined, layered in morning scruff, laugh lines visible, full of teasing. Eyes shimmering with vulnerable hope that squeezed her throat.

John's chest expanded, and his words, an overflow of his breath, released.

"They want a safe place to call home. She makes him want to put down roots for the first time in his life. He works with others to invest in a building so she won't lose her home. So that she won't leave the place that means so much to her."

He reached his hand inside the pocket of his coat and took out a small canvas drawstring bag. "I believe this belongs to you. Here. In this place. Not hanging from a luggage cart in Los Angeles."

Adanne gasped as she pulled out her necklace. What she lost, found by him. "But . . . how did you?"

John shook his head, his own grin wobbly. "I don't know if you would believe it if I told you. But let's just say that a certain manager has a knack for digging up dirt . . . and treasure."

Adanne brushed away the tear that ran down her face with one hand as she held the necklace tightly in her other fist. But the second tear fell quicker than she expected. John raised his hand, tenderly wiping it with his thumb.

"He recognizes that God brings new things, even from hard moments. And new doesn't always mean flashy lights or the big city. Sometimes it's the choice to love and let yourself be loved in return. So"—he leaned in, eliminating whatever distance had remained, moving his right hand from the bridge to place on top of hers—"he says yes to a new project that will put him behind the camera lens and closer to a certain sleepy town." He grinned. "Closer to the woman he found there. Because he loves her."

He gave her the most endearing smile. And as if pulled by a magnet, Adanne's lips tilted up until she felt her cheeks rise and dimples deepen.

"Ah, there they are," he said, his voice thick. He leaned in, kissing each dimple with tender affection.

"What do you think? It's still in development, but—"

Before John could say another word, Adanne threw her arms around him, nestling her head against his neck. His arms wrapping around her waist as she kissed a path to his ear.

"I think the audiences will love it. I know I do . . . love you."

EPILOGUE

*a*danne couldn't remember the last time she'd smiled this much. Although she refused to shed any tears today, she was thankful for the waterproof mascara she'd applied before John picked her up for tonight's festivities. He had raised his eyebrows at her full, high-waisted skirt and fitted blouse. A woman could dress up every now and then. His slow, spreading smile had been worth all the effort.

She stole a glance at him standing with a small group by the drink table. Magnetic even from here, wearing dark-gray slacks and an olive-green button-down shirt. Still looking every bit like a movie star—at least in her book—but she had never seen him more at ease. It was just like Hope Springs to have that kind of effect.

Linen-covered folding tables stood scattered around the gym, balloons gathered in strategic bunches, highlighting the freshly painted slate-blue walls. Strings of lights hung from ceiling beams that had been spray-painted a seamless matte black. Every detail had been considered, from the updated bathrooms to the drinking fountains with filtered water for refillable bottles to the nostalgic smell of wood and leather mingled with scented candles. Her father's name was emblazoned in curvy retro script on the newly polished hardwood.

But the best features of the room were the people. Laughter and the pleasant hum of conversation flowed around tables. These were Hope Springs' finest. Not because of their status, riches, or lack thereof. Adanne's heart swelled with pride. These were her people. She had forgotten, but God hadn't.

This town was still about unity, about pouring out to meet the needs of others, lifting the arms of those who thought they couldn't carry any more.

Those gathered were here for the reopening of the community center, with many of them having put in the resources to make it happen.

Adanne lifted her hand in a wave to Alonzo, who balanced trays laden with Southern soul-food appetizers to replenish empty platters. The sticky-sweet banana scent hinted at bites of fried plantain dispersed among the trays. Her aunt Justine followed close behind with a few healthier options. Uncle Albert diverted from his wife's path to come close to Adanne.

"So proud of you, sweetheart." He placed a fatherly kiss on her cheek before leaving to set pitchers of lemonade on the drink table. It took considerable effort to swallow the lump in her throat. Her fingers instinctively moved to the beloved piece of jewelry hanging from her neck. Oh, how she missed her parents. That would always be, but even that loss didn't diminish what she had in the family that remained.

In another corner, Kenya and a man Adanne recognized from the movie set stood talking with the handsome doctor who had helped during their party at the hospital. The light in her cousin's eyes shone from the other end of the room. Adanne made a mental note to tease her later.

Movement in the center caught her attention. She had to laugh at Daniel and Monica trying to show Mike how to do the latest slide. He was struggling, but she gave him credit for trying.

"Hey, Auntie Dee." Jason waved feverishly from his place on his dad's shoulders, his head bouncing as Daniel went through the steps. His treatment had continued to go well, with the last round of chemo finishing a few months ago. Adanne loved seeing those curls of his again.

"It was all worth it, if just for you," she whispered, blowing him a kiss. She would never fail to be grateful for how God had come through for him. For them all. And she trusted him to continue to do so.

"You have any more where that came from?" John's voice spread warmth from her belly outward, pushing that lump further to the tipping point.

"Not so much. These are only reserved for cute seven-year-olds." Adanne let out a soft cackle as John wrapped his arms around her waist from behind. He placed his chin on her shoulder, the scent of his shampoo filling the surrounding air.

"Anything for the more mature but less cute man in his thirties?"

Adanne smirked. "Maybe, Mr. Pomponio."

"Ah, we need to change that. But for now, come with me." In a well-executed move, he spun from around her back and stood in front of her with his hand held out in dramatic invitation.

She turned back to John with an eyebrow raised, placing her hand on his. "You don't intend to seduce me, do you?"

John smiled, remembrance in his eyes. "Never." He tugged at her hand. "Come on, then."

Adanne knew this facility more than anywhere else, so when John pulled her through the door in the back and down the hallway, she wondered why they were approaching the large storage room.

John beckoned her to stop a couple feet away while he dug in his pocket.

After placing a key in the lock, the door opened into the dark room.

Adanne glanced at John in confusion. The smile on his face softened, but his eyes burned brighter.

"I have a question for you. I thought it would be appropriate to bring you somewhere special."

"To the storage room?" Adanne squeaked, her heart beating with wild rhythm.

"About that. There's been a little plot twist." He flicked on the light.

What she saw paralyzed her feet. Gone were the racks and dusty supplies. The wall facing her held three mirrors rimmed with bulb lights. Underneath those stood three bamboo tables, each with a black, cushioned swivel chair positioned in front of it. The window that used to be blocked by racks stood clear and gleaming, ready to welcome the rays of the rising sun in the morning. No wonder he hadn't let her near the center during the last few weeks of renovation.

Adanne stepped in farther, taking in every detail.

"I'll never forget the look in your eyes that day. Watching you talk about your mom from the makeup chair on set. Thought it'd be nice to work on your passion while remembering how much your mom loved you."

The slight pressure from his hand on her back caused her to turn to her left. On that far wall was brick painted with the words "Her Mother's Daughter" in the same inviting retro script of the gym floor. They framed a large photo of her mama, eyes shining, mouth with the brightest smile. Hair curled the way she always liked it.

"You—you know what my name means?" The lump in her throat couldn't remain. Tears slid down Adanne's cheeks as she stepped toward the photo. She placed two fingers on the glass. Soaking in the words that were not a status to be chased, but an identity to be remembered.

"Now, my love, can you take a seat, please?"

Adanne tried to speak, but her throat ached with oceans of gratitude.

John took her hand again, leading her to the chair right in the middle.

"After all the time you spent working with me on set. Dealing with my annoying behavior. Enduring my feeble attempts to court you . . ."

"Actors and their dramatics." Adanne rolled her eyes but couldn't speak further. Her trembling smile all she could give.

"I need to make you an offer . . . that I hope you won't refuse."

He spun Adanne's chair around as she gripped the armrests. When it came back to a stop, she covered her mouth. John faced her on one knee, extending a ring in the open palm of his hand.

"You've got the job," he said, his voice thick with emotion. "If you want it, of course. There is no one else I want as my wife. No one but you."

Adanne leaned down, taking the thick band with the elegant diamond solitaire in her hand, her soft braids falling like a curtain to the side. She placed it on the tip of her ring finger and extended her hand to let it rest in John's palm, his gentle touch moving the ring firmly into place.

"Challenge accepted," she whispered, millimeters from his lips.

ACKNOWLEDGMENTS

Do I have permission to write? This was the question I asked myself during the first year of my family's move to Iceland. I've been writing most of my life, from scribbling on scraps of paper as a toddler to publishing my first nonfiction book decades later. But in the midst of this huge transition—a new role, new language, new baby—I had doubts about this desire of my heart.

Writing this book is a literal dream come true. The ten-year-old who made up stories about her Barbies is squealing inside of me. I will never get over the sweetness of the Lord to allow me to write these books from this beautiful land of fire and ice. And that sweetness overflows from so many who have played their own parts in making this book a reality.

To you, dear readers, I owe so much gratitude. You are the ones who added *Her Part to Play* to your physical and digital libraries. You join launch teams, read, review, and share with friends. Thank you for loving books and supporting authors in the process.

Thank you to the friends who've listened to snippets of my words over the years and shared in my excitement. So much of this story carries over from experiences I've had with you.

I'm grateful to my church, The Rock Family in Huntsville, for your cover and support of our family. I'm passionate about writing diverse stories because our church and our city have reflected that.

Barb, I'm so grateful to be represented by you. You turned every disappointment into an opportunity to pivot. Thank you for your prayerful wisdom and direction over this process. I'm honored to be your client and a part of the Books & Such literary family.

Rachel, thank you for believing in this book and in me— and for the UTK coaster I set my coffee on when I sit down to write (Go Vols!). You and Kristin have made this book so much better with your thoughtful questions and edits. I'm still in awe of your skills. Brianne, Michelle, Karen, Laura, Erin, and the rest of the Revell team, thank you for your work in making this book the best it could be. Special thanks to David Sluka of Chosen Books who didn't let a pitiful proposal years ago keep him from giving me great advice, connection, and encouragement. Baker Publishing Group is full of incredible people.

Huge thanks to the authors who took the time to read and endorse this book. Bethany, Michelle, Patricia, Rachel, Robin, and Toni, I'm already a fan of your books, and your support of this debut novel has meant so much to me.

To all the ones in the midst who have shared words that guided and challenged along the way, thank you.

To my friends and family-in-love in Iceland, thank you for your love and excitement over my writing journey. The community and friendships that have developed here are an answer to prayer. And we love living down the street from Afi and Amma. ʹÉg elska ykkur.

To my stateside family, my brothers and sister, thank you for your love and support. I'm proud of us and what God has unfolded in our lives. You are the best siblings (and siblings-in-love) that I could ask for. Daddy, thank you for instilling in me a passion for writing and teaching.

Mommy, you showed me not just how to read the Word and know God, but how to cling to his Word as a lifeline. Thank you for your love, sacrifices, continual prayers, and constant encouragement (Isaiah 54). You are the best Mommy and Nana. And thank you for giving me the name for my lead character and making sure it was from the right tribe, LOL!

To my kids, I'm so glad you've allowed Mommy to do this "boring" thing, haha. The sweet moments after bed-time stories and prayers are when I typed the majority of this book into my phone notes. I love you, and like we say each morning, don't forget who is with you (*Jesus!*). I write so you can run.

To my husband, your support means more than I can say. You have pushed me and believed in me more than I believed in myself. You helped silence the voices of doubt and accu-sation. You fanned my call into flame, time and time again. Thank you, my joyful, wonderful Viking. I love you, babe.

Father God, what can I say? You are truly the Author and Finisher. I pray these words, and the words to come, are like oil on your feet, a fragrance of worship that fills the rooms you desire. You are everything, and I love you with my whole heart.

Jenny Erlingsson is an Alabama-born author and speaker of Nigerian descent, who has been an avid writer and reader since her childhood. After twelve years in pastoral ministry, she currently lives and serves in Iceland with her Viking husband and four adorably feisty kids. When she is not running after them or ministering with her husband, she can be found writing romantic Christian fiction and creative nonfiction to inspire deep faith in diverse settings and trying not to read five books at a time with a side of Icelandic chocolate. Connect with her at JennyErlingsson.com.

Connect with Jenny

JennyErlingsson.com

f JENNYERLINGSSON.AUTHOR

⊙ JENNYERLINGSSON

BB JENNY-ERLINGSSON

Be the First to Hear about New Books from Revell!

Stay up-to-date with our authors and books and discover exciting features like book excerpts and giveaways by signing up for our newsletters at

RevellBooks.com/SignUp

FOLLOW US ON SOCIAL MEDIA

 @RevellFiction

@RevellBooks

 Revell
a division of Baker Publishing Group
www.RevellBooks.com